ZOTZ!

ZOTZ!

by Walter Karig

❧ *with drawings by the author* ❧

RINEHART & COMPANY, INC.

NEW YORK ❧ ❧ TORONTO

FOREWORD

The following preface to this book should be skipped entirely. It is boring, full of irrelevant details and allusions to persons and places (most of them perished) nobody ever heard of, and having nothing to do with this story.

W. K.

PREFACE

MY NAME IS John Jones. I am the only person in the world who knows exactly what he is doing—and *why*. I am the only person in the United States, at least, who contemplates the future with confidence and serenity.

I said, my name is John Jones. My father told me I was thus named to challenge me. "In a world," he explained, "wherein millions of Joneses are annually farrowing tens of thousands of additional Joneses in a race of procreation with the Smiths and the Cohens, it will take diligence and ingenuity for *a* John Jones to become *the* John Jones."

My father's father had the opposite idea, and ruined his son's career. Perhaps Grandfather believed that Inigo Jones became the greatest of architects because his name was not William or Henry. He christened his son Ezekiel Zwingli Jones. One fears to contemplate what burden of nomenclature would have been laid on my father had his parent been an historian like himself, instead of the evangelical clergyman he was. Inevitably Father came to be known by his initials, and "E.Z." eventually degenerated to "Easy," in direct consequence of which he never progressed farther than the unsubstantial chair of Ancient History in St. Hubert's Academy, on whose campus I was born, November 11, 1890. Who is going to entrust great responsibility or pay much respect to a man so labeled with tractability and insouciance?

I grew up, a lone child, and even a lonely one in a school of one hundred boys because I was the son of an unpopular teacher. At Harvard I was a history major, following the course of least resistance, because I had been raised intimately with Ashurbanipal and the Tarquinii. I narrowed my specialty to the Asianic cultures, not only because Professor Xceros generously demonstrated his gratitude to the few that enrolled with him, but out of genuine interest in the mysterious people whose best-known personage—with wry thanks to that inaccurate doggerel "Horatius at the Bridge" —is Lars Porsena of Clusium.

In the summer of my third year I was included in the National Geographic Society's expedition to Charchemish and Pethor. I graduated with honors and eventually won my doctorate with a thesis, never successfully disputed, proving that the transmutation of the Latin b to f in modern Teutonic tongues (English included) is of Semitic, and not Keltic, influence!

"So what?" I hear you vulgarly remark, probably unconscious of the fact that that phrase is a literal translation from the Yiddish and consequently of Semitic influence itself.

Well, *that* knowledge could have ended the war a year earlier, prevented ensuing difficulties with the Soviet Union, averted inflation and diverted nuclear fission to exclusively peaceful industrial use.

You will probably not believe that—yet.

I will not vaingloriously set forth the details of my career, although the intelligent reader will by now have identified me as the leader of the Keating-Griggs Foundation Expeditions III, IV and V which proved the Mesopotamian origins of the Tursci in 1924. Suffice it to say that when the recent war forced me to suspend my operations in the Dodecanese Islands (where I had found exciting verification of Herodotus's theory of the origins of Hellenic culture) I returned to the United States the winner of my father's challenge, possessor of incredible knowledge, and $412 in cash. But—

I was *the* John Jones.

In every civilized country, and in some which had fallen from that status, when the name "John Jones" was uttered people would say: "Ah, you mean John Jones, the archaeologist, ethnologist and etymologist!"

I know that Americans scorn "the professor," and I marvel at the paradox in a nation which establishes as the goal of individual success the ability to send one's offspring to college. So, should you have chanced to pick up this book to "kill time" and, having read this far, be tempted to observe that my learning is of vast impracticability, I most especially recommend that you do not lay the book down.[1] You are in special need of it, together with congressmen and brigadier generals.

Of the several posts eagerly offered me I chose the one that you, as a person of so-called common sense, would undoubtedly deem the least desirable—Professor of Semitic Languages at St. Jude's Theological Seminary (Episcopal). The course excluded Hebrew, which had a full professorship of its own. The position offered a living, which was necessary; a vocation, which was desirable, and a considerable leisure in which to work upon the several books I had planned. No theology was required of me. I was one of three lay professors, the others being the instructor in church financing and budgeting and the teacher of oratory. The Seminary was overcrowded, which some of the faculty joyfully accepted as a sign of the long-awaited religious awakening, and a few suspected to be inspired by the imminent Selective Service Act.

I went to work and found it pleasant. In the first semester of my second year the country was ignominiously kicked into a war it should already have won for the world of decent men. Two years later there came into my possession, by a series of not incredible coincidences, the astounding powers of which you shall read.

A full and faithful account of my experiences is owed to humanity, and to the American people in particular. Because I might be considered a prejudiced witness, or even dismissed as a crank, I decided that the appalling history should be written by an impartial hand. I finally chose for that mission an historian of quiet note and open mind, a man of good reputation if inadequate fame, Walter Karig.

[1] This is the only clause in the entire Preface to which I subscribe.—W. K.

xi

I have just finished reading his manuscript. If Karig did not exceed my expectations, neither did he disappoint me. He was given all the facts, and a free hand so long as he told the essential story truthfully and objectively. He has done that, but being a professional (which is to say, a commercial) writer, he has embroidered the narrative with a certain whimsy which impels me to write this preface and insist upon its place of precedence.

The biographical data I have included in this preface is to repair its omission in the narrative. Karig said it was not necessary to the story. I hold otherwise. He said nobody would understand it. I am used to that. I want to assert my utter normality, however above average I am mentally.

I am 5 feet 10 inches tall, partially bald but gray of hair; my eyes are blue, my physique what is known as wiry. Outside of my profession I have few prejudices. Although I was for some years connected with a religious institution, I believe that real religion began to deteriorate when man first created God in his grandfather's image, complete with viscera for which he can have no heavenly use. Religion will not mature while it endows God with whiskers.

I commit you now to Mr. Karig's narrative with the final advice that you heed him well, or as well as you are able. It is a story that should arouse every thoughtful man—and woman, too, for there *are* thoughtful women. I am sure of that, for otherwise by simple operation of the Mendelian law the power of thought would have been bred out of humanity long ago.

I am not content to leave judgment to posterity. There will be no posterity, unless this generation acquires judgment for itself.

JOHN JONES

February 10, 1947

INTRODUCTION

DR. JOHN JONES, the international authority on the ancient civilizations of the Near East and recently professor at St. Jude's, came to my office in the Navy Department in the summer of 1944. He was seeking assistance to put his talents to use in the war.

He was just one in the unending stream of persons with a mission that poured jerkily past my desk; earnest persons, all, terribly in earnest; people who came to Washington at their own expense, burning with conviction.

But he came back, again and again, easy to remember by his habit of keeping his hands always deep in his coat pockets; patient, insistent, secretive. The Navy had no need for archaeologists or linguists, which was as far as Dr. Jones would identify himself, but he always returned, hinting more broadly each time that the vital secret he guarded transcended, although stemming from, his knowledge of Near Eastern antiquities. He would impart it, however, to none but "the ultimate authority."

Now of course in the chain of command my position was to act as a barrier to prevent persons like Dr. Jones from annoying the ultimate authority. Impressed by his great sincerity, I finally gave him unofficial assistance, which he rewarded with greater confidences, the startling results of which are related in the narrative Dr. Jones has authorized me to write. I have chosen that vehicle—almost in the form of a novel although that is a technique of literary expression in which I have small practice—because it enables me to delineate the Doctor's character and personality and to provide the not unimportant background against which the drama was enacted. This narrative form, further, enables the reader to peruse Dr. Jones's story as fiction, if your mind rejects it as authentic fact. I confess that I sometimes find myself not only believing it to be one or the other, but in the uncomfortable position of doubting that which I am believing at the time. I wish I had never heard of Dr. Jones.

WALTER KARIG

Washington, D. C.
January 18, 1947

P.S. I have, as I said, attempted to put this history in the form of a novel. So, *except* for Dr. Jones, the Rev. Dr. Alfred Claverhouse, Mrs. Angela Brant, Miss Virginia Finster and, of course, myself, *all* the characters in this book are fictitious, bearing synthetic names such as belong to no persons known to me. It is possible that, out of affection, I have endorsed some of the characters with the amiable qualities of persons who have blessed me with their friendship. But if anyone should say: "I wonder if he meant that to be I" (for all my friends are grammatical even when excited) or "I wonder if he meant that to be Johnny Walker (or Charley Tompkins, Dick Williams, Boris Shishkin, the very Rev. Dean "Zab" Zabriskie, Admiral Frank Farley, USCG, Captain Atherton Macondray, USN, Colonel "Gally" Galliford, USMC, the Rev. Drs. Mollegan, Brown-Serman or Kevin, or any of their womenfolk)," why the answer is "No!" That is, I don't think so.

W. K.

ZOTZ!

1

THE MOTH APPEARED from nowhere, as big brown moths always materialize in the best-screened home, and proclaimed its arrival by—literally—a headlong assault on the disk of light projected upon the living-room ceiling by the lamp.

For minutes none of the three persons in that room acknowledged the intrusion. But the cadence of the moth's soft pounding threw Angela Brant's knitting out of whack, and she found herself knitting one, purling *two*, in time to the moth's lunges, with disastrous effect upon a khaki scarf— her thirty-seventh since Pearl Harbor Day.

"Alfred," she complained to her brother, "please do something about that creature."

The Rev. Alfred Claverhouse knew better than to waste breath on the sigh of resignation that rose in his throat. He put aside his *Study of the Manicheo-Paulician Heresy of Thonraki*, folded the evening newspaper, and made an ineffectual swipe at the moth.

"Alfred!"

"Yes, Angela."

"You know better than to do that! It will make a big smudge."

"But then, what . . . ?"

"You men, always so helpless! Get the Flit gun."

"Where is it?"

"I suppose if one wants to get something done, it's best to do it yourself. Look at the horrid creature. The powder is coming off its wings and making spots."

Mrs. Brant laid her knitting aside, thrust herself out of her chair, and started for the kitchen. Alfred put himself in front of her, walking backward.

"Just tell me where the thing is, I'll get it," he protested. "Goodness knows, I haven't used it since I don't know when."

"And you don't remember where you left it then," Angela told him. "Out on the terrace where you were using it, I judge, to kill aphids on the euonymus. At any rate, the euonymus leaves are all scalded."

Brother and sister looked at each other through their respective bifocals, his hands contritely folded on his rounded stomach and hers augustly clasped over the same (but more rigidly confined) portion of her anatomy. The nascent dispute was arrested as the eyes of both shifted to the third person in the room. After all, despite his nearly three years of cohabitation in the Claverhouse-Brant domicile, John Jones was not a member of the family.

Not *yet*, the Widow Brant may have thought, unconsciously—or subconsciously.

Jones, who had been musing on the sofa surrounded by his notebooks, was eying the suicidal moth. They saw him slowly raise his right hand, point a doomful finger at the insect. He said: "Zotz."

"Hey, what's that?" Alfred asked.

Jones blinked, dropped his outthrust hand. And, as if in answer to his host's query, the moth plummeted to the floor with a final soft "plop," its wings folded and its six legs stiffened in death.

"Well, it killed itself," Angela observed. "Pick it up, Alfred, and throw it out of doors."

Alfred stooped and picked up the insect gingerly between thumb and finger.

"Just how did you do that, John?" he asked.

"John had nothing to do with it," Angela said. "He didn't move out of his seat. You saw him."

4

"Er, just a coincidence," Jones remarked huskily. "There it was, banging around. And I—ah, I—well, you know. Playful idea. Really quite childish. I—I am as surprised as you are."

"It just beat its brains out against the ceiling," Angela said.

"But, Angela dear, a moth's brains are not in its head, and anyhow its head is quite undamaged. It really was a most remarkable coincidence," Alfred argued. "You saw John. He pointed his finger at the creature and said something, and it dropped—"

"If the horrid thing's head is undamaged it is all the more proof that it beat out its brains, if they are not in its head," Angela retorted. "Throw it out, Alfred."

Still staring at the moth, which he held almost at arm's length, Alfred Claverhouse, professor of apocryphal literature and heresies at St. Jude's Theological Seminary, walked to the screen door and threw the insect forth into the sultry May night. He turned to resume his chair by the lamp, and saw that John Jones, professor of Semitic languages, was sweeping up his time-and-travel-worn notebooks from the sofa.

"Turning in?" asked Alfred.

"Yes," Jones answered. "Yes. It is really an oppressive night. And after this afternoon—I think I'll try to sleep."

"I'd still like to know how you did it," his host and colleague observed.

"I really—I mean, well, it—ah—quite startled me too," John Jones replied, straightening himself under his double armload of notebooks. "Good night, Angela. Good night, Alfred."

2

IN HIS OWN ROOM John Jones sat on the edge of the
tester bed, elbow on knees and lean jaw in palms, sweating
out in retrospect the crescendo of disturbance that had
reached an apex that day.

Ten days before, in the opening week of the spring term,
Jones had received a letter, an event in itself.

It bore a military frank, an Army postmark and a censor's
seal, and proclaimed in the upper left-hand corner that the
sender was Lieutenant Ansel Judkin, 412th Tank Corps,
AUS. Jones had read the letter through before he recalled
that Ansel Judkin was one of several seminarians who had
resigned in December, 1942, to enlist.

Now here was a letter from Judkin which dismissed any
doubts that the receiver would remember the sender, which
glossed over inquiries and reports on health and spirits, and
came to the point in the second paragraph.

Jones had reread the paragraph, cursing with care and
deliberation the censor who hacked out the place name. The
razored gap in the letter mocked like the empty mouth of a
Greek mask.

"Just as we headed into the valley north of —— the 88s
let loose from the ridge. My tank took one on the nose, and
we scrammed out of there, diving for a shell crater about ten
yards distant. We (the crew of four and myself) were happier than I ever will be over anything except the Armistice

6

when we found that the shell had punched a hole in the roof of what seemed to be a cave, and we wriggled down into it. Then we saw it was not a cave but a sort of vault, built of long, thin bricks that had been painted over but most of the paint had flaked off. You could make out some figures and what appeared to be writing. Anyhow, in the middle of this vault which was about six feet square was a sort of altar painted black and on it was a jar that had been sealed, but the smack the shell had given the place had just about shattered this pot. In it was a disk of very hard, red porcelain or something like poreclain, with all this funny writing on it. It wasn't Greek or Latin. There were other things in the crock. Some powdery black stuff and an obscene little statue of a woman which the sergeant immediately claimed as his share, and a small sickle-shaped knife of some metal still shiny which another one of the boys took just for the sake of a souvenir, I suppose. Anyhow, I kept the disk and I am sending it to you because I remembered how cracked you were on funny languages, and if you can make anything out of it I wish you would send me the translation. You can keep the disk . . ."

There was another paragraph or two about generalities of combat life. Jones, at first resentful of the imputations in "how cracked you were on funny languages," saved the letter against the arrival of the trophy. It would be, he judged from the position of the battling armies, a Phoenician relic in all probability. A temple of Ishtar. That would explain the "obscene little statue," another irksome phrase. One generation's obscenities were another's idols, and vice versa. The Ishtarians had with reverence carried into the unknown seas (which they penetrated to England and even Brazil, some say) the figure of a goddess on whom the portal of life and the fountains of nutriment were purposely and religiously emphasized—for some yokel of a Yankee sergeant to guffaw at five thousand years later. Bah!

So he had saved the letter, and yesterday, Tuesday, the promised relic had arrived in the last mail, swathed in a grimy khaki handkerchief which in turn had been encased in a badly worn—and too-long worn—sock. But when Jones held the red disk in the flat of his hand he gasped his amazement so audibly that the guardian of the campus post office inquired solicitously: "Swallow a bug, Professor?"

Incised on the flinty surface was a pentagram, the mystic five-pointed star every new religion has borrowed from the older. Beyond its points concentric circles had been cut into the disk, and between the lines thus formed had been inscribed, by some artist now fifty centuries dead, a rune—in Astyparaean!

There were not twenty men in all the world who could even have identified the inscription, and of that score not one as able to translate it as John Jones.

Jones had pocketed the disk with trembling fingers. The laws of chance, he marveled, sometimes paid incalculable odds. That the German shell should have missed destroying the disk by inches; that it should have been found at all; that it should have been found by a man with curiosity and intelligence enough to preserve it; that it should have been found—of all the tens of thousands of American soldiers in Italy—by the one man who had been a pupil of the one man who could decipher the inscription!

It was almost unbelievable!

Wednesday was a day on which Jones had no classes. Wednesday was warm and sunny. Wednesday was today. A day a thousand years long.

After breakfast Jones took out the notebook that contained his records on Asianic languages, a sturdy, linen-bound, loose-leaf volume whose three hundred pages were covered with his precise, Graeciform writing, with this and the disk he repaired to the back yard of the house.

There was, of course, no space between the words of the inscription, no punctuation; Jones studied the meaningful scratchings, comparing them with notations in his book, until, after nearly an hour's hard concentration, he was able to make out the ward "thaban," meaning "language."

He worked backward and forward from that landmark to find the beginning of the sentence, and was impatient when

8

Mrs. Brant called him in for a luncheon of French toast, gooseberry fool and iced tea.

"It looks to me like a thunderstorm is brewing," Angela observed, passing him the syrup. "I'm going over to Margaret's after lunch to discuss the Spring Festival program for the Women's Auxiliary and will you keep an ear on the phone, please? I expect a call from Eleanor. She wants to have the white elephant table again this year, I know, but I do want her to have the potted plant table because then I know she will contribute a lot of stuff from her herb garden. And if Ruth calls to find out what I wanted—"

Angela rattled on while John chomped his untasted food and made mental resolve that the telephone could ring itself inside out before he would leave his studies to answer it.

He returned to the shade of the big sycamore tree as soon as he could, sprawling on the cool turf with the disk before him, a pad and pencil in his right hand, his notebook in his left.

"That's got it," he told a startled squirrel some two hours later. "It begins right here."

Chin propped in hand, he began to transcribe.

Thus is gained the power of the silent death that strikes without sound, without wound, by night, by day.

Jones translated the sonorous phrases aloud, unconsciously intoning them with all the unction of a bishop reciting a confirmation service.

First prayeth one in the language of the ancient ones thus:

Khatnoth takhath blecho.

Jones shook his head over the phrase. It was in no language he had ever encountered, unrelated by longest imaginable root to any language he had ever heard about. He repeated it over and over again, rolling the words over his tongue and larynx.

Thunder snarled, but Jones was unheeding.

Now draweth one the symbol of the female and upon it the symbol of the male, the whole making the symbol of the unmoving star which is the home of Zotz . . .

9

The pentagram, of course! As his right hand transcribed the inscription, Jones's left forefinger traced the five-pointed star of the Pythagoreans in the sod. "Damnation!" he interjected, as a twinge of pain stabbed him to the elbow. He had gashed his finger on the sharp edge of a bottle cap, halftrodden into the earth. He put his finger in his mouth and continued:

Now cometh the letting of blood and the drinking of blood and thereafter if ye would strike any living thing dead thou hast but to point thy finger and call upon Zotz . . .

Zotz!

As Jones's lips formed the unintelligible word a deluge of rain descended upon him. He struggled to his feet, clawing to retrieve his precious notebook, scrambling for the pad the wind was lifting, when a blinding flash of lightning left him with no vision but that of dancing blue sparks. The thunder, coming immediately upon the lightning, was the loudest sound Jones had ever heard. Its echoes beat through his benumbed ears and as he blinked to see if the bolt had struck the house, he was paralyzed by the sight of the huge sycamore toppling slowly toward him.

How he reached the back porch, twenty yards away, he would never remember. His feet were not on the top step when the great tree crashed upon the spot where he had been blindly kneeling seconds ago.

A gale of wind, driving the rain in parallel sheets before it, wrenched clusters of twigs and leaves from the fallen tree, clusters as big as bushel baskets. It drove the storm before it, too. The almost midnight darkness was suddenly cleft by the mid-afternoon sun and the light was reflected from ten billion million raindrops on every shrub and tree.

Jones stood, dazed and blinking, clutching his sodden notebook and the oozing pulp that had been his pad of translation. The back yard was a mess, an unholy mess. The sycamore had been split by lightning and then had shattered against the ground.

"My disk," Jones had yelped, then, and splashed across the soaking sod. But the spot where he had been working was a

IN THE LIVING ROOM SAT A STRANGE WOMAN

churned mass of mud from which slivers of lightning-riven wood rose like quills of a giant porcupine.

Still in a daze he walked back to the house and entered it.

"Great Zeus!" Jones cried out hoarsely.

In the living room, sitting bolt upright with her eyes closed and her lips closed, sat a woman. A strange woman. And she was quite naked.

At Jones's exclamation she opened her eyes, her mouth likewise.

"Who are you?" Jones exclaimed. "Or what are you?"

"I—I," the woman stammered, at least thereby demonstrating she was human. "I was just hurrying to beat the storm when—when—I think I was struck by lightning. I don't think I'm hurt . . ."

She looked down at herself and screamed at the sight of her nakedness. She leaped up, and sat down again, embracing herself in the instinctive and universal gesture of modesty and concealment.

Jones reached down and snatched a rug from the floor. He tossed it at her. "Use this," he said curtly. "I'll get something better."

He went to the hall and took his own raincoat from its hook.

"Put this on," he said. "I'll turn my back."

Half a minute passed. "I'm all right now," a faint voice assured him. "Thank goodness I still have my shoes."

Jones turned to her.

"Do you live far?" he asked.

"Just down the main road a little way," she answered. "You—I—you are Mister—Professor Jones, aren't you?"

"Yes, but I'm afraid I have never had the pleasure . . ." The stilted phrases came clumsily to Jones's stiff lips.

"Then I won't tell you," the woman said, suddenly smiling, and quickly concealing the smile under the upturned collar of the borrowed coat. "And when we do meet—formally, that is—I beg of you not to remember this afternoon. And now I'm going to *run*!"

She was, Jones now had the composure to observe, a comely

13

person; not a girl but not—Well, he closed his eyes a moment to recapture the vision of her as he had first seen her.

"I assure you," he spoke, still with Victorian phrases, "that I am the most forgetful man this side of Cnossus. And if you hasten, I think no one will mark your departure."

"Of all awful things to happen," the woman cried, babbling now in nervous aftermath of nightmare experience. "But I am all right. I really am. I'm not hurt a bit. I have heard of things like this, people being struck by lightning and having all their clothes torn off without getting hurt, but that it should happen to me, and here of all places!"

Reaction had certainly loosened her tongue. Jones guided her toward the door, his hand at her elbow disguising urgency as helpfulness. "I always have heard," he said conversationally, "that persons hit by lightning were branded by the mark of the bolt."

"Ooh!" The young woman paused and pulled the voluminous coat from her, to give a quick look at what it contained.

"I'm okay," she sighed, and in that slang word Jones detected now a hint of accent, not Yankee, not southern, nor quite British either. But she went on to thank him warmly. "And not only for what you did, but for what you are going to do for me."

"Going to do?"

"Yes, by forgetting all this."

She turned, ran down the wooden steps, and down the hedge-lined walk to the road. She paused there, looking swiftly to right and to left, and then vanished beyond the shrubbery.

Jones shook himself, and turned back into the house. He walked through the hall to the back porch, and surveyed the shambles of the yard. Angela's chrysanthemums were a puree under all that welter of branches. Alfred's precious rustic garden bench, which he had made himself and doggedly used (although it bit into backbone and backside as with fangs), was less than kindling. But the precious, the unique, the irreplaceable disk—better the whole house had been demolished than that it should have been destroyed.

14

A squirrel undulated across the littered lawn, and leaped upon the stump of the shattered sycamore. It chittered with idiotic excitement.

Jones cocked a resentful finger at the mockmaking rodent.

"Zotz for you," the scientist barked back. "Zotz, Zotz, Z-z-z-zz!"

The squirrel leaped as though stung, and fell back upon the stump, its tail and one limp paw dangling over the splintered edge.

Jones clutched at the balustrade, his own knees sagging. He stared at the squirrel. It did not move.

Jones went quietly into the house.

He encountered Angela charging through the front door, with Alfred pounding up the porch steps behind her.

"John! Was the house struck?"

"No," said Jones, gesturing toward the kitchen door beyond. "No, I was."

3

EVIDENTLY ANGELA'S first thought had been that if a man struck by lightning could still walk and talk he should be able also to render himself such first aid as the Red Cross handbook prescribed. She went out to discover and to lament the shattered tree, the chrysanthemum hash.

Alfred, shocked, was the quicker to recover. The Christian fortitude he had preached for thirty years suddenly came to his own aid.

"It could have been worse," he said. "Except for the tree, no damage done that a year's growth won't remedy. Oh, lordy, my rustic bench!"

And then he quite shamed Angela by saying, suddenly: "John! He may really have been hurt!"

Angela wheeled squashily and hastened into the house, up the stairs, to knock at John Jones's door.

"Are you all right, John?" she inquired.

"Perfectly all right, thank you."

"Are you sure you aren't bruised or anything?"

"No, no, I am not hurt at all. Only a little unnerved."

Angela paused irresolutely before the closed door and then went downstairs to prepare what was for her almost extreme unction—two tablespoonfuls of whisky in a tumbler of water. She mounted the stairs again and besought Jones to open the door and receive the stimulant.

She was reassured at the sight of her boarder. He was pale,

yes, and his hand shook a little as he courteously took the glass, but he was obviously unmarred. With a murmur of thanksgiving she turned and went below again.

Jones waited until she was halfway down the stairs before he closed his door and sat down again upon the bed. He drained the glass absent-mindedly and set it on the night table where his sodden notebook rested in a widening aureole of dampness.

He stared fixedly before him at a scattering of dead wasps on the painted floor boards. Presently he lifted his eyes to find the source of a new buzzing. A great, purse-bellied drone bee, thrust from the hive by the company union as a non-producer even of more willing workers, climbed up the screen.

As if hypnotized, the unwinking Jones slowly raised his right hand, forefinger uncurling to rigidity.

"Zotz," Jones said.

The bee dropped.

"Good lord," Jones murmured almost prayerfully. "What has been done to me?"

Rather, what had he done to himself? No, it was beyond that. The gashed finger at the opportune moment in the incantation; certainly that was no willful act or even an action subconsciously motivated. He had not known the bottle cap was there, had not known what were the words he had next to utter.

"The best thing I can do is to forget all about it," he counseled himself. "Go downstairs, that's what. Talk about the storm. Talk about what's to be done over the damage. I'll forget everything else. Forget Zo—" He forced his mind to become a blank before it could reflect the fatal name of the One who dwelt on the unmoving star.

He joined Alfred and Angela in the ruined garden, where a gaping group of neighbors pointed out that it could have been worse. Alfred was standing close to the tree stump, stirring something with a twig.

"How do you feel, John? Where were you when it happened? Lucky it wasn't close because here is a squirrel just about fried to a crisp. It must have been hit in mid-air as the

17

tree went down, because I found it right here on the stump."

"I'd rather not look," Jones said, revealing a sudden and, to Alfred and Angela alike, an uncharacteristic tenderness. "I'm very fond of squirrels."

Alfred flipped the tiny corpse into the shrubbery with his twig. "Make a meal for a cat," he observed. "Well, that was a close one. But we'll soon have it cleared up. We will have a fine store of firewood this winter, and anyhow the tree did shade the garden too much."

"At any rate, there's nothing to be done about it now," Angela said briskly. "There's dinner to get."

The men followed her into the house, Alfred remaining in the kitchen and John betaking himself to his self-appointed chore of setting the table, a division of work agreed upon when the Claverhouse-Brant cook patriotically accepted a job as junior clerk in the War Department at three times the salary for half the work.

John Jones was thankful for the solitude of his task. He placed the crocheted doilies, laid out the knives and forks and spoons, and pepper pot and salt cellar.

There was the episode of the lightning-struck woman as an eerie epilogue to the storm's demoniacal visitation. It was true, as she had said, that persons had been stripped of their clothing by a bolt of lightning, or, more probably, by the vacuum caused by the discharge. A sudden and horrid doubt entered Jones's thoughts, and he hurried to complete his task so he could assuage it.

He piled three plates in front of Alfred's place, set out the tiles for the hot dishes, and then hastened to the front of the house.

Although he searched the shrubbery for a hundred yards on either side of the entrance walk, even peering at the oak branches overhead, he could find no shred of female clothing —nor of any clothing, for that matter. A pants' leg would have been a joy.

Was, then, this dark woman, an Alecto or one of the other daughters of Ge, a by-product of the disk's dark thaumaturgy? He conjured her to his mind's eye again, as he had

18

first seen her, sitting on the sofa with eyes closed and head thrown back, black hair curling about white shoulders, her full breasts outthrust, her navel an inky thumbprint on the taut parchment of her belly. He recalled her conversation: the strange, husky accents of her voice that made the slangy American idiom sound like an alien effort.

An ague seized John Jones. Zotz he could keep imprisoned in his own mind, so long as it remained strong, but if Zotz had sent one of his handmaidens to lure or to force him in the use—the misuse even!—of the Silent Death, then God help him, God help him indeed. In the mythology of every land were folk tales of strange creatures left behind by lightning flash and thunder peal. Even now the newspapers sometimes bore stories, with tongue-in-cheek effort, of such—

"John!"

Jones's muscles jerked at the summons from behind. But it was Angela.

"John, I've called you a dozen times. Dinner is on the table and getting cold."

Calmed by the homely, workaday-world summons, John Jones entered the house and took his accustomed chair. It was with some trepidation that he bowed his head for Alfred's prayer before meat, wondering whether he, himself, might not vanish in a clap of thunder at mention of the Holy name.

"—Amen!" Alfred lifted the cover of the dish. "Well, well, lamb chops," he exclaimed like a character in Dickens, as if he had not seen them on the broiler fifteen minutes before.

"And I expect you to pick the bones clean," Angela warned. "The points I had to spend, and the money too, on those scrawny little chops. But we are lucky to have any meat at all. Mary suggested that we ought to raise goats. She said she ate goat meat in South America and in the Holy Land and she doesn't doubt but what we have eaten it often enough when we paid for lamb, but goodness knows I wouldn't have the heart to raise a kid and then see it served up in chops and roasts, and besides, who would butcher it?"

"I would," John said. "I've killed—gazelles."

"Ugh! I know I could never eat anything I had seen alive,

19

not even a squirrel, and I hate squirrels. Oh, excuse me, John. You love them, don't you? You wouldn't even look at the one the lightning killed this afternoon. But they do ruin our pears."

John swallowed twice at a piece of lamb.

"Are there any new people in the neighborhood?" he asked.

"New people? No-o-o, I haven't heard of any. You want to change the subject, don't you? I never heard you express an interest in the neighborhood before." Angela smiled. "But there! We would both be awfully happy if you took a closer interest in the community, wouldn't we, Alfred? There are some splendid people in the neighborhood, John, even aside from the faculty, I mean."

But John was silent during the rest of the meal, ruminating on the thought of a ripely lovely witch clad in a voluminous raincoat, gleaning the neighborhood's clotheslines for raiment. He helped stack the dishes and to carry in the coffee and dessert, wondering when and how the Nemesis would next manifest herself; and, so wondering, did not hear the doorbell and was unconscious of the brief exchange of conversation with Alfred at the front door.

"A young lady who said she was Virginia's sister," Alfred reported, returning to his coffee. "She brought back your raincoat, John. I hung it in the hall closet. She wouldn't come in. Said she saw we were still at the table."

"Hey, how's that? My raincoat?" John Jones was jerked from his reverie. "Whose sister?"

"Which Virginia?" Angela exclaimed. "There are scads of Virginias in the neighborhood. But, John! What's this about your raincoat?"

"During the storm this afternoon," John mumbled. "I didn't know who she was, but she was caught in the rain and I knew she belonged somewhere close by from—from the way she was—ah—dressed."

"Well, Sir Walter Raleigh Jones," Angela laughed, a little shrilly. "So that was why you asked if anybody new had come into the neighborhood. John, I do believe you are blushing."

20

If he had not been, John promptly was. He felt his cheeks grow hot.

"Well, I'm glad she returned the coat," he growled.

"Virginia's sister. Now, let me see. There's Virginia Buell, but she has no sister, and Virginia Drew, she had a sister visiting her last summer—no, it was a sister-in-law," Angela murmured, ticking off a neighborhood census on her fingers. "I can't figure out who she might be."

John grunted an "Excuse me, please" and betook himself to the living room and his notebooks.

Virginia's sister. "I can't figure out who she might be." Who could? Virginia's naked sister. She sat right there. *Right there, Alfred, where you are sitting now!* Virginia's sister. Virginia's nixie. A witch should have better sense than to pick a person without siblings to claim as sister. . . . Nonsense, John Jones. The heat's got you!

Angela brought in her knitting. The three sat in silence, then, until the moth arrived to meet uncommon death from the remote hand of the most badly frightened man in all America.

So, then, the event leading up to the tragedy. At the moment of the moth's arrival, John Jones had rationalized the day's extraordinary events and was self-convinced that he had been suffering from illusions induced by shock. The controversy between Angela and Alfred over the means of destroying the moth had madly inspired him to make the ultimate test of the Silent Death. He had not expected the moth to fall.

Alfred had seen it fall.

It was all true, then.

He heard Alfred mount the stairs and pause outside his door, then slowly repair to his own chamber. Jones rose from the bed's edge, folded the soldier's letter and tucked it between the pages of a notebook. He went to the bathroom and as he brushed his teeth he was tempted to point at his own image in the mirror and to invoke the Ancient One in the supreme test of all. But a bristle broke off the brush and

21

lodged in his bridgework, and by the time he had dislodged the irritant he had decided that the greater justice would be to find Virginia's sister and, if she could not satisfactorily identify herself, to incinerate her where she stood.

John Jones climbed into bed, and fell into dreamless sleep.

4

JONES AWOKE the next morning, alert and refreshed but uneasy with subconsciousness of change. The small unease in his breast entirely took possession of him. Yes, the dead wasps and the bee were still on the floor beneath the window. Everything was different, and would forever be different. There was a tightness in his throat, and a swelling in his chest, when he went down the ivory-enameled stairs to the dining room where Angela and her brother already were at their coffee.

"Are you sure you feel well, after yesterday?" Angela asked, after Jones had ducked his head over his napkin in obedience to the mealtime ritual.

"Never in better health, thank you," Jones answered across his orange juice. "Just overslept a bit."

There was nothing wrong with his appetite. As was his custom, he breakfasted well and silently while Angela discussed the day's anticipated problems with her brother. Alfred was told not to forget to notify the Students' Self-help first thing to send over three or four young men to cut up the fallen tree.

The mellow summons of the bell interrupted Angela. The two men rose and went forth from the house to merge in the stream of young men oozing toward the lecture rooms of St. John's Hall.

Jones surveyed the thirty-odd second-year students of

23

divinity, dutifully assembled for further instruction on the kinship of Assyro-Babylonic to Hebrew, Aramaic and modern Arabic. St. Jude's, of course had been founded to produce missionaries to the Moslems. Although few of its graduates had gone forth to the lands of the Mussulmans in recent decades, the study of Levantine tongues was still prerequisite to a B.D., and a curate's post in the suburbs of Washington or New York—where some of the young clergymen learned to wish that Yiddish had been included in the course. But Yiddish, of course, is essentially an Aryan dialect.

Jones cleared his throat and thirty-some young men in sweaters, mismatched and baggy trousers, and dirty shoes looked up if not expectantly, at least attentively.

"Yesterday," Jones began, "we considered the transmutations of certain root words from the Assyro-Babylonic. Thus the A-B word for house, *bitu,* appears as *bayeth* in the classical Hebrew, *baytha* in Aramaic, and *baitu* in modern Arabic. It is interesting to note that in its progress through the cycle the word has now returned almost to its original pronunciation. However, as we pursue the study of linguistic relationships we must not be led astray by superficial resemblances. For example, you could build a tremendous edifice of error on the fact that the Hebrew and the Sanskrit words for 'six' are almost identical, although wholly unrelated.

"Can anyone tell us what these two words are?"

Three forearms were lifted, and Jones regarded the hands limply agitated to signal knowledge. He picked the owner of one, and pointed at him with a "Yes, Chipling?"

Chipling started to rise, and then with a grimace of pain straightened out in the embrace of the broad-armed chair. His long, lean, toothy face turned white.

"Sorry, sir," he gasped, "but I got a sudden pain, like— like a stitch in my side."

Jones clutched the desk, and his face was whiter than Chipling's, his eyes dropped to his ring hand and focused on the bony, well-kept index finger.

"D-do you—do you wish to be excused?" he asked thickly. "Perhaps you had better report to the infirmary?"

"I'm all right now, sir," Chipling said, passing a hand over his face. "Whew! Must have been something I ate. The words, sir, are: Hebrew *shesh* and Sanskrit *shash*."

"Yes, yes, quite so," Jones said automatically. "Quite so." He looked at his watch. Twenty minutes to go. Then another thirty-five-minute period with the senior group in Turkish. From 10:15 on, then, nothing to do—nothing to do but to ponder the appalling power concentrated in that digit of his.

The classroom echoed to the sound of scraping feet and creaking chairs as the students shifted about impatiently, wondering at the professor's silent introspection. Again habit prodded Jones into routine action.

"I would direct your attention to other basic affinities of the Semitic tongues," he said, automatic as a jukebox. "Some of these are not phonetic. They are grammatical idiosyncrasies. For example, in all the languages, ancient and modern, in this group, masculine nouns take a feminine number —and vice versa—from three to ten. Thus the word for goat is masculine but *three* goats is feminine—"

The bell boomed, the chairs scraped, the young men left and another group, their elder ditto marks, entered and sat down.

"It is not generally known that Osmanli is the head of a large family of tongues," Jones began mechanically. "The Turkish language in its several dialects is spoken from Central Persia to Siberia. . . ."

Jones did not remember that it was the same lecture he had delivered the previous Thursday but neither did his students. They dozed, took notes, or boned up on the topic for the next class, according to their natures, and when the bell boomed again, Jones was not the last man out of the room.

Hatless, hands clasped behind him, the gray little man strode across the campus, striving to conceal that his soul was in turmoil.

Evidently he had smitten poor Chipling merely by training his finger on the hapless student. The power, then, was not alone in the *word*. The gesture was the noose about the victim's neck; the word jerked tight the noose. The pointed

25

finger poised the victim for the blow that the word delivered.

Jones's long stride had carried him off the campus onto the dusty weed-bordered meadow where the boys played softball or touch-football on Saturday afternoons. He paused at a wild azalea, over whose red-pink blossoms a swallowtail butterfly hovered in giddy debauch.

Slowly, stiffly, as if shackled by arthritis, Jones raised his right hand and pointed.

The insect faltered in the air. Its wings clapped together, and it fell into the cluster of bloom. Jones whipped his hand behind him, and stooped to observe that the butterfly, lying on its side, was pawing for a foothold with its front pair of legs. As he watched, the creature struggled erect, moved its wings experimentally, and resumed its exploration of the flowers as if nothing had happened.

If a part of the power was in the gesture *without* the word then the word without the gesture must contain the balance of potency, Jones reasoned. He moved closer to the butterfly, which, unconcerned, uncoiled its proboscis into one flowerlet after another.

Jones clasped his hands more firmly behind him, and leaned toward the insect, eyes focused.

"Zotz," he said, firmly. "Zotz."

Nothing happened!

Nothing happened! Jones wanted to shout the good news. The butterfly continued to sip, and Jones stared at it with love, and happiness, and—and then he blinked. Was a mist coming over his eyes? Tears of joy? It looked as if a shadow had fallen upon the flowers, although the fore-noon sun shone down without dispute. The flowers became dull and dusty, although the raggle-tailed butterfly still probed them languidly.

Jones withdrew his left hand from the clasp of his right, and made a grab at the insect.

The cluster of flowers dissolved under his fingers in a puff of pink dust as his hand closed upon the struggling butterfly.

Cautiously Jones parted his fingers to examine his catch. His knees sagged and nausea knotted his entrails as he saw that the butterfly, too, was only a palm-full of ashes which moved, however, with a curious sort of stirring as if the bits of powder and husk were struggling to re-unite.

Jones dashed the horrid fragments from his hand, and trod them into the sod, stamping and grinding with his heels, the while his affronted intellect fought the evidence that by itself *the word destroyed without killing.* He scrubbed his tingling palm with his handkerchief.

"Good morning, sir! Did you step into a yellow jacket's nest?"

Jones spun on the heel he had been grinding into the turf, whipped his hands into his pockets as he turned. His blurred vision centered upon a woman, a woman somewhere between youth and maturity, a woman dark of hair dressed in a yellow sweater whose sleeves were pushed halfway to her elbows and which was pulled down snugly over a heather-tweed skirt. A woman, in short, whom he had first seen naked and then bidding him farewell from the folds of his own raincoat; and he had no words for her.

"You don't have to live up to our bargain that strictly," she laughed. "I returned your coat—and thanks for not remembering."

Now, Jones had been fully determined how he would treat with the woman when next they met—no, when he overtook her. But here she was, no more mysterious, no more sinister, no more beautiful, and no more hateful than any of the young faculty wives or the junior matrons of the suburban community that sprawled around the Seminary.

She could be no Ishtar, no Bel-it. Jones's fingers gripped the stuff of his pockets as his dry tongue clacked out the polite lie that he had knocked down a berserk wasp and was unhurt, and that he was obliged for the swift return of the raincoat although from the looks of the weather he would not soon need it.

"We must arrange to be properly introduced," the woman said, still smiling. "Did the storm do much damage?"

"It will take a long time to find out," Jones said, looking straightforwardly at her. "We have never had a storm like

27

that. It seems, somehow, to have been something more than an ordinary thunderstorm."

"I'm darn glad it was unusual," she answered, almost gaily. Or was it mockingly? "I'd hate to have many such experiences—and so would you, I bet."

Jones had no reply to that. Still smiling, the dark woman shrugged, gestured, and strode into the grove. And suddenly Jones was convinced that the shrug and the gesture, like the faint accent, were not of this place, or time.

He watched her out of sight, and then turned to resume his walk; he waded blindly through the weeds to the gravel country road that twisted westward, the gliff of dread and perplexity stronger upon him.

Here was he, the receptacle of incredible power. So far, at least, he was master of that power. It could not assert itself; it had to be summoned and joined: the gesture and the word. The word he could put from him. If ever it showed a disposition to cross his lips unbidden he could, and would, bite his tongue clear through.

But it was a word in whose utterance the tongue played no part! If his tongue were torn out by the root, he could still pronounce it: Z—!

And the gesture—the most instinctive of all gestures. Would he have to sever his hand to restrain its terrible potency?

One or two persons greeted Jones from their dooryards as he strode the road, and he acknowledged their salutations with a stiff sideways bow. At least, he still presented a normal appearance to others, he thought, a belief he was joyed to confirm when he encountered Mrs. Fairleigh, the Commodore's wife, at a bend in the road. She was pushing a wheelbarrow containing a sewing machine, three bunches of spring onions and a turtle, and she was glad to stop for restful conversation.

"I'm returning Mrs. Gibson's sewing machine, and I thought while I was on the way I'd stop in at the Stanleys' and see could I trade my onions for one of their lettuces," she explained chattily. "I'd use the car, but we only have an A card and anyhow the exercise is good for me. How have you been?"

"And the turtle?" Jones asked affably, ignoring the question.

"Oh, I just thought I'd drop him down in the Grove where he couldn't get run over," Mrs. Fairleigh explained. "Now, what are you doing?"

For Jones had picked up the handles of the wheelbarrow.

"Let me push it the rest of the way for you," he said. "I was just about to turn back anyhow."

And, despite Mrs. Fairleigh's protests, that is exactly what he did, and with more happiness than he had felt all day. "This is the way I shall have to go through life," he thought. "With my hands so full of useful occupation that they can never be raised against any man."

He trudged happily down the road, raising his voice against the wheelbarrow's rumble and crunch, gravely exchanging neighborhood gossip with the Commodore's wife. Not that he had much of that stock in trade, to be sure, but he gave a colorful description of the bolt's shattering effect on the sycamore in barter for news of off-campus romances, pregnancies and parties.

Mrs. Fairleigh observed that it must have been the hand of God that deflected the bolt from Angela's lovely home, and Jones was not inclined to argue the point, having discussed the storm at all only in a spirit of self-discipline. He helped Mrs. Fairleigh carry the sewing machine to the Gibsons' porch, saw the turtle started happily on his way through the underbrush of the Grove, and relinquished the no-longer burdensome barrow to his neighbor to enter the Refectory, where he lunched with the students as was his infrequently claimed privilege.

Out of the ingredients of wheelbarrow, housewife, onions and turtle he had compounded himself a formula, and a salutory one the first dose had proved to be.

5

JONES INVITED a healthy mind in a healthily occupied
body by joining the Students' Self-help crew and piling the
cordwood to which they reduced the shattered sycamore. He
raked and weeded and mowed between classes and after dinner, neglecting his notebooks and his manuscript.

Two days of that and Angela, with delight she somehow
felt shyly constrained to conceal, remarked to her brother
that a powerful change had come over John.

John joined—even led, sometimes—the discussions at dinner, and continued them into the normally silent study-and-
knitting sessions in the living room. Even his posture had
changed, Angela noted with satisfaction. He lounged in his
chair, with both hands rammed deep in his pockets, and dis-
coursed like a normal human being on point-rationing, the
rabies epidemic, and the advisability of establishing a community root cellar.

What John was trying to do was to bar the past from his
mind; the immediate past and that antiquity (in which he
had hitherto lived more intimately than with the New Deal)
out of which Zotz had burst.

Sunday's somnolent afternoon found Jones seeking other
refuge, however. One could not very well cut and cart wood
or set out tomato plants, not on a Seminary Sabbath. It was
Angela's custom to pour tea for such students, faculty members and folks of the neighborhood as might drop in for small

30

sandwiches and smaller talk. Danger lurked there, Jones knew. So he let himself quietly out the back door and headed for the Library where, he planned, he would find anesthesia in the bound volumes of *Punch* which were kept as source material for the witticisms expected of the clergy these days in all utterances except funeral orations.

As usual on Sunday the campus was the playground for the children of the community. It would take years of mellowing before Jones would gain tolerance, let alone affection, for children. He conceded their necessity for the perpetuation of the human race, although he had never heard a single parent ever express the slightest interest in the perpetuation of the human race.

As Jones walked to the Library he noted with professional interest that the children at their games pronounced ancient incantations—eeny, meeny, miney, mo; and ibbity, bibbity, sibbity, sab—mumbo-jumbo handed down from child to child through the millennia. Not from parent to child; no, adults were excluded from the secret order of childhood, where the blood rituals of dead races are recited in otherwise forgotten languages; where white magic (and black) are so commonly employed that a child has but to say "I am an elephant" and is instantly transformed, not only to itself but in the eyes of all its companions, into a great, gray, trunk-curling peanut snatcher.

The shouts and chatter of the youngsters were abruptly cut off by the great oak doors of the Library closing behind Jones. The single big room of the Library seemed to be empty of life. The librarian's desk, just beyond the vestibule, was unoccupied. The bookstacks were being explored by no browsers, and the narrow gallery was bare too. Jones walked through the nearest alley of stacks to the rear of the building, where the inconsequential books were stored. He selected two bound volumes of *Punch*, bound in drab linen, and carried them to a reading table.

It was cool in the Library, and quiet, a garden-close of wisdom whose air was scented with the potpourri of ink, paste and paper. It was contagiously peaceful there, although

31

Jones knew that he was surrounded by millions of words of argument from the exalted to the bitter. At arm's length from him, for instance, were rows of works on eschatology, the doctrine of finality, in all its bewildering interpretations from religious fascism to the pious radicalism of those who hold that God permits man—some men—to speculate on what God has chosen to conceal.

He felt, himself, like a person just escaped from levels so low in purgatory that he had been able to see devils. He was a Samson self-shorn. He contemplated his right hand. Forever locked in those lean, hairless and sinewy digits was the secret of gods who had ruled the worlds when Jehovah was still an apprentice deity overseeing an obscure tribe in Asia Minor. Those ancient ones, banished to a purgatory-in-space by the triumphant God of Christians, Jews and Mohammedans, had artfully sneaked past His defenses to make one John Jones the quisling of the universe by giving him the power of life and death. Well, they had picked the wrong man! A weaker person would have used that power to make himself the dictator of the world. How easy the process would —could—be: To mingle with the crowd at a public ceremony; a harmless gesture, a whispered word, and the President and his Cabinet would be obliterated with the president of the Senate and the speaker of the House. Whoever stepped into the widening breach in the nation's leadership would fall before Zotz until in panic and anarchy the sheeplike public submitted.

Dangerous thoughts, John Jones! He scourged his mind for indulging in such reverie. No, while the ancient gods fretted and fumed on their distant Siberia, John Jones would keep their plot locked in his fist!

His quiet self-satisfaction was interrupted by the sound of a door closing, and the unmistakable click of high heels on the waxed floor. Probably Mrs. Phoebe Jay, the librarian, he thought, sighing a little. A gabby, if well-meaning, old hen, Mrs. Jay; a monomaniac on the subject of southern genealogy, which made her archly claim a scientific kinship with Jones as a fellow antiquarian.

The steps came closer and were suddenly echoingly loud as the woman turned a corner of the stacks. She said "Oh" and Jones looked up.

It *was* Mrs. Jay, and Jones blushed as he realized he had been hoping it would be somebody else, even the dark-eyed woman of the storm.

"Why, Professor Jones, you startled me," Mrs. Jay said. "I thought the place was empty, and here you are, more quiet than a mouse. Not that we have mice. I pride myself on that. Nor any kind of vermin. Silverfish and suchlike."

Jones raised his head, nodded and smiled, and returning his eyes to another Partridge cartoon showing an ironclad Britannia rescuing a robed and grateful figure labeled "India" from the tiger Revolution.

"I just stepped out the back door to see if my assistant were on her way," Mrs. Jay explained defensively. "She seems to be late, and I don't want to miss dear Angela's tea."

"I'll keep an eye on the place," Jones mumbled, his insincerity demonstrated by his failure to remove said eye from the book.

"Would you, Professor Jones? Oh, that would be so kind of you. I don't believe a soul will come in before closing time. Except Miss Finster, of course. She should be here any minute, and she'll lock up at six."

"Miss Who?"

"Miss Finster. She took Helen Frazer's place when Helen married Oliver Ordway after his ordination last June. She is one of the old Fairlington Frazers, you know."

"She wasn't so old," Jones observed mildly. "Not over forty."

"Why, Professor Jones! She was scarcely over thirty. But I must run. Miss Finster—oh, here she is now! Miss Finster, this is Professor Jones. This is Virginia Finster, my new assistant, Professor. Well, I really must run."

She walked, however, to the exit, leaving Jones half risen from his chair, his hands braced against the tabletop, looking up at the Storm Woman.

"So, now we really have been formally introduced," she

said, with her ready smile. She was wearing a green, belted frock of linen with a wisp of orange scarf tucked in at her dark throat.

"And that's your name," Jones nodded like a china figure with a pivoted neck. "Virginia Finster! That explains it."

"Explains what?" Virginia came closer and leaned against the table.

"About Virginia's not having a sister."

"Me? I have no sister. What do you mean?"

"Neither has one of the other Virginias, and the second one's is maybe just a sister-in-law. Angela wasn't clear."

The young woman's smile stiffened, and she withdrew a pace. Jones blinked his eyes.

"Excuse me, Miss Finster," he said. "I'm not talking in riddles. When you came to the house the other night to—ah—return my raincoat, my host thought you introduced yourself as Virginia's sister. And his sister, Angela Brant, wanted to know which Virginia, there being several, and it being doubtful whether any *has* a sister so far as is known, anyhow. You can see that, in connection with certain events of the day, it was all most alarming to me."

The woman retreated another step, her smile vanished now.

"I don't get it. If you thought you loaned your coat to somebody's sister, who didn't have a sister, then you might have had reason to worry. But I brought back your coat, didn't I?"

"It had nothing to do with the coat. At least, I mean—by the way, your clothing!"

Virginia looked hurriedly down at herself.

"What's wrong with it?" she asked, hand fluttering from throat to slide fastener at her waist.

Jones felt his neck turning red, but his interest was scientific. "I mean, the clothes you—well, lost."

"Why, I picked them up and hid them under your coat, when I left of course." Now Virginia's throat and face were red, and her manner chill. "They were pretty well soaked but hardly damaged. The zippers were melted, that's all, and yet there was not a mark on me."

34

"Yes, so I—ah—very remarkable. But you found the garments."

"Right where I was standing when the lightning struck," Virginia said. "I suppose you went out and looked for them, to make sure my story was true and that I wasn't a refugee from a nudist colony?"

"I'm sorry," Jones said. "I have violated the compact of forgetfulness. You are here now, Miss Finster. Where did you come from?"

"From the Professional Women's Placement Bureau," she said, and added, "of course."

She seemed to Jones's mind to be a little resentful of his blunt questions, and he thought to himself: She probably thinks I am a lecherous old goat, a semireligious recluse, a reluctant male virgin reveling in an intellectual fornication.

"No, that is not what I mean." He smiled. "I have no doubts as to your qualifications as a librarian. In fact, I have no interest in them. I mean, are you one of the Lynchburg Finsters or the Fayetteville Finsters, as Mrs. Jay would classify you? It is, I might say, an unusual name. I detect from your speech that you are not from these parts. Please excuse me. I do not mean to pry. You see, I, too, am a stranger here, more familiar with distant places. But I came here deliberately, for a positive reason—"

"And so did I," Virginia Finster interrupted. Her cheeks were flushed, and her eyes very bright, Jones noticed, as she pulled a chair from the table and sat down.

"It may surprise you," she began, addressing her clasped hands resting on the table's edge, "that I know more about Horus Apollo than about St. Paul, and that I am more familiar with the ritual of Koromantin obeah than the rites of the church. And yet it shouldn't surprise you, of all people."

She raised her smoky eyes to his bleak ones, and then restored her gaze to her interlaced fingers. Jones, his own hands still flat on the table top, felt his knees sag and he groped for his chair with his skinny backside and was grateful when he felt the pressure of the hard oak, for had the chair not been there he would surely have dropped to the floor.

35

So, he told himself, this was the introduction to the show-down, and he wondered how best to make his riposte.

"I am," the woman continued, "a student of ophiolatry. It is, I admit, a queer specialty for a woman. You know what it means—the worship of snakes."

Jones nodded, not knowing whether his signal of assent had been seen by the woman because he did not raise his eyes from his flattened hands. He thought to himself: She thinks she is sly; she makes half-revelations to sound me out, to test me; she is an agent of Zotz, but a knowing one, not unconsciously one like Lieutenant Judkin; well, I will fight Zotz with Zotz and at the first thrust from her I will impale her scaly spirit on that slightly tremulous forefinger, there.

But Virginia kept on talking: "I have spent a lot of time in the West Indies. Haiti, of course, where voodoo and obeah have become commercialized, tourist attractions. Trinidad and the Virgin Islands are better, and Dutch Guiana even better than those. But the war came and I had to quit. I had to. I haven't any money of my own. I must work. I mean, I have to work for others so I can do my own work.

"I came here. They needed an assistant librarian. I have done research enough in London and Vatican City and Mexico and Washington, to know the system of every library. It was easy to get the job. The salary is fair, but nothing to what a war job pays; the work is easy. Between fetching books and putting them back I have plenty of time to give to my own work."

Jones was puzzled, but he was also relieved. It was a plausible story, one that he could readily and sympathetically understand. If this woman, this confessed initiate in the serpent cult, was an emissary of Zotz as he had first suspected, then she was certainly identifying herself in a most oblique manner. From her terrifying introduction ("I know more about Horus Apollo than of St. Paul") she had retreated into commonplace gossip of personal economy.

He looked up at her, for maybe this obliquity was guile of a proof distilled by the Master of Serpents himself.

Virginia Finster returned his gaze with smiling frankness.

36

"Of course," she said, "I wouldn't tell this to a soul but you, Dr. Jones."

Jones smiled back at her, and felt all his muscles relax. His hands stole back to his pockets. Why, this woman was doing what he himself was doing, for the same reason and in like cause.

"I think," he said affably, "that we are achieving a complete understanding. In fact, almost a partnership, because I am in a like situation."

Virginia's expression became almost radiant.

"Oh, I'm so glad!" she exclaimed. "I am awfully grateful. Honestly it is too generous of you."

"What do you mean?" Jones felt the muscles of his hands grow tense again.

"You won't misunderstand me," the woman said, leaning forward so her full breasts swayed beneath the thin linen. "We are both disciples of science, you might say, and we serve a common master, so to speak, just like these men of religion serve God without hope of getting rich."

"Yes?"

"Isn't that so? I knew all about you, Dr. Jones. Who doesn't? And as I said, you won't misunderstand me even if you think I am too fresh when I tell you I came here because you are here. I've been wondering how in the dickens I could explain that, and how I could make a deal with you, and you come right smack out and talk partnership yourself."

The breezy idiom only made the confession sound more sinister in Jones's ears. Had Virginia Finster transformed herself into a plumed serpent the effect on Jones could not have been worse. Horror congealed his muscles so that it was with stark physical effort that he worked his jaws to speech. Priestess and spy of Zotz, sent to act as his acolyte and yet taskmaster!

"So—so—so that is it," he stammered, and a great rage melted fright and the loathing; he stood up, toppling his chair. He saw Virginia stare at him, and there was still laughter in the depths of her eyes. Jones raised his hand, and Virginia Finster's right hand unlinked itself and rose likewise.

The Word was shaping itself behind Jones's teeth when the Sabbath calm was ripped by a shrill scream, and another, and another that merged with a demons' chorus of yells beyond the windows. It seemed to Jones as if the Ancient Ones had dispatched a commando force of screeching devils to stay his hand, and he had a momentary vision of a writhing column of Furies twisting down over the Seminary's sedate dormers to the rescue of the basilisk Finster.

6

JOHN JONES SHOOK the horrid vision from his eyes, and saw that Virginia was already at the door, tugging at its stubborn weight. But when he moved, it was with a quickness that placed him by her side before the dark woman reached the bottom of the Library's granite steps.

The screaming had given way to a medley of treble gabbling, punctuated by the noise of many doors slamming, and cut across by shouts of inquiry that were masculinely hoarse or femininely shrill, but the cause of all the disturbance was at first not apparent. The twenty or more children who had been playing in the Grove had gathered into an uneasy clot from which arose the chorus of squeaks and chirps. One very small child had fallen, some yards distant from the group, and a weeping little girl was tugging at the youngster's hand, dragging it toward the crowd and effectively preventing the child from regaining its feet and faster progress.

"Just a fight," Jones deduced as he overtook Virginia. "Some nasty little girls' hair-pulling match. . . ."

But now the squealing chorus fell into a pattern of words, and Virginia gave a small scream as the phrase suddenly sounded clear: "Mad dog, mad dog."

"And it is," she gasped, seizing Jones by the arm. "See it, over there by the pines?"

Jones did see it, a feisty little spotted beast with a fringed pretzel tail, and quick as there was terror in that sight there

39

was also pity for the tortured dog that blundered into trees in its delirium and snapped at the lichened trunks with drooling, blood-flecked jaws.

The children, seeing Jones and Virginia so close and the haven of the Library thereby revealed, started pell-mell across the grass toward them. Now there was screaming again, the rearmost imploring "Wait for me-e-e"; and the noise and the motion, in the aching eye and brain of the rabid dog, made new agony for the animal, and it charged toward the little horde.

"Oh, God," Virginia moaned. And again she moved first and fast, running toward the children, and past the first and fastest of these, crying to them to run into the Library.

She was not running to meet the children; that was at once clear to Jones. She was running to meet the rabid dog, to invite and to divert his attack, and Jones, more stung by shame than any male protective instinct, pelted after her through the panicky gackle of children, slapping at the small hands held out to him.

As he ran, Jones looked around for a branch or a billet of wood; confused memory reminded him that a dog will bite at that which is thrust at it. The technique is to kick the leaping beast smartly under the jaw as it jumps to the attack.

But there was not even a twig on the neatly raked campus, and Jones, who felt as if he were running on a treadmill, saw the dog swerve from Virginia's skirts and cut in behind her toward the nearest knot of stumbling, sobbing young-sters. He stretched his arms toward the children in a futile gesture to make the distance between them and himself smaller, and the sight of his own outthrust hands reminded him of the sudden power that they contained.

But how to use it? The dog's erratic course prevented a clear target; there were children between the animal and Jones, and behind the dog came Virginia, and behind her the vanguard of Seminary students raced, brandishing shovels snatched up from aid-raid precaution equipment, and cur-tain rods, and prayer books.

Whatever had to be done had to be done in scant seconds. And all at once Jones knew what to do, for in the onracing students he recognized Chipling and on the instant Jones halted, stretched forth his right index finger, and with lips clamped between his teeth he pointed at the ravening dog although that gesture had of necessity to embrace all between him and the animal, and those who were close behind.

Half a dozen children fell prone, as if wire snares had enmeshed their feet, and a thin wail went up from those helplessly distant at the appearance of the youngsters' sudden collapse in the path of the snapping, snarling dog. But that animal also sprawled, stiff-legged, in the paralysis of Zotz, and even as Jones saw the furry menace made harmless he also saw Virginia pitch headlong to the sod.

For the moment it took Jones to leap over the sprawling children the campus looked like the kodachrome of a battlefield. The gray little man reached the dog, which had begun to twitch and paw for a foothold and he pointed again.

"Zotz," said Jones, and the dog's body became convulsed and then it relaxed in death.

Jones stood over the creature's body, and as his hand dropped an ague jerked at every nerve in his body while nausea clawed at his guts. From under twitching eyelids he saw the tumbled figures of the children stir and rise and resume their running, and as they regained their feet, Jones uncontrollably lost his. He sat down abruptly, jittering like a sackful of mice.

"The dog is dead!" he heard somebody shout. "The dog is dead!"

"The dog is dead!"

The shout was a shuttlecock of joy tossed back and forth, and the children who had achieved sanctuary came crawling back. The students formed a cordon around the dog.

"Stand back, stand back," they warned the crowd. "Don't come too close."

"Is it really dead?"

"Don't touch it."

41

"Get a sack or a box. It ought to be sent to the Board of Health."

"The ground ought to be decontaminated where he's lying."

The Dean pushed through the crowd, his collar a pulp, anxiety making a mask over his kindly face. "Was anybody bitten?" he asked. "Are the children safe? Whose dog was it?"

No, nobody had been bitten. Yes, the children were all safe. Nobody knew whose dog it was. It had run into the Grove acting queerly. Little Robin Smith had been the first to take alarm. No, it wasn't Robin, it was the little Robbins girl. No, it wasn't, either. It was, too! But nobody had been bitten, no, sir.

"It must have been on its last legs. Lucky it dropped dead when it did."

"Yes, it was an act of God."

Jones heard all this as from a distance, as one hears remotely in a doze. He stood up, brushing dust and bits of grass from his suit.

"The lady in the green dress ran out to shoo the bad dog away."

The lady in the green dress? Where is the lady in the green dress? Ah, Miss Finster!

"Miss Finster, that was a very brave thing to do."

"No, not at all. Everybody here was doing the same thing. These boys, and Dr. Jones—where is Dr. Jones?"

"Here he is—there he goes—Dr. Jones! Professor Jones! John!"

Jones found his sleeves grasped. Half a dozen of the faculty were trying to shake hands with him. Alfred, still clutching a chipped saucer (one of Angela's precious Wedgwood "Edme" pattern) stared up at Jones.

"I saw it," he exclaimed. "You were the only one to keep your feet. Splendid, John. Foolhardy, but magnificent."

"Nonsense," Jones said, sidling off. "Miss Finster was there ahead of me."

"Where is Miss Finster? Oh, Miss Finster! Such presence

42

of mind. Such courage. You and Dr. Jones deserve a medal. You really do."

"But what would you have done if the dog hadn't dropped dead right at that instant?" one blonde junior faculty wife asked. "What would you have done?"

"Naturally, I would have bitten him," Jones snapped. Alfred took his arm and tugged him away from his admirers.

"Easy, old man," he counseled. "No time for sarcasm, John. I know you feel all upset, but these folks are only trying to show their appreciation."

"I did speak like a damn fool," Jones grudgingly admitted, as Virginia broke from her admirers and came up to him, two grimy patches on her skirt showing where her knees had dug into the sod in the spasm Jones had had to distribute so widely. She, too, put out her hand but Jones pretended not to see it.

"Quite an interruption in our conversation," he said dryly. "We must continue it at some other time."

"You were very brave," she said formally.

"I only followed your lead."

"But I failed in the pinch. Fancy, falling down like that. Just like the children."

"Almost as if they had all been struck by lightning," Chipling put in. "Bang! Even the dog. But it hit him for keeps."

"I almost went over on my—on my face, too," one of the other students observed. "Felt the funniest stitch in my side. Staggered me, just as the others went down. But I saw Dr. Jones standing there with his hand stretched out as if to ward off the dog that was jumping for him, and I just kept on going."

"You saw Dr. Jones doing what?" Alfred squeaked.

"He just stopped short and held out his hand at the dog," the youth repeated. "Bravest thing I ever saw. But then it dropped dead, fortunately."

"Did it feel like a stitch in your side, sort of?" Chipling asked. "Because that happened to me in the classroom the

43

other day. It was—why, it was in your lecture, Dr. Jones. Remember?"

"I can't be expected to remember all the juvenile belly-aches in this academy," Jones snarled, and he strode off at his most vigorous pace. Alfred started to follow him, but Chipling plucked him by the sleeve.

"Excuse me, Dr. Claverhouse," he said. "But my experience in class, the other day, and Miss Finster flopping over like that, and Shrewsbury said he felt a twinge just from running a few yards—"

"Yes? Well, what of it?"

"Do you suppose there is something wrong around here?"

Jones, departing, heard the question and almost broke into a run. Alfred looked after him, anxiously.

"No, of course there is nothing wrong except with yourselves," he snapped.

"Do you suppose the water supply is quite pure?" Chipling gently insisted. "Or it might be a dietary deficiency, sir. We get an awful lot of spaghetti and starches at Refectory. Maybe we ought to send a committee to see the Dean."

"I suggest you consult the Infirmary. Probably smoking too much and not enough exercise," Alfred snapped. "Certainly before you start organizing any CIO committees you ought to see a doctor."

"Yes, sir," said Chipling meekly, and turned away. Alfred started forth on John's track fuming. As professor of the subject, he could smell a heresy farther than his sister Angela could smell a cake scorching, and to him, twenty-seven years on St. Jude's faculty, any accusation that the Seminary did not take perfect care of the physical, as well as the spiritual, needs of its membership *was* heresy. Contaminated water! Dietary deficiency! Contaminated fiddle-faddle and dietary humbug. It was rebellion. It was communism. Still fuming, he caught up with Jones, who slowed down at his hail but did not turn to meet his friend.

"John," Alfred puffed, "I wonder if you realize the significance of what that lad was saying back there?"

"I didn't hear a word of what he said," John lied.

ALFRED CAUGHT UP WITH JONES

"Well, it's a bad business, a very bad business," Alfred snorted. "Such accusations. Wanted to send a committee to the Dean!"

Oh, so! Mr. Chipling loomed now as a menace, John thought. Well, there was a way to remove him or any other menace. Chipling had complained of a stitch in the side; the next one would be a proper stitch. Heart trouble would be the diagnosis. A clear history of heart disease. As easy as that. But what about the Finster woman? That remained to be settled, too. So she had come to the Seminary only because he was there. We serve the same master, hey? But what was Alfred prattling about?

"But perhaps you are not aware of it, I said, hey, John?"

"Aware of what? A lot of silly talk and loose accusations?"

"No, no, no! I took care of that. I hope I did, anyhow. I mean, the coincidence. Have you marked that?"

"What are you talking about?"

"Weren't you listening to me? I said, the other evening there was the moth. You stretched your hand out, and it dropped dead. And now the dog. I said, it was a strange coincidence."

"Yes, it is. I hadn't marked it, no. But now that you mention it—!"

"This is your second distressing adventure within a week," Alfred continued. "Two very narrow escapes from almost certain death. I am still not sure that you escaped the first one unscathed."

"I am perfectly all right, Alfred," Jones replied. "And in my lifetime I have had narrower escapes at closer intervals. And now I think I shall rest a bit before supper."

But Alfred was not to be denied.

"Please do not misunderstand me," he went on doggedly, following Jones up the porch steps and putting a delaying hand on the screen door. "This is something of which you are probably not aware, if it exists at all. But there they are, the dog and the moth. And that obnoxious pinko, Chipling, although he did not die. It may not be very scientific, but don't you think that you may have become charged with electricity from the lightning, John, and when you point—"

Jones wrenched the screen door from Alfred's detaining hand.

"Damn it, let me alone," he choked. "Don't ask me any more silly questions and stop bothering me, please! Please!"

He stamped up the stairs to the refuge of his chamber, leaving Alfred Claverhouse clutching the porch railing with both hands, his eyes brimming with shock and pain and compassion.

7

IN THE LIVING ROOM Angela and Alfred were in their accustomed niches—she knitting, he reading.

John eased himself back into his favorite chair. "Well, this is a nice quiet evening after a hectic day, isn't it? I certainly need a good, long dose of peace and comfort."

He continued to muse how most good it would be—or could have been, rather—to round out his lifetime in this atmosphere of contentment Alfred and Angela had achieved. Even the tempest of war blew gently here; if it caused them to suffer, it was intellectually because of the badness that was abroad and the sorrow that had come into the lives of friends whom the war had bereaved. But the war would pass, and the sorrows would be healed, and the years of serenity would again wholly enfold this household—and both Angela and Alfred knew that, because they believed implicitly in the invincibility of goodness. He envied them their faith—and their ignorance.

Jones was almost a-doze when a sharp rap of the door knocker sounded with all the effect of a warship's call to general quarters. Angela thrust her knitting into its bag and her hands into her hair. Alfred buttoned his coat, recited his "now-who-can-that-be-at-this-hour" ritual, went to the door. Jones stood up, irked at the intrusion upon his synthetic happiness, wondering whether he could retreat to the kitchen and creep upstairs unseen. But he was dismayed to hear

Alfred say: "Why, yes, he is at home. He is right in the living room. Come in, please."

Alfred re-entered the room and stood aside to usher in two persons. One was a small and hairless man with a very long nose and a very wide mouth, and the other was—Virginia Finster.

"Good evening," said the dark woman. "This gentleman came to see me, and I told him it was really Dr. Jones he ought to talk to."

"My sister and I were just about to retire," Alfred said, "so you can have Dr. Jones all to yourselves."

"No, please stay," John exclaimed, full all at once with unease and foreboding. "Good evening, Miss Finster. And good evening to you, sir."

The hairless man smiled jerkily. "I am from the *Star*," he said. "You know the *Star*, of course."

Sudden nausea was instantly drowned in wrath as John Jones stiffened to the shock of that bald pronouncement.

"Yes," he said thickly. "I know the Star. Why do you come here? Why don't you go back to your damned Star?"

The wide mouth gaped. John heard Angela gasp, and heard Virginia vent a nervous laugh.

"I'm sorry you take it that way," the hairless man said. "I—well, nobody has ever spoken to me like that before. I'm just terribly sorry you feel that way."

Jones sat down abruptly.

"The unchanging star," he snarled. "The star that never moves."

"I admit the *Star* is pretty conservative," the man argued, "but it isn't quite as bad as all that, Dr. Jones. Offhand, I would have guessed that you would prefer it that way. But I've got to turn in something to the boss and if you would just tell me—"

"Tell your boss that John Jones wishes he had been eaten by jackals in the Libyan Desert rather than endure what has befallen him. Tell him that I defy him."

"My God, I can't tell him that!" the man cried. "I'd hate

50

to think what might happen to me—and to you too—if I repeated that."

"I don't care what happens to me," Jones said earnestly. "But I do care what happens to my friends. Why did you have to come here? Couldn't you have summoned me to your accursed star? I would have gone, gladly. Why must these innocent people be involved?"

He glared at Virginia, to make it plain that he understood her complicity and did not include her in his category of innocence.

Angela spoke up beside him.

"John, dear, I really don't mind," she said. "I know how you feel. Indeed, I do. Everything was so tranquil after all that horrible upset. But I am sure this gentleman is only doing his duty, and that it would be all for the best if you humored him."

"Angela, you just don't understand," John said wearily. "I might as well tell you all about it. Then, no matter what happens, you will at least understand and, at the most, you might be able to prevent what this emissary from the North Star—"

"Excuse me," the hairless one interrupted eagerly. "I knew you must be mistaken. It isn't the North Star. It is the Evening *Star*. I don't know anything about the North Star. Never heard of it, in fact. And look here, if you all want to talk like characters in a Thorne Smith novel, it's okay with me, so long as it's on the subject. I might get some good gags out of it, but let's turn the comedy on the dog, not the poor old *Star*. Our local man turned in a couple of sticks on it but the boss thought it was good enough for a suburban feature, so he sent me out to get the piece. But all I get is double-talk."

"I can understand every word you say," Jones sighed, "but their sequence is gibberish. Now let us sit down and settle everything here and now. I suppose that explanations are due everybody."

"That suits me fine," beamed the man.

"Mind you," Jones said, "I am making no apologies.

What I did I would do again, and shall do so long as I am able. I want that understood."

"Why, certainly, Professor," the stranger said soothingly. "But in the interests of accuracy, a moment ago you said you would rather be eaten by buzzards than to have had it happen, and now——"

"He said jackals," Angela put in.

"Huh? What about jackals?"

"Eaten by jackals, not buzzards."

"Oh!" The small bald one gave Angela a long, searching look. "Yes, let's be accurate, by all means. By the way, Professor, do you have a recent photograph of you I could borrow? Of course, we have some stock shots of you in the morgue. . . ."

"Of me in the morgue?"

"No, not of you being—wait a minute! I'm being kidded again. Damned if I don't feel as if I've got mixed up in a Jack Benny broadcast. If you meant that as a gag, Professor, it's the moldiest one in journalism, and if you were serious, 'morgue' means library in newspaper talk."

"That's where Dr. Jones was when he heard the children scream," Angela volunteered.

"Where?" sighed the man limply. "Where?"

"In the Library." Angela put a tinge of accusation in her voice. (In the Library—with Virginia Finster!)

"Oh, to be sure," the bald one choked. "Well, that's a starting point. Just what were you doing in the Library, Dr. Jones?"

"What was I doing in the Library?" Jones almost roared. "Why, I was doing my laundry, of course. I was stuffing animals. What does one do in libraries as a usual thing?"

"Take it easy, Doctor. Excuse me, please. I'm just trying to get a human interest angle. I do wish you wouldn't persist in that hostile attitude. Let's look at it objectively. When a world-famous scientist turns up chasing mad dogs in our circulation area it is a good story whether you like it or not. And it will be in tomorrow's paper, whether you like it or not. And you are more apt to like it if you give the newspaper the straight dope."

"What newspaper?" John asked.

"There you go again. Well, no matter what you think, I believe the *Star* to be the best damn paper in the country. These days I could get a job anywhere and at more money, too, but I like the *Star*. I'm proud of the *Star*. I would rather work for Ben McKelway than—that for St. Luke getting out the Scriptures."

The man stared defiantly at Jones, who at first could only stare back, until he found his voice.

"Why didn't you say you were from the Washington *Star* instead of all that gibberish about Venus?" Jones demanded.

"Sir, I never mentioned Venus."

"Well, that's what the evening star means to me."

"I'm just terribly sorry, Doctor. I thought we were pretty careful on the *Star* but I never encountered such a passion for accuracy. Now, just please tell me, Dr. Jones, how you rushed out barehanded to meet the mad dog."

"I do not think," Jones said slowly, "that I am called upon to abandon my hard-won privacy for the public amusement."

"Look, Doctor," the reporter said patiently. "We have been all over that ground already. A man with your devotion to accuracy and exactitude ought to be willing to co-operate. I told you the story would be in the paper regardless. Why not give it to me straight?"

"May I explain?" Alfred asked with polite eagerness. "I have an idea that it all goes back to a thunder—"

Alfred and his theories! Without taking breath Jones drowned him out with an acceptance of the *Star* man's request as baffling to that person as it was gratifying. "You're right," Jones cried: "Here it is in a nutshell. I was in the Library reading. Miss Finster was—well, at her duties. We heard the children scream. We rushed out. I don't know how she intended to stop the mad dog because, well, I didn't think she had the Word. Anyhow, the dog eluded her. My plan was to pick up a stick and make him worry it. I could find no stick. And then, of course, I suddenly thought of the gesture. All this happened very quickly, mind you. I hadn't thought of using the power when I followed Miss Finster. Anyhow, the dog dropped—"

"Not so fast, please," the reporter begged over his racing pencil. "What do you mean, that Miss Finster didn't have the word? Did you have the word?"

"Certainly," Jones replied. He pushed his hands deeper into his pockets and pinched his eyelids tightly together. "I said 'Zotz' and the dog—!"

He sucked his underlip between his teeth and bit hard. God's teeth, what was he saying?

"How do you spell 'Zotz'?"

"Oh, I don't know. Forget it. It's just a word. Anyhow, that's the whole story."

"Just one thing more. How did you get the word, as you put it? And if it was passed to you, why didn't Miss Finster get it?"

Jones felt sick. Silently he cursed himself for the self-betrayal he had wrought in his impetuous effort to divert Alfred from the reporter—or the other way around.

"Well, never mind," the reporter said. "If you can't remember who it was that passed the word that a mad dog was in the vicinity, I guess it doesn't hurt the story any. I guess that does tell the story in a nutshell. Miss Finster was too modest to tell me of her part in the drama, but she was downright gossipy when compared with the Doctor, here. I know how you folks here at the Seminary feel about personal publicity, but after all it was a pretty brave thing and the public has a right to know. Besides, it will certainly help us in our drive against rabies. I suppose you are in favor of a compulsory muzzling law, Dr. Jones?"

"I am not," Jones replied curtly. "It is fascistic."

"Fa—fa—good gravy! How it is fascistic, Doctor?"

Simply by his determination to oppose everything the Man From The Star advocated, Jones got himself into a corner, and he knew it.

"Start by muzzling dogs," he snapped, "and you have opened the way to a law muzzling people." He had an inspiration: "Then there will be a law to muzzle the press, and how would you like that?"

The reporter shrugged. No matter how Jones felt about it, he had his story, or enough for a story. There was just one little point to clear up, and if he could get Jones to elaborate upon an esoteric remark the moderately good story would become a ring-tailed lallapalooza. And so, in the manner of his profession, he stalked his prey with every appearance of nonchalance.

It was a trick that usually worked with congressmen, but the reporter was matching wits with one who had spent a lifetime playing the same game, in trading with Bedouins, Iraqi and other Semites. Jones smiled inwardly as he watched the hairless one's body relax while a look of bland innocence came over his face.

Then came the expected question: slowly extracted from verbal wrappings.

"I guess that's about all, and thanks a lot," the reporter said. "I'll say again I'm sorry for the misunderstanding. It was all my fault. I can promise you that there won't be anything sensational in tomorrow's *Star*. Just a straightforward, factual account that will—oh, just one thing, Dr. Jones. Earlier you mentioned something about a certain *power* you exercised."

"Power?" John fenced. "Power?"

"Well, I may have misunderstood, but as I recall it you said you had not thought at first about using the power" He shot a quick, sharp look at Jones, who had to summon all his long-tutored self-control.

"Did I say that? The power? I meant, of course, the power of the human will in conflict with the brute," Jones said blandly. "I am sorry if I made it sound esoteric. The only problem was to divert the dog's attention, and the solution was to employ the power of will first of all to impose self-discipline and then to outwit a dumb animal crazed by pain."

"That's very interesting," the newspaperman, if such he was, observed. For quite suddenly Jones's scalp prickled as the thought came to him that perhaps this wide-mouthed inquisitive stranger was what he had at first suspected him to be, and had with sinister deftness assumed the character of a reporter to bait a pitfall when Jones had proved too wary and defiant. Thus the tribesmen of Khairpur, he remembered, trapped the most *zabardast hoshyar* tigers: they would dig a deep pit whose radius was longer than the *sangdil chita's* leap, and fix stakes of sharpened bamboo in the bottom and cover the hole with a lattice of reed covered with grass; but from the center a pole projected as tall as a man, to which a hunter would be lashed, dressed in a woman's sari, who would wail in a high falsetto as if he were a poor old *bhangan* who had become lost while hunting *nimkin machhli*.

Jones came out of his reverie with a start. The room was quiet and its occupants all looked at him as if waiting for an important pronouncement.

"Excuse me," he murmured. "I was daydreaming. Did somebody say something?"

"I just happened to remember something else you said—asked you about the 'word' and the 'gesture' you kept mentioning," the stranger said with an air of guileless nonchalance.

"I don't remember saying anything like that at all," Jones lied suavely. "You must have confused it with something Miss Finster said. She is the authority on words and gestures."

"No, I don't think—" the man said, turning inquiringly to Virginia. John Jones followed his glance. The dark woman turned a blank face to the two.

She would guide the spy from Zotz to him, would she? Jones pressed his advantage home:

"Yes, Miss Finster is an expert in voodoo and obeah, a student of ophiolatry," he said. "That's snake worship, you know. If any mysterious words and gestures were employed, she may have done so. I didn't."

"Is that so?" The stranger turned his whole attention to the woman, who flushed and forced her shoulders against the chair's back as she was pressed to explain. Alfred's eyes grew rounder, and Angela's lips tighter, as Virginia curtly defined herself. Yes, she had gone far afield in Haiti, in Trinidad

56

and Surinam; she had frequently been attacked by dogs; yes, and by snakes. No, her interest in voodoo and serpent worship was wholly scientific and academic.

At last the stranger reported that he had more than enough material for his story and not enough time to discuss more than his sincere thanks to all, and with the promise again that tomorrow's *Star* would do handsomely by all concerned he bowed himself out.

Virginia remained to apologize politely for having abetted the intrusion, although the wrath in her eyes burned through the limpid contrition of her words.

"No need to apologize," Alfred assured her courteously. "In fact, it was an interesting demonstration to me. I did not know that the press so aggressively pursued a subject. With sermons and church notes, for example, one has to take them in to the paper oneself and even then they are not always printed."

If Virginia was waiting for a word with John alone she was disabused of hope when Angela took her knitting from its bag and seemed to settle down, late as it was, for a long stint. But as soon as Virginia left, Angela rolled up her wools.

"Well," she said, as Alfred returned from the hall. "Well!"

"Well, indeed," Alfred replied. "It is well past our bedtime, too, and I am sure we are all exhausted."

"A snake worshiper! A voodoo priestess! A fine scandal that will make when the newspapers get through with it," Angela exclaimed. "I shall speak to Phoebe Jay. Indeed, I think I shall speak to the Dean. I do think, John, that you might have refrained from telling the newspaper person what you had discovered about that woman. You should have told it to us in confidence. Of course, she cannot remain."

"But, Angela, dear," her brother soothed the outraged Mrs. Brant, "Miss Finster is not a worshiper of snakes or a voodoo woman. She is just a student of those things."

"So she says! Of course she would try to explain it that way. John, I think you had better keep an eye on her."

"I'm doing just that," Jones replied with such emphasis that Angela looked at him sharply, to detect a double meaning to his quick assent. She started to say something, and then went silently about the business of preparing the house against the night.

But Alfred lingered, evidently in an unease of perplexity and embarrassment, and trying to conceal both under random observations on the evening's interview. John was not to be misled, however. He made only monosyllabic and indefinite reply, and followed Angela up the stairs. So, there was nothing for Alfred to do but follow John.

At a more propitious time, he determined, he would closet himself with Jones for an earnest talk, a consultation for Jones's own good. There had been much in Jones's amazing responses to the *Star* man that must have been meaningless to the reporter, to Angela, and no doubt, to Miss Finster; it was meaningless, by and large, to Alfred himself, but just the same it held a dark and formless significance in which there was an element of terror. Something had happened. Something dire. Whether it had happened to Jones's mind, or his body, or to his soul, Alfred could not determine, but was determined to learn.

In his prayers that night Alfred Claverhouse made long and especial mention of his friend, and went to sleep with the thought that John had dwelt too long alone and with the past; even in this Christian community he kept to himself while poring over things beyond resurrection or the need for it. What John needed was a vacation with healthy exercise, a fishing trip perhaps. His thoughts merged into a dream of John and himself in a canoe . . . there was tug on his line . . . he reeled in . . . his catch fought and dragged on the line until it broke water . . . not a fish . . . a huge moth that barked like a dog and beat the water to spray with its wings . . . John pointed his finger at the giant insect whose dripping wings blotted out the sun. . . .

8

SERENITY WAS RESTORED the next day, a serenity with certain electric overtones for Jones as his students regarded him with an admiration obviously not inspired by his mastery of Arabic.

It was pleasant to be liked and admired, John discovered, and the discovery was almost as exciting as finding the clue to the inscription on the disk. Respect he had had, and in large measure; respect of the laborer in many lands, whom he never beat and always paid fairly and on time; and respect of the savants of every civilized land. They reverenced him for his knowledge and his authority, but he had walked alone and, except for fair payment, slept alone. Not until the past week had he realized how dependent he was becoming, without knowing it, upon kindly human association. Not until this day—a day externally gray and drizzly—had he discovered the inner warmth that is kindled by amity.

He had his lunch in the Refectory and found the clatter of tongues and crockery cheerful, not aware that he, himself, imparted that cheer to a normally irritating noise; Jones was happy, and did not know it. Pleased he had been, often, and frequently glad—even delighted a few times—but happiness was new to him, and not yet understood. When he entered the house that evening humming, all unbeknownst to himself, one of the livelier hymns ("On Our Way Rejoicing") Angela almost dropped the lemon pie she was carrying to the oven.

59

"Is that you, John?" she called from the kitchen.

"None other," Jones called back. He walked through the hall and leaned in the kitchen doorway. "Hello," he said, "what's cooking?" And chuckled a little to hear himself.

"Lemon meringue pie," Angela said. "With the crust made out of graham cracker crumbs."

"Lovely," said Jones. "I hope it is a big one and that there is nothing else for dinner."

"But look at you, all damp," Angela cried. "You should have worn your raincoat."

"I didn't realize it was raining," Jones replied, touching himself breast, side and thigh. And he hadn't realized it, at all. Now, at mention of the raincoat and the reminder it provided of the opening incident in his week of woe, some of the bleakness of the day entered his soul. He felt his old, gray self as he climbed the stairs in obedience to Angela's advice to "get something dry on before you catch your death."

In his room he emptied his pockets of wallet, spectacle case, loose change, memoranda, handkerchief and fountain pen; he draped his damp coat on a hanger and hung his trousers from a patent spring clip, absent-mindedly picking grass cuttings from their sodden cuffs. Below, the knocker clamored against the front door and shortly thereafter a pair of female voices seemed to duel politely, and Jones decided to put on a fresh shirt against the possibility of a dinner guest. Then his heart seemed to stutter at the thought that the arrival might be Miss Finster and, looking something like a stork in his billowing white shirt and spindle shanks, he opened his door to listen. Whoever it was down there talking with Angela—or talking at her, for the voice was clicking along without interruption—it was not Virginia.

Trousers donned and buckled, John sat swallowing hard against the cud of woe that was more bitter to a palate sweetened by brief happiness. Then Angela called him to come down, if he were not busy, and he descended the stairs to greet Mrs. Phoebe Jay, the librarian.

Angela held out the afternoon paper. "Here," she said, "is the interview with the reporter last night."

60

"You have certainly brought our little institution into the limelight, Professor—you and Miss Finster," Mrs. Jay declared in her starched voice.

"It is not as bad as it might have been," Angela told him, indicating the item with a wedge-shaped forefinger.

Jones took the proffered journal without thanks, the lingering remnant of the day's happiness suddenly defiled for him as a rose is defiled without loss of form or hue when a dog lifts his leg against the bush. He took the paper to the window and saw that

THEOLOGIANS REPEL MAD DOG
CHARGING CHILDREN AT PLAY

A rabid dog, the nineteenth captured in the metropolitan area since January 1, was prevented from attacking a group of children playing on the campus of St. Jude's Seminary Sunday afternoon by the prompt and courageous action of two faculty members, Miss Virginia Finster and Dr. John Jones.

The dog, in the last stages of the disease, virtually succumbed in the middle of the crowd of youngsters as Dr. Jones and Miss Finster kept its attention diverted at grave risk to their own persons. The carcass was turned over to the local health board which today confirmed that the dog, whose ownership has not been traced, was rabid.

Dr. Jones is the world-renowned authority on ancient languages and religions, leader of numerous archaeological expeditions in the Near East. Miss Finster is the assistant librarian, who has been engaged in research in voodoo in Europe, the West Indies and South America and, like Dr. Jones, is accustomed to meet danger with coolness and quick thinking.

Interviewed last night at the institution, both Dr. Jones and Miss Finster modestly refused to discuss their joint heroism. Each tried to give greater credit to the other. They had been in the campus library, a few yards from where the children were playing, when the screams of the latter interrupted their conference.

61

Heedless of their own safety, they kept the dog from attacking the children while herding the youngsters to shelter in the library. Neither had a weapon of any kind, Dr. Jones for once complaining at the efficiency of the groundkeeper in not permitting even a fallen branch to be found to fend off the lunges of the rabid cur.

Asked why they had not stopped to consider their own safety, Miss Finster explained she had often had to battle savage dogs in her explorations of secret jungle temples of savage cults, while Dr. Jones asserted he had complete confidence in the power of the human intellect over the brute after years of experience in the hyena-haunted ruins of desert-buried civilizations.

The dog, a spotted mongrel, was evidently homeless but was known in the neighborhood by the unusual name of Zotz.

Jones read the account through a second time, and some of his confidence and cheer was restored.

"As you say, Angela," he said, returning the newspaper, "it could have been worse."

"And I must say," Mrs. Jay creaked, "that it is an unusual way of becoming acquainted with the unique accomplishments of one's colleagues."

"Such as——?" Angela prodded insinuatingly.

Jones cut in: "Such as the groundkeeper's accomplishment in keeping the Grove scrupulously clean?" he said through the ghost of a grin. Mrs. Jay's feud with the groundkeeper over unmended mudholes in the paths was perennial.

The librarian regarded him coldly. She wet her lips.

"Or," Jones hastened to forestall her comment, "are you as surprised as I am to learn that I used to practice hypnotism on hyenas? I don't think hyenas were mentioned during the interview, do you, Angela?"

"There is no use in you trying to make a joke of it, Dr. Jones, if you will pardon me for being blunt," Mrs. Jay said. "Believe me, we all feel honored to have a layman of

62

your scholarly ability on our faculty, and your bravery yesterday—"

"It was equally, if not paramountly, Miss Finster's bravery."

"And I certainly don't mean to belittle her part in preventing tragedy," the librarian continued primly. "But a student of voodoo, Dr. Jones! An explorer of secret jungle cults and temples! We will not be able to keep a servant on the place, do you realize that?"

"On the contrary," Jones chuckled, "I think you will not only keep them on the place but keep them in order, by dropping a hint that if they don't do better work Miss Finster will put a hex on them."

"Believe me, you wouldn't take it so lightly, if you had dealt with Negroes all your life, the way I have." Mrs. Jay pronounced the noun "negras."

"You know," Jones replied, "I have heard members of the colored races say exactly the same thing." His voice assumed the slightest mockery of the librarian's tones. " 'You wouldn't take it so lightly if you had dealt with white men all your life the way I have.' "

"Of course, you are a Northerner and wouldn't understand."

"Well, do you think there is anything to voodoo?" Jones demanded.

"Certainly I do not. I am a Christian! I do declare, Dr. Jones, you can be most vexing."

"Well, then, one of two things is certain. Either you have —and I don't mean you, personally, but all you professed understanders of the Negro—either you have failed in your Christian duty to convince them that voodoo is a sham and a fake or else they have better proof that there is something to it. Besides"—he raised his hand against Mrs. Jay's indignant I-do-declare—"what you call voodoo is just one small phase of the cult of demonology which has more communicants, in the aggregate, than your—our church, or all Christianity, for that matter."

"Then I take it you mean we should be humbly grateful

that a voodoo woman is connected with the Seminary?" Mrs. Jay snapped.

"Humbly grateful?" Jones shrugged. "No, I wouldn't use those words. But we have Jewish rabbis come here to lecture on the Pentateuch. Why not? And why not a voodoo professor, and a Buddhist and a Mohammedan? We might as well become conversant with what the opposition has to offer They have a lot of customers."

"Dr. Jones, you are making sport of a mighty serious problem," Mrs. Jay protested. "He is pulling my leg, isn't he, Angela?"

"You never can tell with Dr. Jones," Angela observed. "But I do think the Seminary will get a bad name if it becomes a matter of newspaper gossip that there is a voodoo priestess on the staff. I must say I think she ought to be sent packing."

"She's too good-looking, I always said," Mrs. Jay added by way of final damnation.

"Now look here," Jones barked, all humor dispossessed. "Let us get at the fundamentals. This Finster woman is not a witch. She is not a voodoo priestess. She does not conduct occult rites or savage cults. She professes to be a student of them, that's all."

"If she doesn't believe in voodoo why does she study it?" Angela asked. "There are so many worth-while things to study."

"Now, for heaven's sake," Jones protested. "Alfred is a student of heresy. He even lectures on heresy. Does that make him a heretic?"

"That's different," both women chorused.

"How is it different?"

"Well, it's just different," Mrs. Jay said. "You wouldn't understand."

"Oh, Z-z—!" Jones bit his lip. Mrs. Jay smiled brightly at him, gathered her belongings, and explained she had to hurry and she hoped she hadn't delayed Angela's dinner preparations but she had just felt that she had to stop in; and so Angela talked her guest to the front door. But Jones

64

picked up the newspaper and reread the article, and whether it was the printed words or the ones he had uttered in debating the women, he felt good; he just simply felt good.

He might not have felt good later had he been able to pursue this transcript from the minutes of the Board of Trustees of St. Jude's:

"Mr. Grimper requested the Chair to call upon the Dean for comment on the unfortunate publicity the Seminary was receiving as a result of the mad-dog scare of the previous Sunday.

"The Dean said that much as he disliked any newspaper notoriety, he did not believe the current publicity was as unfortunate as might have been the case had anybody been bitten by the dog.

"Mr. Grimper said he appreciated that, and that the thanks of the board were due the employees who had, apparently, driven off the dog at risk of being bitten, but that he was sure the reputation of the Seminary would suffer from publication of Dr. Jones's claims that he had conquered the dog by sheer will power, and especially by the allegations that Miss Finster was proficient in certain black arts known as voodoo.

"The Dean replied that he was sure this was all newspaper talk and that the only interview granted by Dr. Jones and Miss Finster was with the greatest reluctance and in the presence of another member of the faculty.

"Mr. Grimper said that nonetheless the Seminary was being held up to public scandal and ridicule and suggested it might be wise to terminate Miss Finster's services with payment of a substantial bonus and a strong letter of reference, and that Dr. Jones be given leave of absence for a few weeks.

"The Dean said that in his opinion such action would only cause greater gossip and notoriety, in which the Chair concurred. The Board adopted Mr. Grimper's motion that the Dean investigate the allegations that Miss Finster was conversant with voodoo and to make inquiry into her status and Dr. Jones's as professed Christians. . . ."

Jones was happily unaware of those proceedings, also.

Faculty gossip never reached him, however much he contributed to it by his mere being.

But most of the rest of the community heard it, with sundry embellishments. Members of the Board told their wives, who told their friends, who told their hairdressers, and so the news percolated to Holy Hollow that something like a modern trial for witchcraft was in the offing; and so, on the following Sunday, the Chapel was as crowded as it ever was on an Easter Sunday.

9

ST. JUDE'S SCANT SCORE of buildings is loosely
clustered over about as many acres on the slope of a shallow
depression bitten semicircularly from the ridge overlooking
the Potomac estuary. From the lower lip of the amphitheater-
like valley a road dribbles through trees to the trunk highway
to the eastward.

On the flanking slopes of the upland vale, ranged along the
spurs of the trifurcated road, stand about two dozen homes
occupied by families that have none but spiritual (and that
sometimes attenuated) affiliation with the Seminary. They
are, in the main, families of some substance economically,
composed of individuals averaging more than the mental age
of 13.5 years which is the nation's norm: retired service per-
sonnel—most of them reactivated to desk commands during
the war—and upper-bracket civil servants married to ex-
schoolteachers.

Some fifty or sixty adults, then, all known to each other
by their first names, surcharged with self-respect, comprise
the community known to its inhabitants as the Neighborhood and to reputedly jealous outsiders as Holy Hollow.
Their organization is almost tribal. Holy Hollow has no
political entity; no mayor, no fire department, no police
force, and no more in need of such than it needs an airport
or a poorhouse. Its people are happily self-sufficient and
sometimes unhappily aware that the communities beyond

their perimeter deem them smug. At such times they make determined, concerted effort to prove themselves gregarious and cosmopolitan, but whether it is the suspicion with which their sporadic amiability is received or the sufficiency of their own community, the Holy Hollowites soon withdraw their tentacles of amity and return to their tribalism.

Of the same tribe, but a different totem, are the faculty families of the Seminary itself. The females of what may be called the clerical and the secular totems of the tribe mingle indistinguishably. The males display an occasional differentiation when the clericals don the reversed collar, but otherwise these are liberal-minded, pipe-smoking Low Churchmen who can drink as lusty a julep or brew a hot buttered rum with as proper ritual as the other male Hollowites. The latter—always of course eliminating the student body as a transient element—are reasonable men of the world who, in the aggregate, know something about everything of importance, including dogmatic theology. Having by proximity accepted religion as an intimate factor in life's routine (and by that process having come to regard their clergyman neighbors as men working at a job), nobody was ever ashamed to stay away from church or, for that matter, to attend it three times of a Sunday if he so willed.

From that community, however, John Jones was a man apart. He was known to everybody, and knew many of them by name. But he took no part in the endless croquet tournaments or the sporadic stunt nights. The others, being individualists within the tight compass of community, generously and amiably allowed him to walk his solitary path. Although he was not of them, he was with them, and that sufficed him and them both, most pleasantly.

Miss Finster, however, was too recently the newcomer to have achieved any Holy Hollow status. She was an outsider on the inside still on trial. Presently she would be asked to attend a meeting of the Women's Auxiliary, where the First Degree of membership in the Neighborhood would be administered and her privilege to greater intimacies determined.

So, when word got around that Jones and Miss Finster

were "in trouble" as a result of the mad-dog episode, the first impulse of the Neighborhood was to draw up in a tight circle, like musk oxen, to present a solid and menacing front to the outside world. And that they would do, too, if only for the sake of the Hollow's unblemished reputation, but what they would do within the circle for its own abiding comity was something else again, or might be something else. And for guidance everybody went to church the next Sunday.

Unexpectedly they got that guidance from the pulpit.

Normally the sermons, delivered by the faculty members in rotation, were of high literary quality which managed to utilize the Lesson for that Sunday as the rack upon which to hang a philosophical dissertation on some ethical problem which had never bothered any member of the congregation. In short, they were very good Episcopalian sermons, and the students took notes on them as if they were lectures, marking the point at which the preacher folded his hands and leaned over the edge of the pulpit, and at what juncture he reared back and spoke from the chest.

They were sermons satisfactory to everybody: teacher, apprentice and audience. Colonel Johnny Trotter did once remark to the Rev. Dr. Ronnie Cavern, from his secure position as twice senior warden, that all sermons ought to be debates in which members of the congregation could argue back to the preacher. It was a very funny remark, and widely repeated.

But going to church in Holy Hollow had many of the aspects of the old New England town meeting. If no controversies were raised within the walls of the church, many were debated to crystallize the Neighborhood's communal viewpoint immediately outside its walls, after the services. And in those discussions the preacher of the day was usually at his most assertive.

On this Sunday, the day's week since the mad-dog episode, the Rev. Dr. Archer Uzziel took the service, and "Uzzy" was a radical who had been known to convert a text from St. Paul into evidence that it was not unchristian for labor to go on strike. On this Sunday he was even more the iconoclast, for he chose to base his sermon on a local occurrence. That of itself was extraordinary. In fact, under different circumstances it might have been considered impolite by some of the parish. But the sermon was on the theme which every person persent had in mind even during the processional and the creed, so Uzzy could not be fairly accused of introducing temporal problems into the service.

He reminded the congregation that just a week ago a vicious and rabid dog had suddenly been loosed upon their happy, well-ordered community to the imminent peril of its children. It was only by the Grace of God, he said, that this day's service was not one of mourning and of prayer for the bereaved and the suffering. But the Lord had chosen as His instruments two persons, comparative strangers, who had gone forth with what the unthinking might term recklessness and with what all would agree was consummate bravery to avert the greater tragedy at the risk of personal disaster.

With that, several necks were craned to locate Jones and Miss Finster in the congregation, and smiles and nods were directed to them, which Virginia only acknowledged by bowing her flushed face lower. Jones, however, was completely unconscious of the kindly signals, as he was of what Dr. Uzziel was talking about. Church attendance being almost obligatory upon members of the faculty, he had long since learned to insulate himself against the urbane harangue from the pulpit and automatically took refuge within the sound-proof chamber of his inner consciousness at the sermon's start.

He felt Angela's elbow nudge him. "He's talking about you," she said, and Jones, who had mentally been evaluating the benefits of a life as a forest fire watcher in the High Sierras, grunted audibly and focused his eyes on the minister.

The preacher, having made his point, now proceeded to drive it home into the teeth of the scandalmongers and the self-righteous by allegory and metaphor. ("He's certainly piling it on Old Man Grimper," the knowing whispered.)

What Uzziel was saying, when Jones began to listen, was

that there was a mad dog loose in the world; had he been a Methodist he would have identified it as the devil; had he been a Catholic, he would have identified it as skepticism; had he been almost any other member of the faculty he might have identified it as materialism. Uzziel came right out in calling it fascism, which he said was worse than rabies. The Pasteur treatment might cure the bite of a mad dog but there was no cure for fascism except amputation. He identified fascism with the Antichrist, and vowed that all who fought it were doing God's work.

Now, there were persons, the preacher said with calculated and meaningful emphasis, who deplored some of the allies we were forced to embrace in the battle with totalitarianism. There were some who, regardless of cost, would have relished the defeat of Communist Russia by Nazi Germany, for between the paganism of the Nazis and the economics of the Communists they saw little choice. But if God chose atheist Russia as one of His instruments in the extinction of fascism, then it was beyond mortal prerogative to question the fact. Whatever their beliefs, the Russians were fighting bravely, and dying uncomplainingly, in support of our common cause, which we also believed to be God's cause. For us to demand that the Soviets adopt the two-party political system and the Nicean Creed before we acknowledged them as allies, he said, was as absurd as a desperately wounded man inquiring into the political and religious beliefs of the surgeon. It was not the first time that God had employed instruments which to the mortal mind were of dubious and even evil merit in the accomplishment of His ends.

If the preacher had actually had any intention of imbuing his hearers with a more tolerant attitude toward the Soviet, he failed. Everybody, from the pale and tight-lipped Mrs. Phoebe Jay to the acutely uncomfortable Virginia herself, translated that sermon into terms of Jones, Miss Finster, Old Man Grimper, and the nearest feud. Everybody, that is, except Jones. He had heard only the latter half of the sermon and had therefore accepted it as literal in intent, and only accidentally—but most peculiarly—of personal application.

71

He sat on the edge of his pew, erect, eyes wide and fixed on the clergyman as he completed his ritual, and it took another nudge from Angela to make him realize the congregation was standing. As he jerked himself to his feet he seized Angela's arm with a grip that sent tremors all the way to that worthy woman's shoulders, yes, and to her bosom and beyond, to dissipate in most curious flutterings under the stout bastion of her girdle.

And he didn't let go, even in the final kneeling; as the exodus began amidst a hum of voices more vibrant than during any prayer, Jones said: "Angela—Alfred!"

"Yes, John," Angela whispered. Alfred was already out of the pew and in the aisle comparing hypertensions with Mrs. Josie Stonewall.

"Thank you, my dear, for bringing my attention to the sermon," Jones said, still gazing at the now empty pulpit. "It has shown—it has meant—it may change the whole—I can't explain. (Oh, excuse me, Mrs. Clevis; good morning!) I'll want to talk to you. And Alfred, of course. Later. I have to have time to think. (What? Who? Oh, excuse me, Mr. Brooker; good morning!)"

10

ON THE CHURCH LAWN the throng, not yet quite sure of itself, stood about saying "Splendid sermon, wasn't it?" and "How is your dear mother?" until Virginia Finster emerged and Colonel Trotter stepped up to her to say this was his first opportunity to commend her on her bravery, and the dowager Mrs. Macandle (whose great-great-grandfather had once owned thousands of acres thereabouts and indeed had made a gift to the Seminary of the very ground it stood on) introduced herself and asked Virginia to tea someday. Within a very few minutes the confused young woman had been invited to join the Auxiliary and to help tend the fancy-work booth at the Spring Festival.

When John emerged, still holding the arm of a rather pale Angela, some of the Neighborhood people's attention was diverted to him, but Jones only looked vague and said: "Oh, thanks, but excuse me, please." With that he dropped Angela's arm and stalked off through the Grove toward home, which caused some of the women to wonder aloud how things stood between him and Angela, "and, don't you know, all this notoriety might cause him to up and marry the Finster woman. That's the way such things usually turn out, but they are not as a rule happy marriages, my dear."

Angela herself was the most confused person in all that gathering. Dr. Uzziel's allegory had not been lost on her, but what it had meant to John to cause him to react so enigmatically—and excitingly—was beyond her power of deduction. She had not agreed with Uzziel's thesis at all, her opinion of Virginia Finster not being wholly objectively attained. But she saw how the land lay, a vista fair to Virginia and saved from dreariness for herself only by the afterglow from John's strange stammerings—and the clutch of his hand.

She courteously invited Virginia to her Sunday five-o'clock, turning aside the equally courteous declination with: "Oh, bother the old Library! You can get one of the students to watch it for half an hour." And then, Alfred radiant and perspiring by her side, she went home to turn up the heat under the chicken stew and to make dumplings. To her brother's query as to how she had liked the sermon she merely said: "It seemed to excite John strangely. He has gone on ahead to—to think, he said."

The meal was a quiet one even for the Claverhouse-hold (Alfred's ancient pun) with John silent through it all. After the dishes were done Alfred helped Angela make twenty small lettuce sandwiches (oh, the blessing of ready-sliced bread again!), wrapped in towels to await afternoon consumption. The tea tray was made ready and covered with napery, and all this time John sat on the porch, tilted back in a willow rocker, where Alfred and Angela presently, and wordlessly, joined him.

Alfred read, his ears and half his mind alert for some sign from John. Angela knitted, which left her mind free for worry.

She was determined John should have all the privacy he desired until he was ready to speak. Just what it was that had happened to him in church she could not understand, and her guesses were stubbornly pessimistic. He acted almost the way she had seen adolescents behave when they "got religion," but there was certainly nothing in that sermon to arouse a religious frenzy in the most emotionally unstable high school girl, let alone as coldly self-controlled an agnostic as John Jones.

He certainly couldn't be thinking of getting married to

74

MRS. MACANDLE ASKED VIRGINIA TO TEA SOMEDAY

that—oh, dear Lord, no!—that Finster woman out of a sense of duty and protection. The bare thought made her mental monologue incoherent. No, there wasn't anything, not a thing, in that sermon to make John romantic, not even in—not toward—that grip on her arm, that clinging grip, that clutching—it couldn't—suppose it was! Suppose he felt that she—that their—but there was nothing in the sermon, there was nothing in the sermon, to make him—

It was all impossible to figure out, and so Angela sternly commanded herself not to think about it, employing that mental process (with which so many women are gifted) which eliminates the insuperable by denying its existence; thus department store bills which exceed the bank balance are annihilated simply by being hidden under the desk blotter.

That self-hypnosis dulled all apprehension, until Angela found herself saying "Do you know, Eleanor has the best recipe for making summer squash palatable? She puts a little chopped dill in it." And having said it, her voice echoed in her ears like a stentorian shout, and she was forthwith mortified at having broken the silence.

But even if she had said that Eleanor had a recipe for making centipedes palatable by serving them in a kerosene sauce, she would not have elicited comment or notice from John Jones. John was still thinking. He was reaching a conclusion. John's solution did not come with the speed and splendor of lightning, although the inspiration that had ignited his train of thought had been electric. Instead, discovery dawned upon John, little by little, and as each bright facet was lighted his mounting excitement was communicated to the watchful pair who loved him.

Finally he chuckled, and the echoes of that small sound of mirth sent a thousand chimes ringing in Angela's heart. But she was alert now not to intrude upon rhapsody, even to divert any small share of the healing happiness to herself. Alfred, too, only looked up from his book and then exchanged glances with Angela, smiled, and went on reading.

Now John, of course, was not happy, and his faithful

friends were prematurely pleased. But he was contemplating a joke, a cosmic joke; nay, greater than a cosmic joke! An interstellar joke, a practical joke, of such proportions as to make all Jove's previous mirth but a giggle.

He became grave again, his eyes turned ceilingward but focused inwardly. There were practical considerations.

Through the screen all the green smells of a ripened spring sought to lead the stodgy trio by the nose, away from walls more substantial than the bough-barred sunlight. Angela was beginning a new worry, that her five-o'clock guests would begin arriving before John's meditation was completed.

And then, quite suddenly and without changing so much as the position of his eyes, John spoke, and had he spoken Etruscan or behind smoke, his hearers might have been less surprised.

"How can I get an audience with the President?"

Angela snarled her knitting; Alfred dropped his book, and made no effort to retrieve it.

"Hey, how's that?" Alfred stammered. "You mean—*the* President?"

"Yes, I mean the President of the United States."

"But, John, why on earth do you want to talk to the President?"

"Because I want to get into this war."

"Great day in the morning," Angela gasped. Her ball of wool joined Alfred's book on the floor, lazily uncoiling. And then, realizing at once that it would be most unpatriotic to demur and that there was about as much chance of John's being accepted as of herself being drafted, she managed a weak "How splendid, John."

"John, you're too old to fight," Alfred said, startled into bluntness. "You know you are. What put that idea in your head anyhow?"

"Uzziel's sermon."

There was the answer to all Angela's morning worries. Well, at least he was not planning to marry the Finster woman.

"It seems to me," she said, "that you are doing a very important work here, and you will not be easily replaced. But if you want to do something more directly associated with the war, I should think there are thousands of opportunities short of shooting off guns."

"Of course!" Alfred exclaimed. "That's what you want to see the President about, isn't it, John? To get an appointment to some war enterprise like the Red Cross or the—er—WPA, or one of those?"

"How do you get an audience with the President, then?" John repeated.

"I don't suppose it is easy, especially these days," Angela observed. "You probably arrange it through your senator or congressman."

"No, I don't want to get mixed up in politics," John said.

"Well, I always say, do it the simple way," Angela declared. "If I were you I would just write a letter to the President asking for a five-minute interview on a matter of importance, and see what happens. He can't do less than say no, and he—oh, goodness gracious, here come the Clevises and Miss Pealbody already. Alfred, help me carry out the tray."

Alfred rose with alacrity. So did John, but not to assist in the Sunday afternoon rites. He continued through the house and out the back door, and naïvely turned his steps toward the Library, at which the brow of every eye in line of vision was raised. Old Jonesy going to his regular Sunday rendezvous with the Finster gal!

Nobody on earth—not anybody—could have guessed that what was in Jones's mind was a bit of shrewd taunting, and a morsel of anticipatory gloating-over, of (how could he describe Virginia?) a she-demon; maybe not a she-demon, but certainly a creature of Zotz and a not-too-well-disguised *agent provocateuse* of Antichristendom.

When Jones entered the Library and found himself cordially greeted by a somber-faced youth from behind the desk he remembered, too late, that Angela had said something about expecting Miss Finster at her tea. For a moment he thought of returning thence, but the memory of one such chirrupy session served to propel him toward the rearmost bookstacks, there to pluck a random armful of volumes to erect as a barricade behind which to resume his cogitation.

This is what he thought:

Brooding timelessly in their exile on the Unmoving Star, watching, waiting, all the banished old gods had to bide the moment when accident fractured the seal that Jehovah had placed on the earth, to their impotency. Growing meaner, more vindictive, by the century. Celebrating no doubt, with monstrous orgy the imitations of their dark doctrine in Georgia and Mississippi and New Jersey, in China, Russia, Italy, Japan and Germany.

Out of that finally came war, and out of the war-torn earth came the hidden formula for the restoration of Zotz. While Jehovah and Jesus, and, no doubt, Mohammed and Confucius, toiled to maintain the Kingdom of God, the exiles managed by patience, cunning, and perhaps black magic to get that formula to the one man who could decipher it. And so the Red Disk came to Jones.

But the gods would have been mad indeed, and impotent to a degree beyond the survival of evil on earth, had they not provided the inheritor of the disk with some kind of surveillance. It could even be that these servants of the Ancients were not aware of their mission, for he was forced to admit to himself that the behavior of Miss Finster and the reporter person was either bafflingly subtle or caused by a faulty connection with the Source of the Power.

Be all that as it may, there was he, Jones, and he alone, the sole and final repository on earth of that Power; he could slay with a look, a word, a gesture. The gamble the Ancients had been forced to accept was the recipient's ability to overcome humanity's greatest frailty, selfishness.

Well, thought Jones, and he thumped the oaken table, the odds had not paid off. He would use the Power of Evil for good. He would use it secretly, positively, and if need be at cost of his own life. It might even be best for the world if its employment was at such extravagant personal cost.

But—he would need help: the help of one man, and only one man, could help him. The President.

His plan was simple. It would cost the government nothing, in time or money or trouble.

He would follow Angela's suggestion and write a simple, straightforward letter to the President asking for a brief audience. Good Angela, with her sturdy common sense, her direct and forthright manner; Jones told himself he did not know how fortunate he had been to find inclusion in a home so ably managed, his every creature comfort provided without intrusion on the precious privacy of his mind. He wondered what kind of man her husband had been, and whether he had appreciated the paragon he had had to wife.

Am I falling in love with her? he wondered. Or am I, in my middle years, in love with comfort and cleanliness and an endless supply of clean shirts with all buttons intact?

But when he thought of Angela's person his mind pictured only her full, patrician face complete with eyeglasses, and her square, sturdy hands. Whether the balance of her anatomy possessed any attributes of contour and contact to make a man—even of fifty-four—sacrifice brain power to groin power . . . ?

Slowly the chaste image of Angela in his mind's eye became obscured and then dissolved, to reveal a torso blue-white yet somehow rosy too, and shaped to enfold and absorb the lover; a torso erect as an Egyptian goddess's, its proportions Grecian, darkly accented there and there, and again here, and, broadly, below, with the four accentuants of each feminine outcurving. And instantly the vision was gone, as if someone had thrown a rug or raincoat over it.

Jones blinked, and saw nothing except the book stacks, all shadowy now, and somebody coming toward him through the gloomy aisle of embalmed thoughts. He arose hastily, looking at his watch—past six o'clock, and a safe hour to return to Angela's.

"Why, hello, Dr. Jones! I didn't know you were back here."

"Miss Finster! Good evening. I was just thinking about—that is, I was thinking."

"I've been here half an hour, and didn't hear you at all. You should have a light, Dr. Jones. I just came here to see if the back windows were closed before locking-up time, but if you want to stay—"

"No, no," Jones protested. "Not at all. Not another minute. I forgot the time. I came here—I came here—" He fumbled for an excuse.

"I know," Virginia smiled, and as Jones's brows arched she went on: "To escape the tea party of course. I went over to Mrs. Brant's for a bit. She is a grand lady, isn't she? But she told some of us of your decision, and I can understand that it still takes a lot of—"

"My decision?"

"Yes, to take up war work. I admire you for that."

"Why, thank you," Jones replied, wishing Virginia would stand aside or pass on, so he could leave. But she stood as if deliberately barring his way, one hand resting on the top of the reading table, the other on a shelf of the bookstack opposite, swaying a little on her white pumps so that the old-rose colored frock of some sort of imitation silk she wore rippled (flame-like, came to Jones's mind) against her thighs.

"I tried to, myself," Virginia said. "But there's no demand for my particular talents. Of course, I do Red Cross stuff—staff assistant work."

John nodded politely. He felt cross with Angela for having blurted out his intentions, and put heaven knows what kind of interpretation on them. He wanted to announce it to Virginia himself, to study the effect of oblique reference to a particular talent *he* had.

"I suppose you'll be leaving here," the woman was saying slowly. "I wish very much that you would give me just a little of your time before you go." She raised dark eyes to his. "I think I've already confessed that I took this job because you were here. That's really true."

"I never doubted it," Jones said, and Virginia's hands dropped to her side at the flat accusation in his voice. "Of

82

course, I have discussed my plans with no one yet. Not even Ange—Mrs. Brant. I do not know when I shall leave."

"But you're quite sure you're going."

"Quite sure. You see—" and John rose deliberately—"I think I can contribute something toward the winning of this war which no other person can. Does that sound conceited to you?"

"No, no, indeed, Dr. Jones. Of course it doesn't. I know what you have done, and what you can do."

"Do you, indeed?"

"Why, of course I do!"

"And you think that my contribution to war can be effective, and important? You are not humoring an old fossil in his naïve belief that his unique knowledge of dead-and-forgotten language can win the war?"

Virginia smiled, and shook the dark waves of her hair. "I just know you can do it," she said. "I bet if Hitler or Hirohito is fated to have his head bashed in with a Chaldean brick, you'll do it. Oh, I do beg your pardon, I didn't mean to be flippant."

For now it was Jones who had fallen back a step.

"Flippant, my dear? Forget it! It's just that—well, I'll be god-damned if I understand you."

"I don't know what you mean," Virginia cried. "Good grief, what did you want me to do? Weep and beg you to keep out of danger? You don't want me to say that your noblest duty is here, stuffing Arabic into the heads of brats in this ecclesiastical trade school, do you? Just what do you think of me, Dr. Jones? What do you think I am, anyhow?"

"I wish to God I knew," Jones replied fervently. "Well, I'll try to arrange time for the discussion you requested. Why don't you drop around to the house some evening?"

"Thanks a million," said Virginia. "And now I really must close the joint. It's close on to suppertime."

11

"*WE WERE JUST* about to sit down without you," Angela said.

"I am terribly sorry to be so late," John apologized. "I was reading in the Library, and fell into a train of thought."

"Did you see Miss Finster?" Angela could not help saying, suspecting that John might well have fallen into something besides a train of thought.

"Yes, a little while, just as I was leaving. She didn't know I was there until she started to lock up. She told me"—and John made the statement an accusation—"that you had told her of my intention."

"Wasn't that all right?" Angela asked. "Why, we are all that proud of you! Surely you did not mean to keep it a secret?"

"No, of course not," John answered, searching through the plate of leftover and slightly edge-curled sandwiches. "Only I wish that Miss Finster hadn't been told."

Angela was suddenly happy inside, although externally contrite.

"No, no, it's not important," Jones assured her. "I'm sorry I mentioned it. I just wanted to tell her myself. . . ."

Angela felt as if she had bitten into a cockroach. But Jones went on blithely eating, while Alfred silently spooned up his Ozonated Oats to the last vitamin-surcharged crumb.

"You have not changed your mind about it, then?" he asked.

"No, my mind is quite made up."

Alfred sighed gustily through pursed lips.

"I don't know," he said. "I don't know."

"What?" Angela asked her brother.

"I don't know the wisdom of it," Alfred pronounced heavily. "It is not necessary. There are millions of younger men, literally millions, more able physically than you, John. You may be able to dissemble on your age, but suppose you are killed? You would be just another body. But intellectually, there are too precious few minds like yours to have one of them reduced to a bloody pulp on a battlefield."

"Oh, Alfred, you are downright morbid," Angela stormed. "Besides, John is not going to be a soldier. He isn't going to shoot off any guns. He is going into war work in Washington, into an office somewhere."

"I am not," John said curtly.

"But you aren't going to try to kill people, John."

"I am."

Angela brought both palms down against the mahogany. "That is simply fantastic. I absolutely agree with Alfred. You could do a wonderful job in some office, taking the place of some able-bodied man fit to carry a gun. But if you have any idea you're going to tote a gun you're just dooming yourself to disappointment."

"My mind is made up," Jones called back, as he marched out to the porch. Alfred cast his eyes upward, murmured something, and followed.

Alfred's frantic mental search for a gambit was instantly ended when Jones himself renewed the conversation with the statement that he was taking Angela's advice and would directly address the President with his request for an audience. Alfred made a choking sound, but Jones continued:

"How's this? 'Dear Mr. President: In consequence of a lifetime of exploration and research in Asia Minor and Levantine Europe I have acquired certain unique information which, if properly employed, will enable me to exert a decisive influence on the war. I request a five-minute audience which will be sufficient to explain and demonstrate my process and to outline my plan for its application. Needless to say, the utmost secrecy must be observed.'

"I suppose it should be signed 'Respectfully yours.' What do you think, Alfred?"

"What do I think? What do I *think*? I think—I *know* the President will never see the letter," Alfred said thickly. "That's what I think."

"If I marked it personal and confidential, and sent it registered?"

"John, don't be naïve. You know that that would guarantee its interception."

"I'm not so naïve as you think," John snapped. "I assume I would be investigated before the President admitted me."

"Then why not tell him in your letter what you want to do?"

"I can't. I'd have to show him."

"I think you would have to show somebody else first, to prove that it is important enough for the President's decision."

"Well, it is," John cried. "Do you think for a minute they'll think a man of my reputation and position a crank or a self-seeking idiot?"

"They might," said Alfred, leaning over to put a soothing hand on John's shoulder. "Don't be angry with me, my friend. You are still suffering from nervous shock ("I am not!")—well, then, let us regard it objectively. You wish to contribute to the war effort. You have special knowledge. ("You're damn right I have!") You want to know how you can apply that knowledge to help in the war. That is not the President's province, John. He deals only with the very biggest, the most important, problems. With what you have to offer, I think the State Department . . ."

"God's teeth! The State Department! No, thank you. All my life I have battled and argued and fussed with consuls and vice-consuls. Besides, this is a military matter."

"Then the War Department is the proper place to apply.

You could probably get appointed to Military Intelligence in a civilian capacity, but you should work through the senator or our congressman."

"I wouldn't dream of it. And besides, I'm not just looking for a job——"

Alfred's eloquent shrug was lost on Jones in the darkness.

"Then I suggest you forget the whole matter for a while. You are acting on impulse, John, and it is unlike you. Lay it aside, and then reconsider it with proper perspective."

"And meanwhile thousands of men get killed, and Hitler may produce *his* secret weapon——"

"John, God bless you, what could you do to avert that, anyhow? Now, if you were an inventor, if you were as great an engineer as you are an anthropologist. If you had invented a secret weapon, say; even then it would not be the President's function to employ you."

Jones was leaning forward in his chair, each hand clutching the opposite wrist, and he punctuated every one of Alfred's sentences with a snort.

"You know," he said hoarsely, "I could kill you where you sit."

"I am sorry you take that attitude," Alfred said, rising stiffly. "There is, of course, nothing further to discuss. For my part, I apologize for anything I did to cause you to utter such an unkindness."

"Sit down and don't be an ass, Alfred," John urged. "I meant that literally, not as a hyperbolic threat. That is what I must tell the President in secret."

"Ah, yes, to be sure," Alfred whispered, struggling gently against John's detaining hand. "I should have understood. Of course, the President. You know Dr. Hobson, our staff physician. He is a close friend of Admiral McIntire, the President's doctor. I suggest you talk it over with Dr. Hobson, John, and perhaps he could use his influence with Dr. McIntire. Ah, yes. Perhaps we should call him at once."

"Sit down, you big booby," John chuckled, with a mirthlessness that turned Alfred's leg bones into cold boiled spaghetti. "You think I am crazy, don't you?"

"Nothing of the sort, John. Why, you are as sane as I—saner, I am certain. No, no! Please don't get excited."

"Don't *you* get excited. I think I should have undertaken this whole project without consulting anybody, but now I shall take you into my confidence, because it has gone too far. But I pledge you to tell nobody, nobody at all, not even Angela."

"I promise," Alfred said huskily, leaning forward in as conspiratorial an attitude as his stomach would permit.

"Would it surprise you, Alfred, if I told you I can k—stun any living object with a gesture of my hand?"

"No, not at all, John," Alfred squeaked. And then he jumped from his chair as if somebody had driven a hot needle up through the seat. "Oh, dear God, the moth! And the dog!"

"Yes," said Jones from the shadows. "There was also a squirrel. Not to mention the wasps. And a butterfly."

"And it all dates from a week ago Wednesday, doesn't it?"

"Yes," Jones murmured. "It came—last—Wednesday."

"Tell me about it," Alfred said as he reseated himself, his voice and manner unconsciously reverting to priestly persuasiveness.

"Listen," said John. And, succinctly, he told his friend of the arrival of the red disk, his translation of it, how he had fortuitously cut his finger and sucked the blood and how he had spelled aloud the dreadsome incantation which had invited the lightning bolt. But, whether inspired by some inherent quirk of chivalry or out of canniness he himself could not interpret, Jones omitted all that pertained to Virginia.

"And where is the disk now?" Alfred squeaked, mopping his face.

"Ground to dust and driven into the earth by the fallen tree," Jones said. "I wonder if we might dig there and assemble the shards."

"Heaven forbid," Alfred said hoarsely. "And now let me tell you frankly and in all candor what I think. I believe you are suffering from mental as well as electrical shock. You know that a thunderstorm is a local, meteorological phenomenon. The theory that damage by lightning is an Act of God

88

has passed wholly out of religion into the law. Can you argue that, by reading an ancient clay tablet, you caused a column of overheated air to rise some miles distant, which condensed and in its turbulence stored up a great charge of positive electricity which struck back at its source? No, my dear John, it is not tenable. My advice to you is to consult an electrician."

"Damned strange advice from a preacher," Jones snapped. "You might at least have advised me to consult God. Do you believe God could cause a thunderstorm?"

"Certainly I believe God could cause a thunderstorm, but I do not believe He would."

"People pray for rain and sometimes it rains. It's there in the prayer book."

"But you are not saying that God sent this thunderbolt," Alfred snapped. "You declare that you yourself caused it."

"Yet you do not doubt that I can kill?"

"No, I do not doubt it at all. And I told you what I believed the explanation to be, and I advise you to consult a physician. You are the equivalent of a thundercloud. Surely, John, you have had sparks jump from your finger to another object on a cold day. It happens to everybody. The body stores up electricity. You don't feel it. But when you point your finger at something, a spark jumps from it. Even children know that. The same thing has happened to you on a larger scale, that's all."

"Then you would explain my case by natural causes?"

"Why, certainly, and on the basis of your own evidence," Alfred cried, confidence ringing in his voice. "If you wish me to choose between the factual evidence and your assertion that you conjured up the thunderstorm by communion with the North Star, I can only reach the conclusion I have given you. And as a scientific man yourself, you will have to agree that I, as a rational human, cannot choose otherwise."

"As a rational human, yes," John admitted. "But as a priest of the church?"

Alfred pressed his face into his hands.

"Especially as a priest," he said thickly. "I will pray with you—and if not with you, then for you anyhow—that the Lord help you in casting off this affliction."

"Look," John said challengingly. "Let us go down in the garden and find a toad or a mole. And I will call upon my power to destroy it and you will call upon God to prevent—"

Now Alfred did rise from his chair, and there was something majestic even in the silhouette of his dumpy body. John Jones also stood, expectantly.

"No, no, no!" Alfred cried. "John, what has come over you? A contest—what would the bishop—you can't do it. I will not participate in such blasphemy."

"I'm sorry, Alfred. Of course you couldn't."

"Don't you see, John," Alfred argued, but calmly again, "that if there is any truth in what you say, then you would have to surrender wholly to evil in such a contest? I have no doubt how the contest would end. You would win. If you can call it 'win.' I am utterly certain that you could stun or kill a frog despite my most fervent prayers. God would be mocked in such a contest. He would pay me no heed, because, as I say, this so-called power of yours has been acquired by natural, not supernatural, means. I could no more prevent your electrocuting a toad than I could expect the Lord to hear my prayers that the light not come on when you push the switch in the living room."

"But, whatever its source or origin, I do have the power, you believe."

"I am forced to believe it, because I saw it exercised."

"Well, then, to return to the original proposition, why can't I use it in behalf of my country?"

"How do you propose to use it?"

"That is up to the President," John said deceptively. "I could be sent up to the front, and be used like a cannon."

"No, no! The thought is impossible."

"Or as a sniper," John pressed.

"John, I beg of you. Wait! Wait and see if this electricity does not dissipate itself. Think—" Alfred had an inspiration. "Think what would happen if you did persuade the government to send you to the front, and when you were called upon to blast the enemy, nothing happened. Think of the ignominy of it."

"I'll take the chance," John said. "Alfred, I sincerely thank you from my heart for your patience, and for the advice, even though I cannot take it. I am going upstairs now to write to the President."

He turned and left the porch, and Alfred followed him slowly to the foot of the stairs, as if to deter him. There Angela found him, clasping and unclasping his hands, his face creased with woe.

"You did not persuade him?" she guessed at once.

Alfred looked at her blankly, and then spread his arms in a gesture more of despair than of negation. He climbed the stairs a step at a time, to seek not his bed but the hooked rug beside it on which he knelt far past midnight in prayer for his poor, afflicted and misguided friend.

12

SO JOHN JONES wrote his letter to the President, and put it on the hall table for Angela to take to the post office, and Alfred prayerfully stole it.

He stole it with a clear conscience, for he had made his peace with God in advance. Having pocketed the letter, though, he began to worry. Suppose John asked Angela if she was sure she mailed it? He could not make his sister a party to the benevolent crime, for she simply would not understand the necessity of action so drastic.

Wherefore a letter would have to be sent, Alfred decided. Something innocuous; something that would not merit a reply, but if perchance it were answered, something that would produce no incriminating evidence. Wholly astonished at his own sudden talent for chicanery, Alfred retired to his room and composed a short note calling God's blessing and stimulation on the chief executive and tersely stating that if there were any way at all in which the writer could be of assistance he had but to be summoned.

He took some pains to imitate Jones's precise script, and had the whole job assembled before Angela was ready for the daily walk to the combined grocery and post office.

Sure enough, that evening John casually asked Angela if she had posted his letter, and Angela in complete honesty assured him that she had; she had noticed it particularly, she said, and she wondered what Miss Pealbody, the postmistress, would think when she canceled the stamp and put the letter in the Washington pouch.

"What do I care what she thinks," Jones chuckled, and he whistled a Cyprian love song as he performed his small chores before dinner. "Wait till I get my answer. I'll bet she'll hold that letter up to the light!" he said, on his next trip to the cupboard.

Alfred laughed at that. Laughed happily, and guiltlessly. It would be a long wait, he thought to himself. But Alfred himself was naïve. He did not realize, had no way of knowing, the meticulous organization of the New Deal.

Within twenty-four hours his benign forgery had reached the White House together with some two thousand other letters. It was opened, stamped with the hour of its receipt and became part of a basketful dumped on the desk of a senator's brother-in-law in one of a row of basement offices. The clerk, himself a former country judge and unsuccessful candidate for Congress, gave each letter a hasty reading and then flipped it into the box that would take it on the next step to ultimate disposal. Into one container went the obviously harmless crank letters, into another went the crank letters that might merit a look-see by the Secret Service. A third box was for letters which would be given the polite brush-off, and the smallest received the mail some higher echelon would have to classify.

The clerk read the letter signed "John Jones" and started to toss it into the brush-off pile, and then he stayed his hand and gave it a second reading.

It was terse and exuded self-confidence. Jones. Might be some kin of old Jesse's. Offering to do anything to help. It might be—it just barely might be that the guy had some political oomph. So he clipped to the letter the symbol that meant the writer might be worth looking into, and tossed it into the fourth basket.

For this was, after all, an election year.

At its next stop the letter was detoured again, another notation added to the attached sheet. Eventually it reached the desk of the secretary to one of the assistant secretaries, with the documentation that the writer seemed to be a big-shot explorer (Who's Who) with emphasis on Greece, Turkey, Syria and apparently connected with the Episcopal Church in a large way (Note address). The secretary wrote the indicated temporizing reply, and added her carbon copy to the sheaf which had accumulated around the letter, which then went to the assistant secretary to follow through, if follow-through were the order.

Meanwhile:

Meanwhile, all went serenely in the Jones-Brant-Claverhouse menage. John Jones seemed happy and lighthearted, Alfred seemed composed and content, and Angela's small canker of worry was smothered in the unguent of conviction that if the country was so hard up as to take John Jones into the troops, then there would be greater cause for anxiety than the fate of one middle-aged professor.

So Monday passed, and most of Tuesday. The three friends were sitting on the screened porch that night, enjoying the honeysuckled air, when the staccato crunch of gravel changing into heels tapping on flagstone announced the approach of a visitor.

"Hel-loo! Anybody home?"

"We're all here sitting in the dark. Come right in. Who is it?"

"It's me, Virginia Finster, Mrs. Brant. May I come in just a sec?"

"Why, certainly!" The cordiality in Angela's voice would have done credit to Ethel Barrymore, and been an asset to Clare Boothe Luce.

The men rose scrapingly in the dark, the overhead light was switched on, a seat was found for the caller. Her opinion was solicited on the weather, her attention directed to the fragrance of the honeysuckle, the excellent state of everyone's health was confirmed. With these tribal ceremonies completed, Virginia was ready to give, and the others to hear, the reason for her visit.

"Dr. Jones was kind enough to suggest I might drop in some evening," she began.

94

"John, you should have told me so we could have prepared some refreshment for Miss Finster," Angela interrupted. "Maybe I could stir up some lemonade, if you don't mind it unsweetened."

"Oh, please don't bother, really," Virginia protested. "I'll only stay a minute. I do think it is so exciting about Dr. Jones going off to the war. Aren't you all just thrilled?"

"We must all do our part according to our ability," Angela observed, while Jones rudely growled that the neighborhood would have him buried in Arlington with military honors before he needed another haircut.

"I've just come from the Dean's office," Virginia said, with a catch in her throat. "Oh, he is a prince, a real Christian gentleman if ever the phrase had meaning. But evidently the trustees have been yammering to him about me. And Mrs. Jay treats me as if I were a leper or a ghoul, and the students stare and mumble after I pass."

"Come, come now, Miss Finster," Alfred protested. "Surely you are putting a wrong interpretation upon natural interest and curiosity?"

"Maybe I am," Virginia said. "Anyhow, I gave the Dean my bona fides and of course I offered to resign. It made me pretty sore that some of the trustees wanted to fire me and the only reason they didn't was because it might cause more comment."

"Dear me," said Angela. "And was your resignation accepted?"

"No, it was not," Virginia replied. "And I'm sort of glad it wasn't. I haven't been here very long but I am fond of the old place already and the work just suits my purposes to a T. Oh, please excuse me for talking like this. I didn't come here to gripe."

"And what are your purposes?" Angela pressed. "The ones the job so admirably suits? You must excuse my curiosity. If I am prying—"

"Oh, no, you are not! I have already told Dr. Jones. Only it is a sort of lousy paradox that the cause of my trouble was the cause for my coming to the Seminary in the first place."

"My dear, I don't quite understand," Alfred interjected.

"I mean," she said, with laughter, "that it was Dr. Jones's tattling on me to the reporter that got me in Dutch, and the main reason I took this job in preference to several others was because Dr. Jones was on the faculty."

"Why, I did not know you two knew each other before," Angela exclaimed, and her emotion this time was genuine.

"I never met Miss Finster before—before—" John choked, as the undimmed vision of storm-stripped pectoral prominence flashed into his mind.

"Before what?" Angela probed.

"Before. Just before," Jones said. "Before here, I mean."

"I was first introduced to Dr. Jones that Sunday week ago. Mrs. Jay—"

A voice spoke from the yonder dark: "Do I hear my name being taken in vain?"

"Why, is that you, Phoebe?" Angela called out. "Do come in and sit awhile."

Mrs. Jay stumped up the wooden steps. "Have you company? Oh, good evening, Miss Finster. I was just cutting across your lawn, Angela, and how are you, Dr. Jones? I declare, isn't it warm for May? Although it is practically June. Well, what are you all discussing so earnestly?"

"Miss Finster was about to tell us of her work," Angela said. "Her real work, not just the job she gets paid for."

"I am writing a book," Virginia continued. "Actually it is my Ph.D. thesis but the Orchard Hill Press in New York is interested in bringing it out as a book."

"What is it, dear, a sort of guidebook to voodoo?" Mrs. Jay asked sweetly.

"No, it is about ophiolatry—snake worship, you know. That plays only a very tiny part in voodoo, and it really doesn't belong there." Virginia's voice took on the tones of the zealot. "It is much more apt to appear in more acceptable religions. At least, I'm certain everybody here has read how the Israelites once worshiped a snake of brass, and about Moses and Aaron and Hezekiah. So what? You pass it by for something more to your purposes in the Bible. But let me tell

96

you, snake worship is a lot older than Christianity and still going strong. And it gets all mixed up with Christianity, too, Mrs. Brant. I don't just mean the identification of snakes with Satan, like in the story of Adam and Eve, either. You'd be surprised what I have seen in so-called Christian churches down South, where they bring rattlesnakes right up on the pulpit and the minister and congregation wrap them around their necks and go into ecstasies."

"Negras," said Mrs. Jay. "Still half savage."

"Mm-huh, not Negroes, ever," Virginia declared. "White people, and probably the purest Anglo-Saxon strain in America at that."

"White trash." Mrs. Jay pronounced the curse.

"Maybe so," Virginia said earnestly and innocently. "But I'll bet every woman among them is technically eligible for the D.A.R. and the Colonial Dames because they are all descended from Revolutionary veterans who took up land grants in the mountains of North Carolina."

"Ho-ho, North Carolina," Mrs. Jay fleered. "Why didn't you say North Carolina? That's just a swamp at one end and a pile of rocks at the other where the people of Virginia and Carolina have been dumping their trash for three hundred years."

"Well, and what has all this got to do with Dr. Jones, may I ask?" Angela spoke up.

"Oh, I'm sorry," Virginia said. "I got sort of carried away with my hobby, I guess."

"Snakes are a strange hobby for a young woman," Mrs. Jay observed.

"Oh, but snakes aren't my hobby! Honestly, I loathe them. I can't bear to touch them, and I don't know one kind from another. No, it's just the worship of snakes, the religious part. Of course, that's basically phallic, don't you agree? But—"

John's snort at this juncture recalled to Virginia that she had again strayed from the theme.

"Anyhow—" and she gave a little laugh—"maybe you don't know it but Dr. Jones is about the world's greatest

97

expert on ancient religions, and he is just simply famous on the obscurer ones. I guess what Einstein is to mathematics, he is to—is theurgy the word? Anyhow, when I heard he was on the faculty here of course I was most terribly surprised but I latched on to this job hoping I could get him to help me in finishing my book."

"And now Dr. Jones is leaving us to go off to the wars and he won't be able to help you," Mrs. Jay said with finality.

"Well, you did promise to give me a little of your time, didn't you, Dr. Jones? What about tomorrow? Haven't you a little free time in the afternoon just to glance over my manuscript?"

Mrs. Jay dryly interjected the observation that Wednesdays found the Library most busy, not that she wanted to stand in the way of a scientific treatise, and Virginia protested that she wasn't planning to be away from her post one little minute; all she 'oped was that Dr. Jones would stop by and pick up certain chapters of her manuscript.

"If I find it at all possible, I shall drop by," Jones promised. "I may find myself pressed, but I shall let you know either way."

"Good, and thanks a million," Virginia cried, scattering good nights. "And the rest of you folks, you really ought to get Dr. Jones to tell you some of the things he knows about ancient cults and things. They'll simply knock you down, some of them!"

She pattered off the porch, successfully begging them not to turn on the light for her benefit, which is just as well because the illumination would have revealed Jones sitting rigid and glassy-eyed, his jaw dangling, clasping his wrists with numbing intensity.

"Well, well, Dr. Jones," Mrs. Jay tittered. "You seem to have a most devoted disciple. I suppose all celebrities are bothered to death by amateurs."

"Bothered to death?" Jones echoed mechanically. "Yes, maybe so. If you will excuse me, I think I will go to my room and do a little work on my own book, while I have a chance."

98

"And I must go, too," Mrs. Jay cried. "I have shamefully overstayed my time, indeed I have."

Jones did not help Angela and Alfred to deny that obvious fact, but entered the house and climbed slowly to his chamber. *"Get Dr. Jones to tell you some of the things he knows. . . . They'll simply knock you down."*

13

"*YOU HAVEN'T*," Alfred put the question as a statement of assured fact, "told anybody else what you told me, John."

"You mean, about the disk and all that?" John replied. "Most certainly not. And I'll remind you, Alfred, that I told it to you in utmost confidence."

They were walking across the campus together, Alfred to his lecture hall and John, without classes on Wednesday, en route to the Library.

"I just wanted to know," Alfred remarked. "Of course I will cherish your secret."

"Thanks," said John. "Of course, I will have to tell the President. Why do you ask?"

"Oh, nothing. I was just asking to make sure. I thought if, perhaps, you had told two or three other persons and somehow it leaked out, you might believe I had mentioned it."

"Now, whom else would I tell?" John cried.

Alfred's round face beamed. "I wish I had asked you that last night," he smiled. "It would have saved me a little worry."

"If I have caused you one moment's worry, I regret ever telling it to you," John declared, fully aware that he had regretted telling the story to Alfred in any event.

"Oh, it wasn't anything you said," Alfred smiled. "Just a chance remark dropped in last night's conversation, a common and inelegant phrase which I have heard used a thousand times, but never quite so apropos."

"You mean——" John began, and Alfred finished the sentence for him, punctuating it with a laugh: "What Miss Finster said about your knowing enough about strange cults to knock us down. Funny, wasn't it?"

So, John pondered, Alfred too had noticed the startling pertinence of Virginia's slang. Well, there was but one way to handle the situation and that was to batter down subtlety with candor and conquer obliquity with straightforwardness. He would tell her, politely but firmly, that their battleground was not to embrace the peaceful home of Angela and Alfred. Zotz had caused that innocent pair trouble enough.

Thus resolved, John strode into the Library. Virginia Finster was halfway down a book-ranked aisle, returning volumes to their shelves.

"I'll be with you in a moment," she called to him, to the frowning annoyance of a prematurely bald young man poring over Hillel in the original, and presently Virginia hurried up to him, dusting her fingers against each other.

"Good morning," she said. "I'm embarrassed. I did not expect you till this afternoon and all my stuff is home."

"That's all right," Jones nodded. "It isn't terribly important."

Virginia looked at him wide-eyed. "No, I guess it isn't—except to me."

"That isn't what I meant, I meant my coming here. I can come back for the manuscript this afternoon."

"Oh dear, I hate to put you to the extra bother." Virginia's eyelids reefed another notch. "It's nerve enough to ask you to look at my book."

Virginia excused herself to help a student who said he had been instructed to read a certain volume on scatology but he didn't think that could be right because there was no such heading in the card index file. And while Virginia verified the absence of the topic, looked the word up in the dictionary, and consulted the youth to learn if he probably didn't mean "eschatology," Jones mentally stamped on his own corns and metaphorically punched his own nose. The interview was not going at all as planned. Damn it all, he intended, manuscript or no manuscript (and now he doubted that there was a manuscript), to make it plain that she had gone too far the night before, and that he was still defying her and Those who had set her to spy upon him.

Virginia came back.

"Look here," John said gruffly, grinding his hands into his pockets, "I think we understand each other pretty well."

"Oh, yes," Virginia replied eagerly, her pose of the zealous apprentice at the master's knee spoiled, however, by the necessity of brushing a fly off her short, straight nose.

"Well, that isn't quite true," Jones murmured, half to himself. "There are some things about you I can't figure out at all. But in the main, on the fundamentals, I'm sure, there is no misunderstanding."

"Misunderstanding? Oh, Dr. Jones, of course not. Excuse me, there's a fly on your—oops, he's gone."

"I mean, you know why you are here, and I know why you are here, and that's a matter strictly between us."

"Why, of course, Dr. Jones, if that's the way you wish it. I didn't think you'd want it to be a secret. I mean, it isn't worth while keeping it secret, and people might think it funny if you—if I—if we—I mean, well, it is hard to put into words." She thrust out her full carmine underlip and blew sharply. "Bother that fly! You mean you don't even want people to know you are helping me with my book?"

"No, that's perfectly all right. It is something I'm glad to do for what it is worth, because I suppose some such sort of device is necessary. For you, I mean. For my part, nothing is going to stop me from doing what I intend to do. Must I speak more plainly?"

"Well, I honestly wish you would," Virginia said. "Oh, bother! Here comes the boss. (Good morning, Mrs. Jay.) But I'm perfectly willing to do anything you say."

Jones bowed to the librarian wordlessly. Mrs. Jay carefully balanced a smile above her tilted chin, put some new books on Virginia's desk, and returned to her office.

"I don't think you would," Jones said. "And there is no need to make such sweeping promises."

"You don't think I would what?"

"Do anything I say. I can't speak much more plainly in public but this much I can say, here and now: First, you must refrain from saying such things as you did last night—"

"O-oh," said Virginia. She nodded her head energetically. "Yes, I can see that I—but I was sort of peeved. Okay, I promise."

"Second," Jones continued inexorably, "whether your applause was ironical or not, I am going to offer everything I know and can do to the government, and the only thing that will stop me is—well, to stop me for good. You understand?"

"I understood it the first time, and I certainly meant every word I said when I told you what a noble, grand thing it was you were doing when you have everything here, everything! Comfort, security, honor. Of course, I could say a lot more myself if we could be sure against interruption or eavesdropping."

"I mean *this*, too," Jones said, gesturing toward the desk. The bothersome fly had withdrawn to the blotter, where it was grumpily repairing itself from superficial damages received at Virginia's hands.

Jones did not use the Word, just the Gesture. He pointed his lean forefinger at the insect. It stopped in the act of spitting on its hands and sat there in an attitude of frozen prayer.

John casually opened his clenched fingers and picked up the fly. It lay as stiff as enameled metal in the palm of his hand. He held it out for Virginia to see.

The fly unclasped its paws, and buzzed in circles. Suddenly it found its equilibrium, and flew off.

"Why, Professor! How clever of you—but I wish you would have killed it while you had the chance."

Jones smiled down at Virginia grimly. "No, I have pledged myself not to use the Power to kill except against the enemy —the real enemy. Then, nothing will stop me. Except— death."

Virginia blinked soberly.

Then, without a word, she put out her hand to Jones. He leaped backward to avoid the lethal thrust, felt himself collide with somebody, and regained his balance in the embrace of an only slightly more startled Mrs. Jay, and she, in turn, in the embrace of a filing cabinet.

"Dr. Jones! Did you slip on something?" The librarian was solicitous as to speech, which was directed at Jones, but angry as to eye, which was fixed on Virginia. And Virginia, in turn, was wringing her hands and declaring that she did not know what had happened, and was Dr. Jones all right and unhurt?

The savant, fists clenched and arms straight at his sides, made crisp apology for his awkwardness. Mrs. Jay said she would like to see Virginia in her office when she had a free moment, and turned on her heels.

John gave Virginia a level and icy look. "It seems to me fortunate that our meetings can be subject to interruption," he said.

Virginia stared back at him, and suddenly her eyes brimmed with tears. She turned abruptly, and walked swiftly to the rear of the room, opened a door and closed it firmly behind her without a backward look.

Jones saw her out of sight. He marched out the front door and so through the Grove to the lane, and the road behind it, his mind again in tumult.

Had Virginia Finster raised her hand to strike him down with the Power of Zotz in the moment of his supreme defiance? No, it was preposterous, on second thought. The Power was not in her. Maybe she had only wanted to shake hands, and yet that would have been a curious thing to do, for he had promised to return the same afternoon to pick up the manuscript.

If there was a manuscript! That he would like to see proved. Maybe it was a device to get him off alone somewhere where he would be given instructions and choice of following them or becoming guest of honor at a funeral.

Angrily he plodded the weedy shoulders of the gravel

road. Once a great, yellow-and-black spider agitated her web in protest at his proximity, and he Zotzed her with a vehemence that blighted the giant pokeweed on which her snare was hung. A blue jay cursed him from a near-by fence post; Jones whirled and paralyzed the bird with a gesture. He bit his lip to dam the Word that was forming there, suddenly remembering his vow not to employ it except for the ultimate purpose.

"But that was foolish of me," he said aloud. "Naturally, I'll have to demonstrate it to the President."

"Nyaa-nyaa-nyaa," screamed the blue jay, suddenly recovering. Jones paid it no heed as it fled screaming through the pines.

"In fact, the President will probably ask me all sorts of questions," Jones mused, all rancor vanished as his mind became engrossed with fact. "He will want to know how far the Power extends, I am sure, and I don't know if it works at a greater distance than ten feet or not. Let's say twenty," and he smiled a little at the memory of the young men who had been bowled over with a "stitch in the side."

Yes, if Jones was going to present himself as a weapon he would have to know his own potentialities as well as limitations. Was there any insulation against the Power—glass, brick, stone, wood, darkness? The President was said to be a Navy-minded commander in chief; suppose he asked what would happen if Jones were standing on the bridge of a ship when an enemy vessel appeared on the horizon? Would the Power carry that far? Would it penetrate armor plate?

Jones found that one worry had only been succeeded by another. He turned his steps homeward, and before the screen door closed behind him he had called out to Angela whether there was any mail for him. He was relieved to be told no, although he had calculated that if the President answered his mail the day he got it, the reply should be in the day's post. Angela, knowing his expectancy, had been almost apologetic in telling him there was no letter; when he exclaimed "Good!" and went to his room whistling, the bewildered woman began to hope that Jones had changed his mind and was himself hoping his letter would be ignored.

But what on earth is the man up to? she wondered, brought to pause in her chore of shelling peas by the sound of his tramping back and forth overhead and manipulating windows.

At last she called up the stairs, to ask if she could find something for him, and he called down a cheery negative. But in fifteen minutes, just as she was about to pour the boiling water on the luncheon's tea, John shouted down to her.

"Where's the what?" she called back. "Just a minute."

"Where is that glass cigarette box that girl who's forever riding horseback sent you from New Mexico or some place?"

"It's in my room on the dresser, full of hairpins. What in the world do you want with it?"

"I just want to borrow it for a few minutes, that's all."

"But lunch is ready."

"I'll be right down."

It took a second call, however, to fetch John to table, where he ate fresh asparagus on toast moodily and rapidly. From there he went to the basement to return with Alfred's tin can of assorted nails; he paused in the kitchen to scoop up the big cardboard box of parlor matches. Presently he was down again from his room, and poking around in the rear of the back yard, from which he returned with a brick and something else clutched in the concealment of his pocket.

"John, what on earth are you building?" Angela, burst by curiosity, asked as he stalked past to the stairs.

"Building? Nothing! Oh, say, do we have a wooden box anywhere? A small one, but the stouter the better."

"A small wooden—let me think. What do you want it for?"

"Oh, just an experiment. I won't harm it."

Angela flushed. "I didn't mean to pry," she explained. "I just wanted to know whether it should be waterproof, or with a lid, or what."

"It really doesn't make any difference," he said. "Waterproof or not, lid or not. Do you happen to know if there is one around?"

106

HE DROPPED AN INDIGNANT TOAD INTO
THE BATHTUB

"No, I'm sure there is not, not any kind of wooden box. There is a little celluloid soapbox in the trunk closet that I used to take—"

"Good, that's swell. Can I borrow that?"

"Why, of course. I don't know exactly where it is, though. On one of the shelves. It's pink."

"I'll find it. But no wooden box?"

"No, only the one in your room that your books came packed in. It's under your bed—"

"Just the thing! I should have remembered it."

He climbed the stairs two steps at a time, and hurried into the bathroom.

There he took his hand from his pocket and with it an indignant toad which he dropped into the bathtub. He washed his hands and repaired to the trunk closet, from which he carried the pink celluloid soapbox to add to the array of ill-matched containers on his desk—a tin-bound glass box, the cardboard matchbox (its contents dumped on a piece of paper), the tin nail can (its contents on another sheet), a milk bottle in which a dozen flies and a couple of beetles protested confinement, and a Victorian chamber pot of glazed and garlanded chinaware the pink-tipped handle of whose lid was, on second look, a ceramic rosebud.

From under the bed he produced the cedar box in which his notebooks had been shipped from the Dodecanese; for all its simplicity, an admirable piece of small cabinetwork. To John it was a shrine of sorts, for it had contained and safely conveyed all the salvageable fruits of his last decade of research in the incubators of civilization.

He put it on his desk, too, and surveyed his homemade laboratory with satisfaction. It looked like the tailings of a country auction but it would serve him as well as the whole Bureau of Standards could.

I ought to have guinea pigs and white mice, Jones thought as he contorted himself in the recapture of the toad. Downstairs, the knocker whacked the front door, and Jones heard, without noticing, Angela's slow tread through the hall and the sound of colloquy that followed. Likewise he marked

109

Alfred's return from classes only subconsciously, if at all. Jones was very busy.

It was at dinner that Angela told him: "You had a visitor this afternoon."

"I? I had a visitor? Did he leave his name?"

"It wasn't a he. It was Miss Finster. She left that big brown envelope for you that's on the hall table when I told her you couldn't be disturbed. She asked when it would be convenient for her to stop around and I told her you would get in touch with her yourself."

"Oh, the manuscript," John said. "Please pass the pickles, Alfred."

He had forgotten about the manuscript, or his doubts that one existed. He had, in fact, forgotten there was a Virginia Finster.

14

THE LETTER FROM the White House arrived in Friday's mail.

Miss Pealbody, the meringue-topped postmistress, observed to Angela that some mighty important people seemed to be writing to her house these days.

Angela herself carried the fateful letter by itself in her right hand. It seemed to weigh five pounds by the time she reached the house, and the small bundle of letters in her left hand had by contrast been forgotten. She debated whether to interrupt John at his classes with the presidential communication, or to put it on his dinner napkin, or carry it to his room. Finally she decided to leave it normally on the hall table and to direct his attention to it as soon as he came in.

Or else, she might tear it up. Letters got lost in the mail lots of times. It was just a plain, squarish envelope with "The White House, Washington, D. C." embossed in black. It had come by ordinary post. But there was that nosy Pealbody woman! She had seen the envelope, and had probably told every living soul, white and colored, about it already.

Angela was sitting in the kitchen still fretting when she heard the front door open and close, and she called out: "There's a letter for you on the hall table." Thus it happened that John, arriving two or three minutes after his host and colleague, found Alfred with his foot on the bottom step of the stairs, staring, with quivering cheeks, at an envelope he held at arm's length.

"Bad news, Alfred?"

Alfred thrust the letter at John without a word, and went up the stairs suddenly assailed with consciousness of guilt. He heard the envelope rip, and the crackle of bond paper. As he opened the door to his room he heard John vent a reverberating snort.

"Ba-ba-bad news, J-John?" Alfred quavered.

"Bad news? Bad news?" Jones bellowed. "Great creeping Je—um!—rusalem, no, I could take bad news. This isn't any news!"

Angela leaned against the doorframe of the kitchen, twisting her apron: "No news? Wasn't there a letter in the envelope?"

"There might as well have been none. Listen to this. Are you listening, Alfred? Belshazzar's b-bub-britches!"

"Mercy sakes, John," Angela squealed. "Not from the White House!"

"What do you mean, 'not from the White House'? Of course it is from the White House."

"Such language? I have often heard that the President is an unconventional person but to write—"

"I don't know what you are talking about. I haven't even begun to read," John broke in. "Here goes: It's from his secretary:

" 'The President has instructed me to convey to you his personal thanks for your recent expression of confidence and offer of assistance. Coming from a person of your attainments, both are highly appreciated, for the President is not of course unfamiliar with your great contributions to human knowledge and welfare. Please be assured that, as soon as conditions permit, the President will take advantage of your patriotic offer, and will invite you to discuss with him how it may be best utilized.' "

"Why, I think that is perfectly lovely," Angela cried. "Aren't you proud, John?"

"Proud?" roared John. "Proud? Of what? Of living in a

country governed by a genius of such dimensions that *he* will let *me* know when conditions are right for *him* to hear *my* —Balaam's ass!"

Upstairs Alfred was silent.

"I don't care, John," Angela said. "I think it is a wonderful letter. To have the President of the United States talk about knowing your contributions to—what was it again? Anyhow, I'm proud enough to burst myself. Where are you going?"

"To Washington," John said, pulling his hat down over his brow. "To the White House."

"But, John, at this hour! It is nearly dinnertime."

"I'll get some dinner in town."

"I mean, the President will be at dinner and his secretary will have gone home and you won't get in."

"I can try, can't I?" Jones snapped, and was gone. Angela wailed "Alfred!" but that agitated gentleman slowly pushed shut the door of his room, carefully releasing the knob so the latch would not click.

Although Angela found herself excuses to potter about the kitchen until half past bedtime, only Alfred heard John come home an hour later because Angela had nothing on her conscience to keep her awake once she was in bed. In his mind's eye, as he tossed in his bed, John's reception at the White House had been re-enacted time and again to Alfred: Jones, having argued his way into the President's presence, sitting in front of the littered desk; the President calling for Jones's letter; the forgery detected. Of course John would know who had committed the crime. He would be too loyal to accuse Alfred to the President's face, but that personage might well become irate that anyone should tamper with his mail. He would order an investigation, despite Jones's protests. Alfred wished he had worn gloves to avoid fingerprints; he regretted having ever left his fingerprints on file that time he made the tour of the FBI. The guide had been very persuasive; he had pointed out that if one were ever murdered and left stripped of all identification, the FBI fingerprint file alone could save you from Potter's Field. Now Alfred knew that that had been hocum; the agent knew very well that the chances of murder were fewer by far than the probability of the visitors themselves succumbing to the human predilection for wrongdoing.

Alfred resolved that he would suffer what punishment was decreed and that cheerfully. What tortured him was the disgrace he would bring to the Seminary and to the church on the day he was hauled away from Holy Hollow in the black prison van. He would ask not to be handcuffed.

Perhaps he could still avert that fate by making a complete confession. He would write to the President, himself. He would certainly tell the story to the Dean. The Presiding Bishop was—was-s-s—s-s-s-ss zzz. Alfred slept. That is, his body did, although it quivered in shame at the striped costume in which Alfred's dream clothed it.

Wretchedly he descended to his breakfast, to hear Jones in converse with Angela.

"I was just saying," Jones addressed him, "that my trip was not wholly in vain last night. At least, they know now that I am not to be put off. I went direct to the White House, and by God, do you know you are not allowed to walk on the sidewalk in front of it? A public thoroughfare, Pennsylvania Avenue, and you have to cross the street to get by.

"Well, never mind that. I marched up to the guard just the same and I took the letter out of my pocket—"

"You know, about that letter you wrote," Alfred interrupted bravely, "I have to confess—"

"Well, it is too late now for second guessing," Jones cut him off. "I told the guard, very politely, that I had written the President for an appointment and had got a reply asking me to call but without specifying a date. And, I said, the matter was so urgent I had come forthwith on the chance that the President could spare me a few minutes after his dinner. But the guard explained that the President had some very important guests, with whom he was having a conference after dinner. He hinted that something pretty big was in the making."

"Isn't that exciting," Angela said, turning the eggs.

"He said," John went on, "that the President's time was

114

accounted for every minute for weeks in advance, and even when Winston Churchill was here he had to wait his turn. You know, damn it, it sounds reasonable enough. Anyhow, he suggested I wait a week or ten days. I told him how terribly urgent it was, and he said, yes, but even if it was a way to end the war overnight the forces already set in motion could not be halted, or something like that. He was a very intelligent, well-spoken fellow for a policeman."

"Don't be simple, John," Angela said. "Bring in the coffee. He was not a policeman, you big bunny! He was a Secret Service man, of course. Don't forget the tile."

"Maybe so," John observed, picking up the frying pan and carrying it to Angela's place at the table. "I thought what he said was pretty significant. I asked him, however, please to get word inside the White House that I was particularly anxious, and gave him my card, and he—coffeepot? I brought it—well, I could have sworn!"

The breakfast fare was eggs and introspection, and when the eggs were eaten the three persons went about their Saturday chores; Angela to her housework, Alfred to his basement workshop, and John to his manuscripts.

Not *his* manuscripts, exactly; on his desk was the stout manila envelope left by Virginia Finster. Jones carried it outdoors, deliberately choosing the site of the Zotzian manifestation for his perusal of the thesis.

His eyebrows went up as he regarded the neatly typed title page: *Agathodaemon, or, The Cult of the Serpent in Modern Times, With Special Inquiry into Its Survival in Christian Symbolism.*

Jones's curiosity flared. Not because a lusty young woman should devote her time and talents to research so unimportant to the perpetuation of the race. No, what made him decide to devote his closest attention to this gratuitous labor was the title-word. If the thesis were, as she said and as it should be, an objective history, why did she entitle it with the name of the benevolent Greek serpent-god? Agatho-daemon, "good spirit," was the jolly snake to whom, Aristophanes relates, every Greek drank a toast at the meal's end. Would anybody write an *objective* critique of cereal foods and entitle the work "W. K. Kellogg" or name a history of dentistry "Painless Parker"?

Jones turned to the first page:

"Eve, the first mother of men, was a snake. Cain was a bastard, the fruit of his mother's dalliance with the Serpent in Eden. . . .

"Eve, whose name in Hebrew is *Hawwah*, or Snake. . . .

"Where was Eden? One Semitic tradition (Gen. 2:8) places it far to the eastward. Yet Ezekiel and Isaiah confirm the Babylonian assertion that Eden lay beneath the unwinking eye of the North Star."

The sheets crackled in Jones's fingers.

The North Star! He swallowed against the dryness of his throat.

"Perhaps there is confirmation of the Genesis geography. Due east or due west, half the world around from Judea, is Mexico.

"Wherever the Nahuatl tongue was spoken, the priests taught the descent of man from the first woman, Cihua-Cohuatl. . . .

"*Cihua* . . . woman. *Cohuatl* . . . snake . . .

"Eve . . . Cihua-Cohuatl . . . Hawwah . . . Mother of men . . ."

She wrote, this dark woman of the storm, as if her words were to be recited to the accompaniment of a drum, Jones thought.

He read on: About Quetzalcohuatl, the longed-for redeemer of the Toltecs, Quetzalcohuatl the Plumed Serpent; about the Worm of the Vikings, the Dragon of Han, the serpent Mersegret who guarded the tombs of Egyptians. And while Jones wrestled with Miss Finster's snakes like some literary Laocoön, Angela gathered up her ration books and went out to see what Miss Pealbody could provide by way of mail and groceries. Miss Pealbody dispensed both in the establishment that was Holy Hollow's one concession to commercialism, and engaged likewise in a lively barter of gossip. There was nothing in the externals of the Store to suggest

the market place, although once an enterprising tobacco salesman managed to nail a metal advertisement on the side wall
which displayed, to the embarrassment of the good ladies, the
modern successor to the ancient phallic deity Apis. The sign
was removed with much more difficulty than the ladies had in
persuading their husbands not to ever, ever smoke Bull
Durham.

To all appearance, the Store was an old-fashioned off-
campus white frame house. It was, and is, entered through
a conventional front door from which one turns left into what
had been a parlor, but breakfast cereals and canned vege-
tables line the walls instead of crayon enlargements. One
picks up a hickory basket and fills it with the articles of one's
choice, passing thence into the former kitchen now become
the meat department, and so into the dining room on the
right side where clotheslines, soap, toilet paper, and such
accessories to civilized living may be picked up before the
day's purchases are wrapped. Then one stops at Miss Pealbody's counter to pay the bill, she having already looked
through the mailbox bearing one's initial and waiting with
your *Southern Churchman, Harper's,* and electric-light bill
in hand.

"Nothing from the White House today," Miss Pealbody
greeted Angela.

"Well, Angela," added Mrs. Blattiday, wife of the professor of economics and parish finance, "I must say we are all
excited about Dr. Jones being summoned to the White House
on some war business. Did he go?"

"Yes," Angela replied, in strict truthfulness. "My, what
a dull lot of mail."

"Well, do tell us about it," Mrs. Blattiday urged. "Or is it
all a big secret, like everything else these days?"

Mrs. Blattiday's directness visibly irked Miss Pealbody.
That was no way to wheedle news, especially out of a person
with Angela Brant's taciturnity.

"If Dr. Jones is leaving you soon," Miss Pealbody said, to
show how it was done, "would you be renting his room again?
I know a very nice young naval officer, the son of a cousin of

the district manager for Coca-Cola, so he's no fly-by-night, you can be sure. But," she said, baiting the trap thus disguised with verbiage, "he has to have the room by the fifteenth next."

Three other shoppers had now joined the group, all good gregarious girls who would, Angela knew, put news into circulation with such dispatch as to force the gabby Pealbody to be a listener instead of a purveyor the rest of the day.

"Dr. Jones," Angela said, as she had planned to say all along, "was told at the White House that something of tremendous importance was going to happen very soon. It won't be until after that, that he will be, I guess you'd call it, put to work."

"But what is going to happen?" The question came in chorus.

"I don't know, and I didn't ask," Angela answered with just an acid drop of reproof in her voice. "The less one knows about secret war plans, the better, I believe."

But of course nobody there *believed* that she so believed, or believed in her avowedly self-imposed ignorance. That night, there was not a home in the Hollow but kept its radio on till past bedtime. Two or three men—like Commander Aspinwall Macandle and Commodore Fairleigh—who really knew that something of tremendous significance was impending, curtly told their wives to keep their tongues between their teeth and that was the trouble, by God, of confiding any item of military security to a goddam civilian and especially a goddam long-haired professor.

Probably of all communities in the United States, Holy Hollow was least surprised by the hysterical proclamation of D day on June 6.

John Jones was wholly heedless of the added respect paid him by the people of the Neighborhood in look and speech. Except for that one guileless reference to the North Star in Virginia's manuscript there was not a word, a line or paragraph of sinister portent or intent, and he was baffled.

He was even more baffled by the conduct of some man in a gold-lathered cap, whom he vaguely recognized as a member

118

of the community. This person, deliberately dawdling on the campus path, fell into step with Jones. He did not employ the usual gambit of observations on the weather. He just said: "Professor, it is usually best not to tell all you know."

Jones, his right hand twitching, stopped in his tracks.

"A word to the wise, you know," the uniformed man said, capping the cliché with a quick smile. "Well, nice to have seen you. Great weather, isn't it?" And with that he strode off, leaving Jones standing there speechless, and with his overworked adrenalin glands once more toiling in response to fear and anger.

15

VIRGINIA FINSTER overtook him in the meadow beyond the Grove (as she had some weeks before when the terrible potency of the Word and the Gesture had been demonstrated upon a butterfly) and thanked him all over again for his labors on her manuscript.

Jones said: "It was nothing. I found it all quite interesting."

"I couldn't ask for a higher compliment," the dark woman cried. "You found it interesting! You give me courage to ask if you will write a preface. If you don't, I warn you, I shall dedicate the book to you."

She fell in step beside him. "Your notes were too wonderful. For example, the Seraphim in the Bible; I didn't know that they were half serpent. And all those other Biblical references I never would have found, like the Dragon Gate of Jerusalem and the stone Zoheleth. As you say, it is only in our religion that snakes get a break."

Jones did not remember having ever said that, but, also forgetting how disturbed he had been a quarter hour ago, he chattily said that he sometimes agreed with some of the early Christians who held that it was God, not Satan, who posed in snake's clothing to educate Eve in the facts of life.

Thus conversing, the two strolled slowly across the meadow. They were observed, too, from many a window. What conjectures the sight inspired can be guessed, but none who saw would have guessed the topic of that earnest conversation. Who could believe that a man would go walking in spring with a beautiful young woman just to discuss snakes—and mythological ones at that?

"You should go to the Zoo some time," Virginia said. "The biggest crowds are in the monkey house and the snake house. But the monkey house is a palace of fun. People go there to laugh, and the monkeys laugh with them. But the snake house is quiet. People act as if they were in church. Even the kids."

They were back on the campus, now, and Jones felt his feet lagging, reluctant to carry him away from the woman he had suspected to be of evil origin and more evil intent. Then a sudden remembrance brought him to pause.

"Why," he asked suddenly, "did you use the phrase 'the unwinking eye of the North Star'? What has the North Star got to do with snakes?"

"Oh, but it used to have everything to do with snakes," Virginia said. "Don't you know that, oh, five thousand years ago the North Star was in the constellation Draco? And isn't a dragon a serpent? Really, it's only in historical times that the North Star is found in the Little Dipper. Perhaps I should have explained that more clearly. I only put it in because I thought it was cute."

"So then," Jones snapped, " 'the unmoving star' did move, eh? And what about"—he shut his eyes—"Zotz?"

"Zotz?" she repeated. "Isn't that what the paper said the little dog was named? I don't understand you, Dr. Jones."

"Sometimes I really believe that you don't," Jones replied. "I wish I knew. You are quite certain that the North Star used to be in a constellation named for a serpent—"

"Of course! You can find that in any elementary textbook on astronomy," Virginia assured him. "I'll expand that sentence if you think it's so awfully important."

"I don't know what to think," Jones said. He gave her a stiff little bow without removing his hands from his pockets, and strode off, his brain in turmoil again. His agitation accelerated when he recognized that they had paused on the exact spot where the gold-braided personage had stopped him not an hour earlier to warn him not to tell all he knew.

Who the devil was the fellow? Had he ever seen him before?

But, by all the snakes, he would find out who he was and why the warning!

Jones found Angela, as yet happily unaware from whose company he had just parted, down in the basement taking a census of her remaining canned goods.

"Who," he demanded, "would be a man in a gray suit with brass buttons, with little flat gold-striped things on his shoulders and gold fig leaves on the visor of his cap?"

"It sounds like a naval officer," Angela said, "unless you are asking me a puzzle that requires a clever answer. I am not good at those. I hate to listen to those quiz programs on the radio for that reason. John, does the cap on this jar of tomatoes looked puffed, to you?"

"No, it doesn't. I don't want to know what this man in the costume is, but who—who?"

"What did he look like? Was he tall and heavy-set with solid gold dinguses on his shoulder, or was he younger and slender, with stripes?"

"Stripes," John said, after a moment of concentration. "About as tall as I am. A bit younger, maybe."

"How many stripes?"

"How many stripes? How the dev—why should I count—when a man comes up and smilingly insults you, do you stop to count his buttons?"

"No man has ever insulted me," Angela said, maybe a little wistfully. "Who in the world has been insulting you, John?"

"That is what I am trying to find out," Jones answered patiently.

"Well, then, what did he say, or do? And where did it happen?"

"It happened right here on the campus not an hour ago, and never mind what he said. Anyhow, it is somebody I have seen around here before."

"Well, there's Commodore Fairleigh, and Commander Macandle, but it could not have been either of them."

"Why not? Why couldn't it have been either of them?"

"John, don't be so—so bellicose! Because I'm sure neither one would insult you, especially in language you can't repeat. They're both gentlemen. And I doubt if it could be Captain Sack. I don't know the Sacks so well. They're just renters, but he does something at the White House. Assistant first aid, or something like that."

"That's the man, then," Jones said grimly. "Sack, hey? I'll sack him, all right."

"But how do you know it is Captain Sack?"

"Because he works in the White House, of course."

"Oh, John! You don't know which one of three men it is, but when I mention that one is at the White House you decide he is the one who insulted you. And yet they always blame women for jumping at conclusions!"

"Who says women jump at conclusions? They do, don't they?"

"Oh dear," Angela sighed. "I think I will jump to the conclusion that we will have these snap beans for dinner. Will you carry up the jar for me, John?"

John did. And he moodily ate his lunch. Then (for it was Wednesday and he was free from classes) he put on his hat and headed for the bus line, leaving Angela to guess, if she so minded, where he was going. But Angela, knowing that John Jones was "in one of his moods," gave his absence no thought until Mrs. Jay dropped by in the late afternoon and inquired after him.

"He was out walking with that woman this morning," she mentioned casually. "They seemed to be having a very earnest conversation."

"John has been helping with that manuscript of hers, you know," Angela said. "It must have been quite a task, too."

"Angela!" Mrs. Jay put her teacup down with a clatter. "You remember our last talk, don't you? I told you that woman was up to something, I wasn't sure what, but she was obviously going to use Dr. Jones to her own end."

"What difference does it make, Phoebe? Heavenly days,

if she wants to marry him, she probably isn't the first who tried."

"Marry him! Hmpf," Mrs. Jay snorted. "Angela Brant, that woman is a spy!"

"A spy!"

"Yes, it is all plain as day now. Of course, I didn't know last time that Dr. Jones was close to the White House, and that he was going to do some very important war work. But mark my words, she knew it. She knew it all the time. That bluff of hers, writing a book about voodoo snake worship! Who would ever want to read such a book, let alone write it? And if 'Finster' isn't a German name, I'm a Yankee. I tell you, she's a spy. Why else would she cozy up to him and flatter him? And why else would she praise him for going into war work, and encourage him?"

"It does look kind of funny," Angela admitted slowly. "If she were really in love with him she wouldn't want him to go, would she?"

"Of course not," crowed Mrs. Jay. "I think she ought to be reported to the FBI."

"Well, how would you go about doing that?" Angela asked.

"The number is printed right in the telephone directory," Mrs. Jay said eagerly. "Right up in front together with the police and fire and ambulance numbers. They wouldn't do that if it wasn't to encourage people to call them up. Why don't you call them up right away?"

"I? Oh, no, I couldn't do that."

"Why not? I think it is your patriotic duty to warn them."

"But what would I say?"

"Just tell them the facts, thats' all. Tell them you have no proof, but it is up to the FBI to get proof, isn't it?"

"No, no, no, Phoebe. No, no! You do it. After all, it was your idea."

"Well, I may do it at that," Mrs. Jay said.

So Phoebe Jay took herself off, inwardly thinking that her dear friend Angela was something of a fool; and Angela added mental postscripts to her affectionate adieus that

Phoebe was a good friend, but Lord deliver her from ever telling the librarian anything she didn't want anybody else to know.

Anyhow, Angela thought as she took the tea things to the kitchen, she wouldn't want to be in the Finster woman's shoes. Something, she was sure, was about to happen to that woman, and somehow Angela could not feel sorry for her. It wasn't her obvious yearning over John, exactly, but the manner of her yearning. Take away her manuscript and her brassiere, thought Angela, and what would she have left? Nothing. And to Angela that was a pleasant thought.

Mrs. Jay planned Virginia's destruction along more practical lines. As soon as she reached her home, and without removing her gray rayon gloves, she took note paper from her desk and fountain pen from her purse, and addressed herself to the task of informing J. Edgar Hoover that there was a viper in the midst of St. Jude's.

16

JOHN JONES walked up Pennsylvania Avenue from the bus terminus, still pondering: Outside of Alfred Claverhouse not a soul had been told about Jones's acquisition of an awful and unwanted power. And yet that woman of unwomanly intelligence had crowded herself into his orbit almost on the instant of that acquisition. If she were innocent of all complicity, then the laws of chance and the long arm of coincidence had been extraordinarily stretched. And if she were guilty, then the game she was playing was too subtle for Jones to solve.

Now a man in the Navy's disguising uniform had stepped out of the background like a suddenly activated puppet to speak his portentous and ominous lines, warning Jones not to speak of the things about which he had not spoken. Except to Alfred.

Was it possible that Alfred had found the burden of confidence, so laden with significance to the world, too heavy to bear?

If Alfred had felt compelled to tell, he would have told Angela first, Jones knew. And it would be like a woman, as Jones estimated women, to tell Mrs. Sack about himself for the sake of letting the wife of a White House functionary understand that she, Angela, was also privy to the secret business of the Executive Mansion.

You can't. Jones angrily concluded, trust anybody. That

Alfred should betray him to Angela, and for Angela to nourish her ego by making common gossip of things too terrible to contemplate, was a most shocking brace of episodes. Was it worth while to save a world from conquest by evil, when the kindest of its inhabitants showed themselves to be already corrupted?

Jones's meditation and progress were both halted at that point by a policeman who said: "Excuse me, mister, but you'll have to stay on the other side of the street."

Jones indicated the iron gate to the White House. "But I'm going in there."

"Do you have an appointment or a pass?"

Jones said he had neither, but that he did have a letter which indicated that the President wished to consult him, and he was, he said, merely presenting in person his acknowledgment. And when the policeman demanded to see the letter, Jones showed him the envelope but cannily allowed no perusal of its contents, pointing out that it was a personal letter and thus the property of the writer and not to be read without the author's permission—especially because it concerned certain secret military operations.

A short, stocky man in brown civilian attire came out of the wooden shack just inside the gates and listened to the conversation.

"I'll tell you," he said, as the policeman groped for fresh argument. "You go around the corner there to the executive office gate. This is the entrance to the residential part of the White House. The offices are in the yonder wing there."

Jones thanked him and walked off. The man in brown turned to the policeman. "Always be diplomatic, Joe," he counseled. "Don't stick your neck out. You never can tell when a seedy-looking old nut like that is a V.I.P. Christ, you ought to see the British ambassador."

The policeman nodded his acceptance of the Secret Service man's advice and went back to his duties of keeping tourists off the south side of Pennsylvania Avenue. Jones had disappeared. That did for Jones.

At the mouth of the alleylike street which separates the

White House grounds from the State Department's symbolic architecture Jones was stopped again, and again the envelope worked as a passport to the next gate. But now he was within privileged precincts, and word of his coming was telephoned ahead a half block; he slid like a bead on the taut thread of scrutiny from sentries posted along his route, and was halted again at a wrought-iron gate locked from the inside.

Another and forewarned policeman accosted him between the bars. Jones produced his open-sesame, but here the talisman did not work as readily. Between offending an old geezer and irritating his own boss, the White House cop knew where the odds of greater discomfit fell.

"I'm only obeying orders, mister," the policeman said. "You show me the letter that says you can come in here, and I'll let you in."

"And if you will get the permission of the writer of this letter to read it, I will let you see it," Jones retorted. It was a bluff, he knew. A bluff that had so far worked so well that its final potency could not be doubted.

"You see," he added, with an air of smiling confidence, "I have to obey my orders, too. Captain Sack personally warned me to maintain silence."

"You know Captain Sack?"

"I spoke to him only this morning."

"Well, you wait here a minute."

The policeman climbed the short flight of concrete steps behind him and went into the wooden booth at their head. There he laid his problem before his superior. "This guy out there is a nice old gent but ornery as hell in a polite sort of way. He's got a letter he won't let anybody see, on account of he says Captain Sack told him not to. His name is Jones, Dr. Jones." Who was the letter from? "Well, he won't say. Just that it was from the President's secretary, and God knows how many of them there is. He ain't a crank. He just takes something too serious."

The sergeant took a fresh chew of tobacco to stimulate his mind. "Look, I'll call Captain Sack, and you go and pry out of Jones what's in that letter. You can't tell, it might be

128

important, and first thing you know the newspapers will be razzing us."

By the time the sergeant had learned that Captain Sack was home with a cold and put in a call for him there his colleague was back with the information, reluctantly given by Jones, that the letter was only from Mr. Famulus. "If he was important he'd have a letter from Early or Hassett or 'Pa' Watson." But simultaneously with the receipt of that advice the sergeant had Captain Sack on the telephone and was being told that although the Captain could not personally vouch for Dr. Jones, he was known to him, and he certainly had some kind of White House connection. The Captain thought that Mr. Jones talked a little too much, though, having predicted the Normandy invasion after a visit to the White House some weeks ago.

"If the Jones that Sack knows talks too much, this guy ain't him," the first policeman said. "I never seen such a clam."

"Well, play it safe, anyhow," the sergeant said. "Take him in to Famulus's office. Hell, the President ain't here, so what's the difference? If he is a big shot, we don't get into trouble. If he ain't, maybe we do. But if we keep him out, we get into trouble both ways. It ain't as if this wasn't an election year."

So the gate was unbarred and Jones was escorted onto the hallowed ground, and up the steps to a cemented courtyard, where he was guided right into the vestibule of the annex and his presence explained to a man who sat on a back-tilted chair beside the inner door. And that man said sadly that Mr. Famulus wasn't in.

But Jones, finding himself actually within the White House, or at least an extension of it, said he would state his business with Famulus's assistant in that case (confident that each barrier he passed brought him that much closer to the President). Accordingly he was taken into a large waiting room, in the center of which stood a huge and badly cracked round table with water buffalo carved on the knees of its bandy legs, where he was directed to sit on a leather

129

sofa, under the eye of a desk-enshrined policeman. His guide disappeared into an anteroom.

Jones suppressed a sigh of attainment. If necessary, he would Zotz his way into the executive presence, thereby giving the most graphic proof of the talents he wished to lay at the disposal of the Commander in Chief.

He began a mental rehearsal of his audience. It would have been far better if he had prepared himself with some laboratory apparatus, he realized. Then he could have produced a mouse or frog, and dramatically blasted it to kingdom come on the presidential desk. Then, while the President was examining the corpse with awe and amazement, Jones would swiftly have outlined his plan.

"I have found by experiment" (he imagined himself saying) "that the power can be made to penetrate any substance that was known to the ancient Astyparaeans. Thus it will penetrate glass, lead, clay such as bricks or earthenware, and bronze; but it will not penetrate cardboard, or modern plastics, or steel."

The President, Jones thought, would lean back in his chair and ask him just how he proposed to employ this amazing power. And Jones knew exactly what he would say: "Drop me in a parachute over Berlin. I will allow myself to be captured. I will be the American Rudolf Hess, you see. Eventually Hitler will want to see me. Then I will raise my hand, point my finger—"

"But," the President would cry, "they will kill you!"

Jones saw himself throw back his shoulders and reply: "Mr. President, what if they do? Thousands of younger men than I are being killed every day. My life will be a small price to pay for the victory . . ." Mm-m, no. Something more terse. "I regret that I have but one life to give to my country." No, that had already been used by somebody, sometime; one of the Greek heroes, probably.

Meanwhile there was much to-do behind the closed anteroom door.

The dossier on Jones lay on a table over which heads were bent.

130

"I think," said one, "that we had better call Warm Springs on this. It might even be important enough for Harry Hopkins."

A finger was placed on a typewritten sheet, tracing the inscription: *JONES, John (dr.) Member Faculty St. Jude's Seminary. Explorer Greece, Syria, Turkey, Arabia, etc. Author of a lot of books re same. See Who's Who. Letter rec'v'd 23 May; ans'd 25 May.*

Telephones were brought into action. Warm Springs. Democratic National Committee Headquarters. "Hello? Who is this? Chip? Ed? I can't hear you. Listen to this . . ."

Jones's reverie was abruptly terminated by a tall, heavy-set man who suddenly appeared in front of him, dulcetly inquiring: "Dr. Jones?"

Jones heaved himself from the sofa's embrace, was gently pressed back; the man sat down beside him and introduced himself as Mr. Pilotfisch.

"I am sorry you were kept waiting," he said, and Jones raised a deprecatory hand. The policeman at the desk on the opposite side of the room said: "Ulp!" and sagged, white-faced, in his chair. Mr. Pilotfisch failed to notice the seizure. Jones hastily returned his hand to its pocket and watched the policeman anxiously, thus failing to comprehend anything that was said to him in the first two minutes of Pilotfisch's earnest speech. When the policeman's color returned and he got up to take a drink at the wall fountain at the door, Jones sighed in relief and turned his attention to the man beside him.

"And so," that worthy was saying, "if you would be able to go to New York tomorrow for the conference it will be greatly appreciated. Greatly. We will, of course, arrange about airplane priorities. In fact, I am having reservations arranged now. I was sure you would agree to go. Of course, if it is inconvenient . . . ?"

"But the President?" Jones asked. "I would like, of course, to give him a demonstration. I am not quite prepared to do it today."

"As I said," Pilotfisch smiled, "the President is out of

town. I tell you that in confidence, of course. Officially or un-officially, that is as much as anybody knows. But in wartime, you know . . . ?"

"Yes, surely!" Jones exclaimed. "You do not have to ex-plain. I think I can arrange to go to New York tomorrow."

"Thank you, sir! Then you can decide, of course, as to plans for later. I imagine that you will not be called upon until the end of September or October, but it is all a matter of your convenience."

"September or Oct—but, my dear sir, we can't waste that much time. I want to get started as soon as possible."

"That is most generous of you." Pilotfisch spread his hands in an embracive gesture. "But there are certain aspects of, shall we say—strategy? Yes, strategy. But of course it is all out of my hands. That is up to you and the managers of the campaign to decide. Now, just a minute, and I will find out about your reservations."

He was back in the minute specified.

"If it is convenient for you to take the ten-fifteen plane tomorrow—it is? Good! Your tickets and all will be at the Information Desk. I will have a letter to Mr. Demourgos there for you, too. After all, 512,614 Greeks are not hay, hey? Or shall we say, ztromberry pie? Ha, ha! Well, sir, it was certainly good of you, most co-operative. I am only sorry that Mr. Famulus was not here. He would apologize to you himself for not having written to you sooner. Good-bye, Doctor."

Jones found himself being talked out the door. Guard passed him to guard with respectful affability, and presently he was back on Pennsylvania Avenue, not quite sure to what he had been committed short of flying to New York the next morning.

17

JOHN JONES, complete with a jar of white mice purchased from Schmid's pet shop, reported to the information booth at the Washington Municipal Airport. He was received with deference, supplied with two envelopes—one containing his ticket and the other addressed to Mr. Demourgos in Room C-987, Waldorf-Astoria (introducing Dr. Jones)—and shown where to sit until the loudspeaker announced the all-aboard for his flight.

Permission to absent himself from his classes for the two remaining recitation days of the week had been cheerfully and unquestioningly granted by the Dean. Alfred and Angela, too, had been most incurious about Jones's preparations for an unexplained departure. Jones could not, however, feel anything but nettled that Angela asked no more than "You will be back, of course?" He would have added no information to his "Yes, in a day or so," had he not bethought himself of the undeniable dangers of air travel. To save himself from an unmarked grave if the worst happened, he casually included the mention he was just flying to New York.

Angela had seemed to turn a little pale at that, and so to prove he had small choice in the matter he had added: "At the request of the White House."

To that Angela had replied, rather than asked, that, then, was where he had been all afternoon; Jones's silence was his assent.

So now he sat waiting for his debut in aviation—and in war.

Somebody touched him on the shoulder.

"Excuse me, sir. Your flight is ready. We did not want to call out your name." The uniformed woman nodded significantly. "Through that door, sir, and right down the ramp. Show your ticket and priority to the man at the gate."

Jones looked around for his suitcase and remembered that it had been taken from him at the desk and swallowed up by an aluminum-jawed trap door. Clutching his jar of white mice in the crook of his elbow, under his coat, Jones took the course directed and presently he was being buckled into his seat by a stewardess. In the comforting belief that the webbing belt was a parachute harness, Jones left it fastened all the way to LaGuardia Field.

The ninety-minute passage in the blacked-out plane was smoother, Jones concluded, than riding camelback. It was amazing, to climb into an aluminum tube on the banks of the Potomac, therein to be sealed, shaken, and then decanted on the banks of the Hudson. There was a fourth-dimensional aspect of the whole business, a dreamlike quality even to the processes which ended with his being suddenly reunited with his suitcase in the lobby of the hotel.

There display of his addressed envelope procured Jones directions to an elevator from which he was gently ejected by the pilot gnome into a carpeted corridor whose walls were bedecked with portraits of Mr. Roosevelt and much bunting. He was, he knew immediately, in the right place. He gave his envelope and his card to a young woman seated behind a desk, and she gave it to the young man who was seated on top of it. "Okey dokey," said the youth. "Ztromberry pie!" It was the same code word that the man in the White House had employed, so he gravely repeated "Ztromberry pie."

"Uh-hunh," said the youth. "Cupsa cawfee. Biffa ztew."

"Oh, scram," the young woman interrupted. "Start chasin', Jason."

The young man ducked through a curtained glass door, from behind which he abruptly stuck his head.

"Let's mate, Kate," he whispered, and vanished. Jones pondered the significance of the cabalistic repartee. It sounded flippant, but then so much that was said and done these days wore a superficial coat of irreverence to conceal lofty purpose and deep significance. Under the tawdry title of "New Deal," for example, changes had been wrought in the United States beside which the Code of Hammurabi amounted to a don't-walk-on-the-grass ordinance.

The young man came back and lifted two fingers at Jones. "Wun minnot," he said. "Bin zoop."

The door emitted a full-breasted, dark-complected young woman whose most prominent feature, above the neck, was a magnificent delta-shaped nose, the organ of a Praxitelean Venus of heroic size implanted on the face of a girl whose inky eyebrows were on a level with Jones's scarf pin.

"Dr. Jones? We have been expecting you," she said. "I am Miss Podopsistron, receptionist for Mr. Demourgos. He will see you in a minute. Won't you come in and wait?"

Jones picked up his bag, his coat and the paper-wrapped mouse jar and followed the young woman through the glass doors into a large room whose walls were lined with gilt chairs, except where they were pierced by white-painted doors.

"We're still kind of upset for a campaign headquarters," Miss Podopsistron said apologetically. "We haven't really got started, and we won't until after the convention, really. This is Mr. Demourgos' office."

She opened one of the blank doors and Jones found himself enclosed in a cubicle containing a metal desk, and a swivel chair, an armchair and an odor of cigar smoke. He put his suitcase on the floor, his jar on the desk, himself in the armchair, and his head in his hands. This was, he concluded, a most singularly unmilitary establishment. It must be, he thought, a superb job of camouflage. What Nazi spy would believe that a campaign for the conquest of Greece would be plotted in a hotel suite, whose tenants could ostensibly be visited by consulting a porter?

Of course that explained the significance of the code in

which the young man and young woman at the door had conversed. The youth was an Intelligence officer, the girl either an American spy or one of these new female soldiers.

Jones opened the sack in which his mouse jar was concealed. The occupants stood up, pink noses quivering, rosy paws pressed against the glass. They were hungry, Jones concluded, and so was he. His watch told him he had reason to be. It was one o'clock.

There was a clatter of heels on the bare boards outside, and the door swung open to admit a short, swart, stocky man in civilian clothes, exhaling cigar smoke whose reek was not improved by adulteration with garlic.

"Hah! Dr. Jones! How do you do? I am sorry I was delayed." The newcomer pulled in his paunch with both hands to permit his passage between wall and desk, producing a belch thereby which testified as to the cause of his delay.

"So," he went on, leaning back in the chair. "You have come to help us, yes? My God, what is that?"

"Mice," Jones said. "I have a letter here . . ."

Demourgos fumbled for the letter without removing his eyes from the jar.

"Do you take them with you everywhere?" he asked. "Pets?"

"No, they are not pets," Jones snapped, quickly returning the jar to its sack. "I use them to demonstrate my process." Demourgos shook his black-topped bowling ball of a head, and scanned the letter.

"So," he said, as one relieved of doubt, "you are Dr. Jones!"

"Yes," Jones replied. "Do you wish any other identification? I have membership cards here . . ." He reached for his wallet.

"No, no, never mind," Demourgos protested. "Well, I am delighted to meet you, but it is a little early yet to talk business. We do not expect to get started for nearly four months. The strategy is to let the opposition stick its neck out as far as they like—then, chop!" His gesture was graphic.

136

"I appreciate your confidence," Jones said. "I suppose that is a secret?"

Demourgos laughed, his eyes like ripe olives. "Yes, it is a very big secret."

"Do you expect a very bitter fight?"

"A push-over!" The diamond ring on each of Demourgos' hands flashed as he demonstrated the push-over. "But only if it is done right."

"Well, of course you have better information than I," Jones admitted. "But the Italian campaign, it seems to me, goes rather slowly."

"Pah!" Demourgos repeated his gesture. "They need better organization, that's all. Organization and strategy. And leadership. Most important, leadership. And, of course, it depends on who heads up the opposition. That's most important too."

"What about Eisenhower? He's putting up a good fight, isn't he?"

"Don't you believe it, Dr. Jones! That's just newspaper talk. He isn't even interested. But General MacArthur, now! Keep your eye on him."

Jones was a little aghast, not so much at the intimation that General MacArthur might displace General Eisenhower as at the casual way the mysterious Mr. Demourgos volunteered such momentous information. He did not quite know how to respond, except to cluck his tongue and shake his head.

"However," said Demourgos, "that is none of our business, hey? I promise you, Dr. Jones, when the time comes you will be associated with one of the most important, one of the most practical parts of the campaign."

"Granted, indeed," Jones said. "But if we are to be practical and businesslike, when do we see the President?"

"You come up here from Washington and ask me that?" Demourgos spread his hands on his chest. "We are small people, Dr. Jones, like the mouse that repaid the lion by gnawing the ropes. You know Aesop? Anyhow, you like mice."

"Then the President is not in New York?" Jones asked coldly.

"I should know where he is? New York, Africa, Canada. Did they tell you in Washington he was in New York?"

"Not exactly. I had a letter which said he wanted to see me. So I went to the White House. Next I am told he is not in Washington, but instantly it is arranged that I be flown to New York. You will understand that I am a little confused."

Demourgos' fist hammered the desk. "Like I told you, it is all a matter of organization, and they ain't got it in Washington even. But this letter, it says you are to discuss the business with me, Dr. Jones. Look."

He tossed the letter over the desk. Jones read it at a glance:

This will introduce the celebrated Dr. John Jones, explorer and lecturer, who has volunteered his services. He is eminently qualified to fit in with your plans, and will probably be used elsewhere as the campaign gets under way, as he comes highly recommended in several fields of influence.

Montgomery Pilotfisch, Assistant to the Special Analytical Assistant.

"I am," Demourgos said, "very anxious to have a man of your importance associated with me in my work. But we are not yet quite ready. You can see for yourself. We just moved in here Tuesday."

"That is the one fault with democracy," Jones replied. "Too little and too late. I am not content to wait. I want to get started at once."

"No, my friend, I cannot wholly agree with you. Did we have too little too late in nineteen-forty? Unh-huh. But I can sympathize with your eagerness to commence. Maybe it can be arranged. You speak Greek, yes?"

"Yes, that is relatively unimportant," Jones said.

"Unimportant? My god, Dr. Jones! Listen, my friend,"

138

and Demourgos lapsed into Greek: "Just exactly what is it that you proposed to do for us?"

"That," Jones answered with a strong Cycladic accent, "is something I am determined to tell nobody before I discuss it with the President himself."

"You speak very well indeed in the dialect of the fishing people of the eastern island." Demourgos beamed. Then his face fell as he continued in English: "But I am distressed that you think you got to talk with the President first. Excuse me, I think that won't be any cinch even for you. How about seeing Mr. Ed Flynn, if you do not think it is me who should arrange matters for you?"

"I am sorry," Jones said. "It places you in an awkward position, of course. But it may be that when the President hears my plan he will agree that it fits in better with some more immediate operation than the Greek campaign."

"No, my friend, I beg you," Demourgos protested. "Look, we will start the campaign among the Greeks at once, the minute you are ready. I don't know what this plan is, but I got confidence in you. At least, Doctor, you can try it out on the Greeks first, no? If your plan works there, you got proof to lay before the President when—you see him."

Jones pondered the suggestion. It was plausible. He could be dropped by parachute into Athens, and quietly eradicate the indicated Nazi and collaborationist leaders, probably even without detection or suspicion.

But, no! If he could do it in Athens he could do it in Berlin.

"Again I appreciate your confidence in me, and your willingness to advance the whole campaign on my account," Jones said. "However, I earnestly believe that this is something I must lay before the President and his top-rank advisers. I hope I am not offending you."

He reached across the desk to return the letter of introduction, and knocked over the mouse jar. The taut, perforated paper over the mouth of the jar burst as it struck the arm of the chair, and, with that, six hungry, bruised, but agile white mice scattered over the floor. Jones snatched frantically to retrieve them, and, his first astonishment and impulse to

139

anger overcome, Demourgos joined him in the roundup. There have been quieter fox hunts that covered ten thousand times the territory.

The thumping of furniture, the slapping of hands against floorboards where a mouse had been, brought Miss Podopsistron to the door, which she opened at an inopportune time for all concerned except the mice, who leaped across her feet and vanished into the gilded expanse of the room beyond. Miss Podopsistron was not afraid of mice. What she screamed at was the sight of Demourgos and Jones running around the floor on hands and knees trying to catch them, and, perhaps, at the words that followed the mice through the door.

"Shut that goddam door! There go the son of a bitches!"

The scream brought the outer guard to action. The female half opened the farther door to see a squadron of white mice charging at her across the inadequate barrier of Miss Podopsistron's feet. Her own instant impulse to retreat was reversed by the young man behind her, who entered the affray carrying everything before him.

On the whole, it is best not to describe what happened in the next few minutes. At their lapse, the two women were found standing on gilded chairs, Demourgos was speechless because he had a bleeding thumb stuffed into his mouth, the youth stood triumphant holding a stunned mouse by its tail, while Jones was bearing down upon an inverted wastepaper basket under which he had managed to trap one of the escapees.

Nor is the conversation that ensued worth recording. It was frivolous, on the women's part, and vulgar in the young man's contribution; monosyllabic and somewhat profane on Jones's part, and Demourgos said nothing. The two recaptured mice were transferred to the jar, which was retopped with fresh paper.

"I think," Jones said, "I will return to Washington."

Demourgos bowed, and took his thumb from his mouth. "Yes," he said. "Thank you for coming up."

"I am sorry about the mice," Jones continued.

140

DEMOURGOS JOINED IN THE ROUNDUP

"I do not understand about the mice," Demourgos said. "But please do not explain."

"I would have needed them to demonstrate my plan," Jones said. "However, as you say, there is no need to explain."

"I know," the young man put in. "Mice are to scare elephants with. The G.O.P. Elephant, get it?"

Nobody laughed. Jones put his jar in the crook of his arm, arranged his raincoat, picked up his suitcase.

"Good-bye," he said, and marched out to the elevator. It seemed an inadequate termination to a hideously wasted day, and yet Jones did not want to leave the quarter feeling humiliated at his insistence upon negotiating with higher authority. After all, it was natural for Demourgos to believe his Greek campaign to be the most important operation of the war; natural, and desirable. Maybe Jones's own secrecy, in the face of Demourgos' astounding frankness concerning plans and personalities, would impair the man's morale. Jones wished he could make some more amiable and intimate gesture of adieu than the brusque good-bye, and a happy thought came to him. The code-word! The slogan used by Mr. Pilotfisch and by the young Intelligence officer-in-disguise. Jones turned back, reopened the glass door, and saw the four huddled at the entrance to Demourgos' office.

"I say," he called across the room. "See you later. You know—*Ztromberry pie!*"

He stretched his face into the most amiable smile he could synthetically produce, and then wheeled to catch the elevator, content at having made his departure amiably, incurious over the source and nature of the sounds of violence that reached him through the closing door. Whatever it was he heard, he hoped it was the last of Demourgos.

18

TAKING STOCK on the day after his return from New York, Jones was self-assured that he was correct in refusing to deal with underlings. One valuable hint he had acquired from Demourgos, at any rate: "organization and strategy." He had been too importunate, too naïve, in making a frontal assault on the White House. Not that his efforts had been wasted. At least, he was known within those precincts now.

So, the first thing to do was to get word crisply to Mr. Pilotfisch that the trip to New York had been of no use to either the authorities or himself, because he would disclose his plan to no one else than the President or someone expressly and personally deputized by the President. Probably that information would filter through to the Executive. Undoubtedly, Demourgos' report that Jones had refused to divulge his plan also would percolate. Mr. Famulus, too, would have to be further prompted. There, then, were three crevices in the wall erected around the President by the Janizaries of the modern age. They were not enough.

He wrote two notes. One, to the Pilotfisch: "By this time you are probably aware that my interview with the gentleman to whom you sent me was unsatisfactory. It is probably my own fault that I made the journey under misapprehension as to whom I would see. I can only repeat that the information I possess must be presented only to the very highest authority."

And to Famulus: "I called at the White House and regretted very much that my visit should coincide with the absence of yourself and others I was desirous of consulting. Mr. Pilotfisch tried to co-operate by providing me with transportation to New York, a journey I undertook with too much optimism. I can only repeat that the information I have is so vital to the national welfare that it can only be communicated to the President personally, or to somebody in highest authority specifically deputized by him to hear me."

Now let those simmer awhile, Jones thought, when he posted the letters; now to light a couple of other fires.

His metaphor was inadequate.

The position Famulus occupied in the secretarial hierarchy at 1600 Pennsylvania Avenue is hard to define. He was not so high that his name was deliberately left out of the newspapers, nor was he high enough to have his name deliberately inserted in press analyses of White House operations. The rank he did have, however, enabled him to command Pilotfisch's presence.

"What the hell is all this Jones business?" Famulus asked, tapping a dossier on his desk.

"Oh, that nut! He worked himself inside here last Wednesday. I thought, from your letter and what he said, that he had something. So I got him a ducat on TWA for New York to see the head of the Greek division at campaign headquarters."

"Yes, go on."

"Well, he turns out to be a nut. You ought to be more careful whom you encourage to come around here. This old guy barges into headquarters with a lot of double-talk, turns a lot of white mice loose which scares the girls into hysterics, and tops it all by yelling 'Zdrom . . .' "

"Pipe down! You're just too goddam ambitious! And maybe I can guess for what. Now I'll probably have to get this guy in to see the Chief to clean up the mess you've made, you and your refugee friends. This guy Jones is a big shot in the religious circles, and you may not know it, but we don't have too many friends among the Episcopalians even if the

145

Boss is one himself. And Jones is a big-shot explorer. We don't have a single explorer on the team. The Republicans are lousy with them, naturally, because the explorers get the dough to do their exploring from the fat-cats like the duPonts and Fords and Rockefellers. And Jones isn't just a Greek expert. My God, here in Who's Who you can see for yourself he's an expert on the Assyrians, the Chaldeans, the Turks, the Etruscans, and God knows how many other minorities. Now, goddamit, after this you stop reaching over your head. You got too much to learn."

"But I tell you the guy is a nut. He lets a lot of mice . . ."

"You didn't think he was a nut when you sent him up to New York, did you?"

"No, but . . ."

"Well, but . . ."

"Well, don't give me any such fancy excuses then. Do you think for a minute Who's Who would have a nut in it? You go back and peddle the fish you're given to peddle, and don't try to horn in on the big game."

Pilotfisch, fists clenched and face crimson, slammed out of the room. Famulus propped his head in one hand and addressed himself to the job of placating the powerful Dr. Jones.

Jones, removing himself from intrusion upon his slowly maturing plans, went walking on Saturday. Now that summer was in the weather, if not yet on the calendar, he stuck to the road to avoid the plague of chiggers that infested the grass and thus it was that he was politely stopped by a young man who inquired the location of the Seminary Library.

Half an hour later, and more than a mile distant, Jones's progress, on foot and in mind, both, was abruptly self-halted.

Who was the strange man and what could he want at the Library? Was he, by chance, in search of Virginia Finster? Some casual encounter, perhaps, the excuse for a visit to promote the relationship? The girl ought to be warned against such tactics. She was too unsophisticated, too real and direct, too much the scientist, to understand that a frank

146

smile would be misinterpreted as an invitation by an urbane and lecherous young male.

A woman was not safe on the streets of wartime Washington! The city was full of smart young men, in and out of uniform, money in pocket and consciences left behind; all of them intent upon actively proving that a breakdown of feminine morals was inevitable to the times.

Jones reversed his course and lengthened his stride. The man he had met, as he recalled him now, was certainly mature enough to be married and to have a considerable family.

He reached the cool fragrant sanctuary, hot and tired, moist and angry. A blur of yellow in the dim interior resolved itself into Virginia, smiling delightedly at him from her desk near the door, crisp as a jonquil in butter-hued linen.

"Hel-lo!" she said. "I haven't seen you for simply days and days. Do sit down and cool off."

"Just dropped by to see how the book was progressing," Jones said, panting a little. As he wiped his forehead he looked around the room. As far as he could see, every man in the place was known to him as a student. "It's a wonder you do not have more clients, it is so cool and quiet in here."

"I have just the right number," Virginia laughed. "Any more, and I would be too busy. Any less, and I probably wouldn't have a job."

"Don't a lot of strangers come in, people who have no connection with the school?"

"No, never since I have been here."

"Well, just be careful of strangers," Jones advised her. "Especially of men. There are all sorts of loose characters around, on account of the war, of course."

Virginia's lashes drooped against her cheeks, and she pressed her lips together against the upcurving of their corners.

"Thank you, Dr. Jones," she said, almost demurely. "I shall be most careful."

Jones remained beside her desk in silence; one couldn't, he felt, come right out and ask her if a young man had been looking for her, had found her, what his business might be.

The young man might have been, on second thought, an electrician or a plumber or a book salesman.

"Well, if there is any further help I can give you on the book, just let me know," he said, at last, and thus awkwardly made his departure.

It was good advice, anyhow, Jones told himself, as he sauntered toward home and luncheon. And then he gulped. Walking toward him, as if it had taken him the last hour to cover two hundred yards, was the man who had been looking for the Library. He passed Jones with a courteous inclination and polite murmur, and went directly to the Library as if the directions had been given him that instant.

"The things that happen around this place," Jones said aloud, "are beyond my understanding. I'll be so damn glad to be parachuted into Germany! At least I'll be up against reality then."

19

SPECIAL AGENT PAXTON D. McJAVERT
felt much the same way.

He had received orders to run off a routine check on an
anonymous tip that a woman of mysterious antecedents was
behaving suspiciously in the environs of St. Jude's Seminary. The tip-off was a letter, so obviously written by a woman
that it ordinarily would have been dismissed as a piece of
jealous spitework. But the FBI could take no chances in wartime, and the bizarre accusation of voodoo made an inquiry
indicative. It was just the sort of approach the Nazis would
employ to provoke disaffection among the Negroes.

So, Special Agent McJavert, looking his most inconspic-
uous, arrived at Holy Hollow early this glowing Saturday
morning. The first person he met, a dreamy-eyed parson-
looking old duck, pointed out the Library where his suspect
was reported to lurk. A few rods farther, the investigator
came upon another elderly gent even more palpably the
preacher, doing things to iris with canvas-gloved hands.

He had courteously inquired if he was correct in assuming
that the horticulturist was connected with the Seminary, and
was politely informed that the iris gardener was the Rev. Dr.
Alfred Claverhouse, twenty years on the faculty and at his
service.

"May I speak to you privately?" the special agent asked,
and Alfred, assenting, mentally girded himself against the

always overwhelming arguments of insurance agents and magazine salesmen.

"I am Special Agent Paxton D. McJavert," the investigator said, exhibiting his credentials in hand. To his surprise, the plump little clergyman paled and his jaw went slack; the trowel dropped from his limp hand.

"I—I have sort of been expecting you," Alfred gulped.

"You have?" McJavert concealed his astonishment. "Well, we do have a way of turning up. Do you want to tell me about it?"

"Yes," sighed Alfred, stripping off his gloves. "Do you mind if we walk up into the Grove, where we will not be interrupted?"

McJavert noticed the apprehensive roll of eye at the tidy little house as the request was uttered, and inwardly resigned himself to an afternoon of digging up its basement for the remains of a choir singer. He followed Alfred to a rustic bench under an ancient campus oak a hundred yards distant.

"I suppose you found my fingerprints," Alfred said, trying to work his stiff lips into a smile. "I didn't think of that at the time, but, of course, there was no evil intent."

"Yes, it usually starts out that way," McJavert commented soothingly. "Why did you do it?"

"I did it for his own good, of course," Alfred answered. "But, then, you should have seen the letter that he wrote. I wish I had saved it. Then you would understand."

So that was it—blackmail! The poor old codger. If only he would have come to the FBI in the first place; if only all victims of attempted blackmail would do that, McJavert thought.

"Yes, you should have saved the letter," he said gravely. "It might have lessened the penalty."

Alfred shuddered, and closed his eyes.

"I don't care about myself," he said slowly. "I did wrong, and I expect to be punished for it. But is there not some way we can avoid publicity? It would break the Dean's heart, and impair—unjustly impair—the reputation of this institution."

"I suppose it could be arranged," McJavert said. "A complete confession, a plea of *non vult*, perhaps. Of course, I cannot promise you anything, nor can I bargain with you. Suppose you accompany me to Washington, and you talk it over with the Director."

Alfred sighed gustily through pursed lips. McJavert smothered a sudden feeling of pity for the round little clergyman.

"Tell me," he broke the pause, "did you have any accomplice? Did anybody help you?"

"No, oh, no," Alfred answered vehemently. "If you found Angela's fingerprints on the envelope, that is because she took the letter to the post office. She had nothing to do with it, I promise you. She doesn't know I did it. She must never know."

Who, McJavert wondered, was Angela? The third party to the triangle? It was a plot for a French novelist, he told himself. To hell with keeping this out of the newspapers!

"You see," Alfred said suddenly, "it isn't as if he were not able to do something. Only he thought he had supernatural powers, and that gave him the idea he had a mission in this war. If it were all an illusion, you understand, I would have taken other measures, perhaps. I did suggest he consult a physician, or an electrician."

"Take it easy," McJavert counseled. "Who are you talking about, now? We were discussing Angela last."

"She saw it, too," Alfred groaned. "But she thought it was a coincidence. I mean, about the moth."

"Look here," the G-man said in all kindliness. "You better take a grip on yourself. If Angela saw it done, she becomes a party to the deed, you see."

"Angela is not remotely connected with what I did," Alfred spoke up indignantly. "She was in another part of the house."

"She did not help you dispose of the body?" It was a shot in the dark.

"Not at all. She told me to pick it up and throw it outside. I remember, there was quite a little discussion as to where its

151

brains were," and Alfred chuckled reminiscently. It made McJavert's scalp prickle. The sanctimonious old bastard, giggling over a murder of such devastating effect that there was a question of finding the contents of the victim's skull!

"Look here," he said, "you had better come along with me at once, and tell me, too, where we can locate this Angela if we want her."

"She's down there in the house," Alfred said. "She is my sister, of course. But I tell you, she had nothing to do with the forgery. I, alone, am guilty."

"Forgery!" McJavert sat down again abruptly. "My God, will you please tell me the story here and now, leaving out the electricians and the moths? After you threw the body out, what then?"

"I can't very well leave the moth out," Alfred protested. "Or the squirrel, although I didn't see that happen."

"If you think you can establish insanity as a defense by this line of talk, you are mistaken," the special agent declared. "If you want to make a voluntary confession, you had better come along with me now. Forget anything else I asked you."

"You won't handcuff me?" Alfred pleaded. "I'll just go in and get my checkbook and tell Angela I have to go to Washington. I am sure it will not be necessary to confine me overnight. I will pay the fine, and that's that. It will only be a fine, won't it?"

"That is not my business," McJavert answered. "And under the circumstances I do not think I can permit you to communicate with this Angela in any way. If you will promise to come along with me quietly, we won't need handcuffs."

"She is bound to see us go past," Alfred argued. "And if I don't show up for lunch she will worry."

"As I said before," McJavert said, "you should have taken that all into consideration before you killed him."

"Before I—what? Killed whom? What are you talking about?"

"What are *you* talking about?"

"I'm talking about the letter I wrote."

152

"This is the first time you mentioned any letter you wrote. Look, Claverhouse, you promised to come along quietly."

"Not as a murder suspect, no, sir," Alfred said doggedly. "I did not kill anyone, and if you think I did you had better show me your warrant to arrest me. I think you are crazy, that's what I think."

"Now, now," the G-man soothed. "It's no use, you know. You have just as good as made a confession. If you won't come with me voluntarily, I shall have to call upon the local police to arrest you, and there goes all your chance of hushing it up."

"Whom am I suspected of killing?" Alfred cried. "Answer me that!"

McJavert frowned.

"I didn't accuse you of killing anybody," he admitted. "You accused yourself."

"I did? I accused myself? You are mad!" Alfred panted, his face empurpled. "I suppose you have an unsolved murder on your hands, and you are trying to accuse me of it so you can close your books. Well, sir, I defy you. I will not move from this bench. Call the police if you will. Call out the Marines if you like. I have never in my life laid violent hands on a fellow human being, and I can prove it."

"Please, please wait a minute," McJavert protested. "First you beg me to arrest you, and now you are going to fight the whole Marine Corps if I try it. Will you please, for God's sake, tell me what's biting you?"

"Suppose you tell me first why you came to see me?" Alfred demanded, his wrath still lending him boldness.

"I came here to make a routine check on a letter, a certain letter, that came into our hands," the agent said. "Before I could explain, you were jabbering about bodies, brains, blackmail and—"

"Exactly, the letter!" Alfred interrupted. "I wrote it. That is what . . ."

"You wrote it? You wrote it?" McJavert's voice cracked.

"That is what I have been trying to explain," Alfred said.

"I thought you had found my fingerprints on it and traced it to me."

"There were no fingerprints on the letter at all," McJavert declared. "I had no idea you were its author when I first spoke to you. But will you please, please tell me what all your talk about bodies and brains and Angela was about? You can't blame me if I thought you were confessing a murder. Maybe I still think so."

"It was the moth's body."

"Oh, to be sure. Of course it was the moth's body. Any fool would have known you meant the moth's body. Except me. And I still don't know what in hell you are talking about. Will you please explain before I start chewing up the grass?"

"There is no need to curse or to shout," Alfred protested. "The moth flew into the living room. Angela said for me to kill it. But Jones just pointed his finger at it, and it dropped dead. I carried the body out and threw it away. Angela, my sister, insisted it had dashed out its brains on the ceiling. I told her a moth's brains were not in its head. Later on, much later, Jones told me that he had acquired the power to kill things by looking at them and saying a cabalistic word. That I could not, and do not, believe. I think he is full of static electricity, from being hit by lightning. As you know, and as I explained to him, your body can become charged with electricity just by shuffling your feet on a rug. But he still thinks he has. Oh, Heaven forgive me, but I promised him I would not tell anybody about it. Please, I beg of you, keep what I have told you in confidence. I am ashamed that I broke my word just to save my own skin. You won't tell anyone, will you?"

The G-man, whose eyes had been unwinkingly fixed on Alfred during his simple, straightforward recital, inched away from the clergyman.

"No," he said hoarsely, "I certainly will not. I promise you that on a stack of Bibles. Wild horses couldn't drag it out of me."

"Thank you," Alfred said, laying his hand on the other's knee. "And now that everything is explained and understood,

154

I am prepared to go with you and accept my punishment for the letter."

"Oh, no," the gray-faced McJavert said. "Oh, no! I hereby declare you null and void of any statutory offense in writing the letter, so help me God. *Nolle contendere, habeas corpus* and *de lunatico inquirando.* Go thou and do likewise."

"You mean to say that I am—that I did not—I won't be arrested?"

"Look, Mr. Claverhouse, you go back to your garden. Stay out of the sun. Keep away from fountain pens. Don't stoop over so much, either. Just take things easy, and forget you ever saw me. I will try to do the same. Good-bye."

"But won't you come to the house and have a lemonade?"

"Oh, no! No, thank you. I have to go shuffle my feet on other rugs, if you know what I mean. Good-bye."

He strode off, up the winding gravel road. Alfred watched him for a while. With a shudder he went back to his pursuit of iris thrips.

Special Agent McJavert, pacing swiftly toward the Library, saw the man from whom he had earlier asked directions and murmured a passing greeting. Whoever he was, the man looked startled when he recognized McJavert, and the agent increased his pace. He knew what that look in the eye of a theologian meant, and he was having no more of it, so soon!

He did not have to make inquiry for Miss Finster in the Library. As soon as he saw the dark-haired young woman whose secondary sexual characteristics were of such primary interest, the detective knew that she was the victim of the anonymous letter Claverhouse had confessed writing. Flat-chested blondes never provoke suspicion or jealousy. And so he walked up to Virginia and greeted her by name, introducing himself with the swift legerdemain of wallet-encased credentials.

"I am making a routine check on some individuals whom the government is considering for certain purposes of a confidential nature," he explained in the smooth double-talk of his calling. "Your assistance will be appreciated, and your

155

opinions, of course, will be treated with utmost confidence. Are you acquainted with Dr. Alfred Claverhouse?"

"Yes, I am," Virginia replied. "There isn't a more gentle and respectable gentleman around. He's an old sweetheart, he is."

"Aha, that might explain it," the G-man said, half to himself. "He is not married, apparently. Is he a widower or a bachelor?"

"I don't think he ever married," Virginia said. "But if you want to know more about him, you ought to speak with that gentleman who just left. You must have met him near the door. That's Dr. Jones, who lives with Dr. Claverhouse."

"Dr. Jones, hey? He is a bachelor, also?"

"Yes. You can find out all about him in any newspaper library, or Who's Who, or a dozen places. He is a very famous scientist."

"And what about yourself?" McJavert smiled. "Just for the record."

"Oh, I'm just a nobody," Virginia smiled back. "I am the assistant librarian here, and trying to write a book on the side. Dr. Jones is helping me."

"Aha!" That explained a lot more to McJavert. "You are unmarried?"

"An old maid," Virginia confessed. "Age twenty-eight. Orphan. Antecedents unknown, as they say. I was a foundling."

"Is that so? How did you get your name?"

Virginia's eyes widened. "Why, I never thought of that," she said. "I really don't know."

"There would be ways of finding out, if you are interested," McJavert said affably. "I would like to discuss it with you, informally of course, and outside of line of duty."

"Well, it never bothered me," Virginia said. "A person is who she makes herself, not who her ancestors were, I always say. Of course, my boss thinks differently. She is sort of a crank on genealogy, and I don't think she is particularly fond of me because I never give her any satisfaction when she gets nosy about my ancient history."

McJavert dismissed the boss librarian forever with a wave of his hand. "If you don't mind, I'll call you up sometime and maybe we can get together and do a little ex cathedra sleuthing, so to speak."

"That would be awfully nice," said Virginia.

The special agent went back to the Department of Justice and wrote his report: The letter impugning subject Finster, Virginia (N), was admittedly written by one Claverhouse, Alfred, Rev. Dr., a former suitor of subject, inspired by jealousy of one Jones, John, Rev. Dr., but motive given "for his (Jones) own good." Case closed.

That subject Finster's telephone number was JUbal 700, Ext. 3009, was however recorded only in McJavert's private file.

20

CAPTAIN JAMES ARDMORE SACK, USNR,
was assistant liaison officer between the President's chief of
staff and the President's naval aide.

The Sacks had rented what was locally known as "the old
Hubert place" on the perimeter of Holy Hollow, and on the
perimeter of the Neighborhood's activities they remained.
Thus they were both rather surprised to see the shyest and, of
late, most prominent denizen of the Hollow turn into their
front yard.

"Why, Professor Jones, sir! We are most happy to have
you aboard, sir. Oh, don't sit there. You'll get all covered with
cat hair. Here, take this chair. We were just about to splice
the main brace. Will you join us, sir?"

Jones put on his most affable face, unable to interrupt the
flow of oral hospitality, took the indicated chair and nodded
his acceptance of the drink. While Mrs. Sack darted in and
out bearing bottles, glasses and ice, the Captain offered pithy
comments on baseball, politics and the war as samples of the
conversational merchandise he was ready to offer his guest.

"I have come to you for advice," Jones was finally able to
say. "I am emboldened thus to appeal to a virtual stranger
because you volunteered some sage counsel to me on the
campus the other day. I would be interested in learning what
it was that prompted your warning to me?"

"I am only a blunt, seafaring man," Sack said, "and I'll
tell you plain: Mrs. Sack overheard some scuttlebutt at the

158

store that had you predicting D day right on the nose from some information you got at the White House."

Jones did not know whether to laugh out loud with relief or angrily deny the impeachment, for all that most of it was as unintelligible to him as Chinese. The resulting grimace was accepted by Sack as a rueful confession of error.

"Well, well, I am glad you accepted my advice in the spirit it was given," the Captain said. "Mum is the word, then."

The comment left Jones not only uninformed but more baffled than ever, but it had also left Sack seemingly in the best of humor and self-esteem, so Jones decided not to press his inquiry.

"Now, then," the Captain said, caressing his hairless scalp with a hand burdened by an enormous signet ring, "you said you wanted to consult me on something."

"I'm sure you men will want to be alone," Mrs. Sack said, rising. "I know how it is, these days."

Jones did not deter her. Alone with the Captain, he proceeded forthwith to prepare another crevice in the blank wall erected around the President.

"I will state my question hypothetically," he began. "Suppose a person came into possession of a new and unique—ah —shall we say, technique of warfare—"

"Just a minute!" Sack raised a pancake palm. "Is this person in the Army or the Navy?"

"Neither one," Jones answered. "He is a civilian."

"A civilian who has discovered a new technique of war?" Sack's disbelief was patent.

"Yes, that is the difficulty," Jones declared. "If he were in the Army or Navy he would have no trouble getting his idea adopted."

"That," Sack said into his glass, "is what you think. But go on, sir. What else?"

"This hypothetical person, then," Jones continued, "has in his possession a technique that could materially shorten the war. He himself considers it so important, and of necessity so secret, that he can confide it only to the President. How does he do it?"

Sack blinked and pondered.

"He couldn't do it," was his eventual conclusion. "He couldn't get in to see the President without stating his business, that's plain enough. I guess this hypothetical civilian of yours will just have to let the war be fought in the old-fashioned military and naval manner."

"Now that," cried Jones, "I find incomprehensible. Do you mean to tell me nobody ever tells the President a secret?"

"No, he tells secrets to others," Sack replied. "He makes 'em, not hears 'em, I mean. I guess this person you are talking about will have to go through the chain of command, seeing it is a military matter."

"What does that mean?"

Sack arched his hairless brows. "Chain of command? Why, you know, the chain. You tell A, and A tells the next higher B, and B tells C, and so on up to CNO and JCS."

"Good lord," Jones groaned, "can't we escape all those alphabet agencies even in wartime? The CCC and the WPA come in, somewhere, too, I suppose?"

Again Sack flushed, and his voice was stern. "No, sir! There is no connection, not remotely. The CNO is Chief of Naval Operations, and JCS means Joint Chiefs of Staff, sir."

"I beg your pardon," Jones exclaimed. "I meant no frivolity, I assure you, Captain. But I am of the opinion that the plan I told you about might not appeal to the orthodox military mind. Especially in the lower levels of your chain. It would take a man with the imagination and the authority of the President to appreciate it. I think, if it were brought to his attention that such a scheme existed, that he might summon its proprietor to the White House for an explanation."

"He might at that," Sack admitted. "Why don't you get the word into the White House yourself?"

"I have," Jones declared. "But I can't get to the President. The best I could do was to get this hypothetical person permission to try his plan experimentally when Greece is invaded four months—but I suppose you know all about that campaign."

160

Sack, who had started from his seat is if stung by a wasp, relaxed. "Invasion of Greece!" he exclaimed. "I never—I mean—I trust you have not discussed that around the neighborhood, sir?"

"Certainly not," snapped Jones.

"Just how much do you know about this forthcoming Greek invasion?" Sack asked. "Do you know who is going to command the naval units?"

"No," Jones said. "And General—I take it he was a general—Demourgos, didn't tell me. And I told him nothing about the technique in question."

"A general, hey? Is this technique something that only the Army could use?"

"Not at all," Jones said. "It would certainly require at least Navy co-operation."

"Then I would advise you to go to—to tell your friend to go to—the Navy Department," Sack said. "For one thing, the Navy does anything the Army can do, and sails ships besides. Where would the Army be in the Pacific, for instance, if it weren't for the Navy and Marines? In Schofield Barracks, that's where the Army would be. Let's have another drink."

"Not for me, thank you," Jones said. "Then your advice is that this plan be laid before the Navy. Who in the Navy?"

"Well, being a civilian, I suggest he—you—he talk to the Secretary."

"Thank you," said Jones. "I certainly appreciate your advice. Meanwhile, I think if the President could be informed, he might be grateful to the person who made it possible for him to come into possession of the facts."

"Maybe we could get Tommy Corcoran to play it for him on the accordion," said the Captain. "Well, sorry you won't join me in another drink."

Jones left, satisfied. He was sure Sack's curiosity was piqued to the point where it might produce another crack in the White House barrier, and, meanwhile, the advice to broach the Navy was not without merit.

Accordingly on the following Wednesday he presented

himself at the main entrance of the gimcrack building that was the home of the most powerful Navy on earth.

Jones approached one of the desks in the vestibule, and told the policeman behind it that he was in search of information.

"What kind of information?"

"About the Secretary's office."

The policeman opened a paper-bound directory. Under the heading "Office of The Secretary" he ran his finger down the columns until he came to "Information, Office of Public."

"Put on this badge," Jones was told, being handed an oblong of green celluloid stamped in black with the number 3403. "I'll get you an escort." Presently a tall, sad-faced and gray-haired officer with two small, frivolous-looking gold leaves on his collar said gruffly: "Come this way," and Jones was ushered past the Marine guards down a long, gloomy corridor and into a large room. At a double battery of olive-green desks men in uniform, and women both uniformed and becomingly dressed, pounded typewriters and sipped black coffee from thick, chipped mugs. No one looked at him, as he sat down at the end of the row of men and women roosting in chairs against the wall, all of them with the green celluloid badge that made them look like criminals in a line-up. One by one, these were summoned into an adjoining office by a tall, daintily freckled young woman and all the visitors moved up one seat.

As Jones moved closer to the door, chair by chair, other green-placarded visitors were admitted to fill up the row. At last Jones found himself in the ultimate seat, his buttocks cramped from having instinctive recoil to the body warmth adhering to each chair from its previous occupant.

The door opened: "Will you come in, please?"

Jones rose and entered the adjoining office. He half expected to see a dentist's chair in it, and a white-coated man waiting with forceps and drill. Instead, he saw a narrow room containing two desks, a khaki-clad figure at the farther one silhouetted against the room's one window. The man at the

162

desk was holding a telephone to his ear, intermittently saying "Yes, sir."

The young woman sat down at the nearer desk. "What is your name, please?" She made an entry in a small, cloth-bound notebook. She stood up. Jones dug his hands deeper into his jacket pockets.

The officer replaced the telephone on its cradle and thoughtfully wiped the perspiration from it with a hand-kerchief. He looked up, and Jones saw a burly, pink-faced person, his forehead creased with a deep pucker between the brows.

"Commander Karig, this is Mr. John Jones," the young woman said. She sat down again, and began shuffling papers.

The Commander stood up and extended his hand, which Jones pretended not to see as he sidled into the chair beside the desk.

"How can I help you, Mr. Jones?"

"I wish," Jones said, "to speak to the Secretary of the Navy on an urgent and highly confidential matter."

The officer nodded. "It is," he said, "somewhat difficult to arrange. Can you give me any idea what you want to talk to him about?"

Jones said: "I would first like to know if this is the proper place to initiate such a meeting."

"Well," said the Commander, rubbing the back of his head, "it is the routine point of departure, let's say. I mean, this is the main entrance, but I suppose there are ways of creeping under the tent."

"I have no intention of obtaining admission by stealth," Jones replied stiffly. "I wish to be instructed in the proper procedure."

"Well," said the Commander, "first of all you have to convince me that you've got to see the Secretary. Maybe one of the assistant secretaries is the proper person for you to see anyhow, or one of the Bureau chiefs. Then I've got to convince him he's got to see you."

"No," said Jones, "this is a matter for the Secretary, and

for him to lay before the President. It is on a matter of urgency having to do with the prosecution of the war."

"Oh," said the Commander, trying to catch the young woman's eye.

"I suppose it is necessary for me to assure you that I am a responsible person," Jones continued. "If you will consult Who's Who, either the British or the American, you will find me adequately identified. I can tell you that I am an archaeologist who has spent most of his life in the eastern Mediterranean. I know the terrain from the Adriatic to the Suez as intimately as you know the top of your desk."

"That isn't saying much," the officer remarked. "I never expect to get through these papers to see the top of the desk. Can you speak any of the languages of that neck of the woods?"

"I can, but that is relatively unimportant. I speak Greek, Arabic, Turkish, to name but a few. I can read Sanskrit, cuneiform, hieroglyphics, demotic. And that too is relatively unimportant, although it all pertains to my mission with the Secretary."

"Well, I'll tell you," the officer said. "You know, in the Navy everything is pretty well regimented, and channelized. From what you say, I judge that if the Secretary accepted your idea he would give it to the OSS to execute. So then, the proper approach is via the OSS, don't you see?"

"Frankly, I do not," Jones said.

"Well, that's the way it is." The Commander sighed. "If you had an idea about ship construction, you would have to approach the Secretary through BuShips. Then he would refer your idea back to them. From what you tell me, the Office of Strategic Services is the outfit to deal through."

"Why can I not arrange to speak to the Secretary directly?"

"That, Mr. Jones, is what everybody wants to do."

"But this is a matter for top authority to—"

"Excuse me, Mr. Jones. I'm really doing my best to get you to the Secretary. I wouldn't kid you. If this one doesn't work, we'll try another approach. Now pardon me while I do a bit of telephoning."

He dialed a number, asked for an extension, identified himself. "There is a man in my office who is right down your alley, I think. By name of Jones. John Jones. He's in Who's Who. Yes, of course. I don't know. Okay."

He scribbled an address on a slip of paper.

"Go down here to Twenty-third Street and turn right to the old Naval Hospital grounds," the Commander told Jones. "Kenmuckle is the man you start with. Good luck."

The girl rose automatically and opened the door to the hall.

21

JONES'S BRISK ADVANCE upon the dolmen where
the wizards of OSS performed their rites did not pass un-
noticed; the sight of anybody walking fast in Washington
immediately suggests that the speeding pedestrian knows
where an apartment is about to be vacated, or a furnished
room may be shared. Several persons encountered or over-
taken by Jones fell in line behind him, so by the time he
reached Twenty-third Street he was heading a small but
hopeful parade of men and women who did not know what
they were pursuing but knew it must be desirable.

Of this, Jones was happily unaware. The Office of Strategic Services! From its name, the agency promised to be
exactly the vehicle for his endeavor. He almost jigged with
impatience when he was halted by the sentry, at the entrance
to the walled covert. His troop of followers dispersed with
black looks, resentful at having been defrauded, as Jones,
provided with uncommunicative escort, was led up a steep,
curving drive. In one of a quadrangle of gaunt brick buildings he was passed from guard to guard like the baton in a
slow-motion relay race and delivered finally into the presence
of a tall, frosty-haired man dressed in crisp gray double-
breasted mohair.

"Ah, how do you do, Dr. Jones? Warm, isn't it? My name
is Kenmuckle. Do sit down. I imagine you find Washington's
heat more enervating than the Arabian Desert. The only

166

thing on earth Washington weather is fit for is conversation. . . ."

Jones sat back in the embrace of the leather-covered armchair, grateful for the coolth of the air-conditioned room. Kenmuckle whirled a cane-bottomed armchair from behind his gleamingly naked desk and sat down in front of Jones, his back to the slatted window. There ensued a conversation during which Jones realized he was being most expertly interrogated. Resentment swelled his throat.

"Excuse me," he said thickly, "but it is perfectly apparent to me that you are not going to accept me on my own evaluation, so all this subtle cross-examination gets neither of us anywhere. The proof that I am who I am, and what I am, is abundant. It is, furthermore, objective, impersonal and accessible. I went to the Navy to see the Secretary, so he could lay before the President a simple, practicable plan I possess which will hasten the end of the war. I was sent here, assured it was the first step in that process. Is it, or isn't it?"

Instead of answering, Kenmuckle rose and crossed the room to a door through which he vanished momentarily, to return with a short, ruddy man in white linen whom he introduced as Colonel Merlin. The Colonel sat down in the Commander's chair and to Jones's surprise addressed him in fluent Turkish with assurances that he was personally and officially honored to receive so distinguished a savant. A bit grimly, Jones uttered the proper amenities, which seemed to give Merlin disproportionate delight. He leaned closer, clasping his hands between his meaty knees, and suggested that Jones *Effendi* possessed a great talent which might be gratefully employed by his country in its present emergency.

"That's what I am here for," Jones replied, in idiomatic Osmanli.

"Good! Very good! You would not object to travel?"

"That is also the object of my visit."

"Delightful! Would you be interested in going to Turkey . . . ?"

167

"Not remotely," snapped Jones. "I have already refused to go to Greece."

"So?" Merlin reverted to English. "Who wanted you to go to Greece?"

Jones gave him stare for stare. "I am not at liberty to say."

Merlin looked disappointed. "Next to Japanese," he said, "Turkish is the one language fewest Americans know how to speak fluently. Where is it you do want to go?"

"Germany."

"Ah, you speak German as well?"

"No, I don't. Not above a dozen words, and those badly."

"Oh, I see! You were making a joke. Yes, we all want to go to Germany eventually, to be sure. Quite an army of us, if I may make a small joke myself."

"You may, of course," Jones said as he stood up. "So long as it is a small one. But by the eyeballs of Eblis, I am getting tired of being considered a big joke myself. I want to see the Secretary of the Navy. Can you get me in to see him?"

Merlin and Kenmuckle ranged themselves on either side of Jones, clucking soothingly throughout his tirade.

"Why do you wish to see the Secretary?" Merlin asked. "If you wish, I will try to make an appointment with our director. But the Secretary has no cognizance of this office. It is not a part of the Navy, you see."

"Is it part of the Army?"

"No, Dr. Jones."

"Well, what is it, then?"

"That is hard to say. Call it a fact-finding agency. That is why I suggest that you—"

"Go to Turkey! Well, sir, I will not make the vulgar suggestion where you can go."

Merlin's face became so encrimsoned his eyes appeared to steam in their sockets. "I don't know why you came here . . ." he sputtered, and Jones retorted: "Because I was sent."

Kenmuckle did not lose his urbanity. "I take it," he said soothingly, "that what you have in mind is not a contribution to orthodox warfare, but something wholly new?"

Jones assented, grudgingly because he was suspicious still.

"Then," Kenmuckle continued persuasively, "you will make no progress with the agencies of orthodox warfare, either Army or Navy. Obviously they must stick to their own methods. That is why the OSS was established, as an agency of modern, psychological warfare; not the medieval methods to which Army and Navy cling. We would be glad to hear your idea, and to use it if practicable. You would be surprised how many ideas we use that the military authorities ridiculed."

Jones leaned back in his chair, plucking at his chin, convinced against his own will.

"Very well," he said slowly. "You may take me in to see your director."

Kenmuckle and Merlin exchanged smiles.

"That's fine," Merlin said with renewed affability. "But of course, Doctor, whether he will receive you or not depends on what you wish to discuss."

"I told you," Jones declared. "I wish to demonstrate my technique to end the war. At least, to shorten it materially."

"I understand. But he is a very busy man, directing complex operations all over the world. You must be more explicit."

"You mean, go through channels?"

"Well, in a way, yes. Can't you, in utmost secrecy, demonstrate your method to us?"

"Yes, I could," Jones said slowly. "By god, I could, and with pleasure. But I won't. I doubt if I would show your director, except in the presence of the President."

"Then I am afraid we cannot help you."

"Help me? Help me? I am trying to help you."

Merlin's eyes became hot again. "You have a strange way of being helpful. My God, man, you have to go through channels just to talk to the manager of a filling station."

"The only channel I'm interested in this minute," Jones said, rising, "is the one that leads to the street."

There was no exchange of farewells as Jones followed the guard who responded to Kenmuckle's buzzer. Once in the street Jones encountered the only bit of luck and co-operation that was his share for the day: a cruising taxi dawdling at the curb. He jumped in and asked to be taken to the Navy.

It is a good wind, also, that blows nobody ill. Neither chance nor Providence had provided that cab. Its driver was an honor student in the OSS sophomore class in Sleuthing, alerted on signal to shadow Jones. When Jones learned at the Navy Department that no Public Information was dispensed after 1730, and then learned that 1730 was 5:30 P.M., he was cheered to find the same cabby completing some sort of repairs under the hood of his motor, and immediately agreeable to overtaking the bus Jones would otherwise have missed. Thus Jones was able to get home in time for dinner, and the student sleuth to finish his assignment in time to keep a date with a Department of Agriculture stenographer suspected of being a Soviet spy, but who really was a Wac major in Military Intelligence who believed the OSS man to be a draft dodger.

Of that Jones knew nothing of course, as he knew nothing, either, of Kenmuckle's telephone call to Karig complaining: "The guy is crazy. He has a million things we want, but won't tell us what he wants. He talks Turkish like the Sultan himself. Christ, we could put him to work in Ankara or Istanbul tomorrow. But would he go? No! We could use him in Crete, but he told us in advance he had already turned down a chance to go to Greece. God knows who offered it to him. He wants to go to Germany and admits he can't talk German, but he won't explain to anybody but the Secretary of the Navy. Well, it's your secretary, and your Jones from here on, my lad. Don't wish any more of your cranks off on me. How about lunch tomorrow? Harvey's, upstairs, at 1230? Roger!"

22

ON SATURDAY Jones was back at the Navy Department, again progressing slowly, chair by hot-bottomed chair, until he had gained the presence of the dispenser of information.

"I must say, Commander," Jones said as he was seated beside the cluttered desk, "that you sent me on rather a wild-goose chase the other day."

The officer rubbed the back of his head vigorously, and leaned far back in his chair.

"Not to mix any metaphors," he said, "I was sure I was putting you on the right track. In fact, Kenmuckle called me up and complained that you were a person of extraordinary talent, and they could have put you to work on a job of major responsibility at once, but you would not accept it."

"That crowd is interested only in the obvious," Jones replied. "I have neither ambition nor talent to sit outside the German consulate in Istanbul disguised as a Turkish peddler of *lakhoum*."

The Commander leaned his elbows on the desk and began a complicated doodle on his memorandum pad.

"I don't want to pry," he said slowly, "but if I knew more about what you wanted to do, I could probably find you a shorter path. You haven't"—and here the Commander's eyes narrowed as he regarded Jones over his left elbow —"invented a secret weapon, by any chance?"

"What I possess," Jones said earnestly, "is a technique. I don't know any other name for it. Let me tell you with all the sincerity I command that it is simple, practicable, and of tremendous importance both militarily and politically. It is something I learned from a source now destroyed, which entails forgotten and forbidden forces that were widely employed when the world was ruled by other powers. More than that, I am sorry to say, I can't explain. I may appear to be rude. Believe me, I am not."

"It wouldn't make any difference whether you were or not," the Commander sighed. "Well, if this technique of yours is of military and political effect, derived from sources that used to govern the world, then maybe the Office of Military Government is the channel for you. Kitty, would you get me Captain Shilling's office?"

The colleen dialed a number. Jones said: "Remember, it is the Secretary I wish to reach, and him only as a means to see the President, young man."

"Yes, I know." The officer was curt. "And I explained to you about going through channels, from the lower to the higher."

"Is Captain Shilling higher than you?"

"Doctor, going from a reserve commander to a senior captain in the Regular Navy is a jump in altitude that almost requires an oxygen mask—thank you, Kitty." He lifted his phone, introduced himself over it, and asked permission to send around a distinguished gentleman who wished to submit to the Navy a proposition of military and political importance, thank you, sir.

"Kitty, would you ask Chief Sudol to step in, please?"

To Jones's surprise, Chief Sudol proved to be a small, trim and rather icily self-composed young woman in the uniform of a chief petty officer in the WAVES.

"The Chief will escort you to the Captain's office," the Commander said, and Jones obediently arose and followed the young lady out of the office to the designated door. He was ushered through it to be consigned to another young woman in uniform who relayed him to a young man in khaki,

172

who passed him into a farther office where a tall, heavily-browed officer greeted him and inquired how he could be of service.

"Are you Captain Shilling?"

"No, sir, I am Commander Solon."

"I have already seen a Commander," Jones said. "Now I wish to see the Captain so I can meet an Admiral who will gain me access to the Secretary. I think that is how the channel operates, is it not?"

"Yes. I am sorry, though, that the Captain is tied up. If you could tell me what you want?"

"My name is Jones. I am at present on the faculty of St. Jude's Theological Seminary. Before that, I was engaged in exploration and research in Southeastern Europe and Asia Minor. By a combination of events—"

"Well, Southeastern Europe and Asia Minor, now. I'm sorry but they are in the ETO," the officer said. "That is under Army jurisdiction."

"I have already discussed my idea with an Army officer, and he recognized immediately its importance and application," Jones declared.

"And did this Army officer tell you to come see us?"

Jones shook his head: "No, I came here of my own accord."

"And most wisely, sir," the officer cried warmly. "After all, where would the Army be if it were not for the Navy?"

"I know," Jones said. "In Schofield Barracks."

"Schofield Barracks? Why, sir, they could not have got out there without the Navy's help."

"Well, that's what Captain Sack told me."

"Unfortunately," Solon continued, "compared with the Pacific the ETO is just a suburb."

"Oh, that's all right," Jones said. "The geographical aspect is unimportant."

"Good! I am glad to hear that. Now, then, what is it you have in mind, exactly?"

"I am not sure I am in the right place," Jones observed.

"Oh, I wouldn't say that," the officer protested. "After all, the most important part of an operation is the organization of the conquered territory. I mean, of what earthly use is it to capture an atoll if it is not immediately organized under an efficient administrative program so it can become an asset in the next operation?"

"I don't know," Jones said honestly. "I have never given the matter any thought."

The Commander stared at him. "It's pretty obvious," he ventured.

"Maybe so," Jones conceded. "However, your method of governing atolls is wholly irrelevant, so far as I am concerned. It is wholly remote from the technique I wish to present to the Navy."

Commander Solon struggled to choke down his wrath. He remembered the warnings he had received at the Academy that while the average civilian thought he knew more about running the Navy than its officers did, as taxpayer and voter he was also in the superior tactical and strategical position to have the Navy run the way he wanted. So now the officer spoke soothingly: "I do not say our system is perfect. It was devised by experts, including the best civilian professional advice we could obtain, Dr. Jones. I am quite sure that the religious aspects are well considered, and ample provision made for freedom of worship, with chaplains present to further the interest of Christianity. Every little atoll—"

"I don't give a damn about any little atoll," Jones barked. "Blast your little atolls. Blast 'em, I say! But what I'm trying to do is blast places you haven't got yet."

Now it was the Commander's turn to interrupt, and he held up a compelling palm.

"Why, that explains everything," he beamed. "You were sent to the wrong place after all. Those feather-merchants in Pub Info! You don't want Military Government. You want the Bureau of Ordnance."

"Bureau of Ordnance be damned!" Jones raged. "I want to see the Secretary, not any Bureau of Ordure."

"Bu Ord has cognizance over blasting," the Commander said firmly, pushing a button on his desk. To the white-clad sailor who immediately opened the office door, Solon said: "Kapusta, take Dr. Jones to Captain Shambels. Good-bye, sir. It was a privilege." He seized Jones's hand and used it to propel him to the door.

As the plywood portal closed behind him, Jones planted his feet on the linoleum and told the sailor bluntly that he did not want to see Captain Shambels.

The bluejacket looked at the mutinous civilian with gaping eyes, his mouth open.

"I repeat," Jones said to the sailor, "I do not want to see Captain Shambels. Get me out of here!"

A few minutes later Jones was walking away from the Navy Department. Anger gripped him by the throat like a rawhide noose, and he sat down on a vacant bench in the park behind the White House to recover breath and self-composure.

However, the morning had not been wholly wasted. Commander Solon had made it clear that the Navy had small interest and less authority in the European area, because the President, by some obscure application of politics, had awarded that continent to the Army. Logically, then, the Army was the channel through which he had to aspire to achieve his plan. . . .

23

NEXT DAY was Sunday, and after dinner Jones prepared his usual escape from the afternoon tea. He would,
he decided, visit the Library. It was a long time since he had
seen Miss Finster—Virginia. John smiled as he stood, crisp
in white linen, between the hedges bordering the front walk
of the house. How unfounded had been his fears of the
woman, how groundless his suspicions.

Alfred stepped down from the porch, patting his brow
with a folded handkerchief.

"I'll certainly be glad when the war is over," he remarked,
"and the Seminary gets back on normal schedule, with no
summer sessions. We used to go to Rehobeth Beach for a
month. A pleasant place. Yes, it will surely be pl—ug!"

"Surely be what?" John inquired. He looked at Alfred,
and saw his colleague, brow sweat-pimpled, sidling toward
the porch steps.

"Got to help Angela," Alfred mumbled, and darted in-
doors. Curious behavior, thought John, as he strolled down
the path to the winding drive and turned toward the Library,
his stiff straw hat on one side of his head. Ahead of him
walked another man, white-clad, fanning himself with a
Panama hat, but John carefully measured his pace so as not
to overtake him.

Angela certainly dominated Alfred, he mused, to make her
brother feel so guilty at stealing a few moments from the

weekly preparation for tea-and-gossip hour. And then all such mild wonder was driven from his mind as Jones saw the man ahead of him turn into the barberry-bordered path to the Library.

Jones quickened his pace. He would, he swiftly planned, make such demands on Virginia for obscure works of reference as to discourage the visitor from remaining.

In the Library's cool twilight he saw Virginia standing in front of her pushed-back chair, the stranger leaning familiarly toward her over the desktop that separated them.

Jones advanced briskly, his heels ringing on the waxed floor. Virginia turned a smiling face toward him.

"Good afternoon, Miss Finster," Jones said energetically. "Excuse me, but I am in need of some books. I'd like Marmoronstein's *Old Rabbinic Doctrine*, and Salmond's *Christian Doctrine of Immortality* and Horowitz's *Examination of the Koran* with Muhammad Ali's English translation and . . ."

He gulped. The man facing Virginia was the mysterious stranger, the very man Jones had warned Virginia to regard with suspicion, and, come to think of it, the man whose mere passing seemed to cause Alfred acute unhappiness.

"Just write those names on a slip," Virginia said brightly, "and Abercrombie Baines will get them for you in a minute. He is taking my place here this afternoon."

"Er, Mr. Baines?" Jones addressed the stranger inquiringly.

"Oh, no, Mr. Baines is one of the students," Virginia laughed. "Excuse me for not introducing you. Dr. Jones, this is Mr. McJavert. He is with the—"

"With the government," interposed the FBI man. "How are you, Doctor? I've heard a lot about you."

"We'll miss the bus if we don't hurry," Virginia exclaimed, snatching a broad-brimmed hat from the top of a filing cabinet. She seemed to Jones to be in a state of extraordinary agitation, as she hurried to the door, McJavert making a wide circuit of Jones to join her.

Jones stared at the vacant doorway, confused and confounded. At his elbow a mild voice inquired: "Yes, sir, what books did you want?"

"I would like," Jones said bitterly, "a good, standard reference work on the care and prevention of women."

"Excuse me, sir? I don't understand."

"Neither do I," said Jones.

He stalked out of the Library and paused on the steps at the sight of Virginia and McJavert walking briskly, and closely, down the drive toward the highway.

24

ALTHOUGH IT MIGHT be said he had spent most of his life solving them, Jones hated a mystery. It is one thing, however, to solve the time-obscured mystery of the Etruscan Tursci (for one example) by matching a potsherd found in Tuscany with a fragment of amphora found in Thessaly, and relating them to a tomb painting in Mesopotamia. And it is mystery of another quality when a young woman, who owed as much to Jones as Virginia did, nonchalantly disregards advice volunteered in her own best interests and defiantly accepts the attentions of a man of dubious, if not sinister, behavior.

Cutting cross-lots to avoid the neighbors converging on Angela's tea party, Jones balefully left the campus.

Could it be that the man was a spy?

It was possible, between the gossip reported by Captain Sack and Jones's unconcealed visits to White House, New York and Navy, that some enemy agent's interest had been aroused.

Of course, that could explain the man's curious behavior on the occasion of Jones's first encounter with him. He had asked Jones, practically on the threshold of the Claverhouse home, for directions—an obvious subterfuge. Two hundred yards was the distance between house and Library, and it had taken McJavert an hour to traverse the distance.

He must have spent that hour in entry and search of Jones's quarters!

And why should Alfred turn pale at mere sight of the man's averted face? Had Alfred been tricked or coerced into aiding the search?

"It is all beyond me," Jones confessed to himself. "If he is a spy he is a damn poor one. But what does that make Virginia? Is she being used by him to cover up his dirty work? Or is *she* a spy, too? Are they a team? And if so, in whose service?"

With the birth of the dismaying new suspicion, and the rebirth of the old one, John Jones experienced only a firmer resolve to force the laggard government into granting him the opportunity to end war.

Jones wore his memory-inhabited raincoat when he made his trip to Washington next morning. (He had easily received permission from the Dean to suspend his classes for the next few days.) The nor'easter, he gratefully noted as he was ushered into the now familiar Office of Public Information, had a discouraging effect on the clientele. The long row of chairs was empty. Several of the room's occupants looked up at his entry, and some of them smiled in recognition of an old customer. The Wave chief petty officer who had been his guide greeted him by name and brought a wire hanger for his dripping coat. A petite blonde with a nostalgic Yankee accent introduced herself as Marion Goldstein and asked if he wouldn't like a cup of coffee which, at his happy assent, was mysteriously produced hot, black and unsweetened from the bottom drawer of a filing cabinet.

The skipper, he was told, was at the morning staff meeting. Could Commander Howe or Commander Miller be of assistance in his absence? How about another cup of coffee?

"I'll wait, if it won't be too long," Jones said. "And, yes, I will have another cup of coffee." It was not thirst he wanted to satisfy, but curiosity. The filing cabinet produced again.

"How do you do it?" Jones demanded.

"Well, you see," volunteered the tall, gray officer with the gold leaves on his collar who had escorted Jones to the office on his first visit, "it's another case of Navy tradition in conflict with rules and regulations. And tradition wins. It always does. It's a tradition in the Navy always to have coffee on tap. Always. The Navy is never without hot coffee. But the rules say you absolutely can't plug in an electric coffeepot because it overloads the electrical circuit and makes a fire hazard. But there is no rule against having electric dictation machines. And also there is no tradition about having electric dictation machines. So we just rewired our ediphone and ran a connection from it to a percolator in the filing cabinet. It's practically fire-proof and if there's an inspection—here's the Commander now."

Jones was invited to bring his cup of bootleg into the inner office, where he gave the Commander a biting résumé of frustration.

"I must have action," Jones concluded a little sharply. "I have been butting my head against the stone wall of bureaucratic indifference. Your very loyal staff tells me that if you cannot help me break through it, nobody can. I just want to tell you that if you cannot get me an audience at once I propose to go to the Army with my plan."

The Commander's normally pink face turned geranium.

"I think," he said, rolling an agate eye at Jones, "that you might find it interesting to try. But no cheating, now! You must promise not to give the opposition any more clue than you gave me."

Jones dug his fists deeper into his pockets. "The trouble with the Navy," he said, "is that it is burdened with tradition."

"Could be," the Commander admitted. "I haven't been around long enough to learn 'em. But the Army has a few, too. You'd better apply to the Army Air Forces. They haven't been in existence long enough to acquire many."

Jones bowed stiffly. "I shall follow that advice," he said.

Scant minutes later Jones was clinging to a stanchion in the khaki-glutted bus that lurched over Memorial Bridge across the historic Potomac, creaking and groaning and rattling as it negotiated the elaborate maze of recurved highways on the far shore toward the vast sprawl of the Pentagon. Presently he was being pushed willy-nilly by the

181

throng up a steep flight of ironshod steps and squeezed past an iron railing, to be flattened against a long counter, behind which a crisp blonde with corrugated coiffure demanded to know whom he wanted to see.

"Whoever is in charge of aviation," Jones replied.

"Have you an appointment?"

"No, of course I haven't, but . . ."

"What did you want to see him about?"

"Well, about a new invention."

"Just a minute, please." The young woman leafed through a directory. "See General Bullblank in 3C-4L-3-S-19."

"I beg your pardon?"

"General Bullblank in 3C-4L-3-S-19. I'll write it down for you. Here is your badge."

Jones stared at the slip of paper thrust at him with his large, numbered celluloid badge.

"Look, it is really very simple," the young woman said. "The building has five sides, A, B, C, D, and E. Three-C means the third floor of side C. The next number tells what corridor you take, the fourth. I don't know what the L means, but the three means the third court counting this as one, and then S-19 is the nineteenth stanchion on your right, and that's where the General is. You can't miss it, and besides the Sergeant will escort you."

25

THE FAIR-HAIRED young man with the eagle on his collar rose from his chair and extended a cordial hand with the fluid self-possession of a mortician's receptionist.

"Colonel La Fesse," he said, simply. "How do you do, Mr. Jones? You wish to see the General? Will you tell me what about?"

"No," said Jones. "I do not wish to appear rude, but that is the simple fact. My business will be briefly stated. I repeat that I have nothing personal to gain in any way, financially or otherwise. What I have to say is, of necessity, to be imparted only to the man in ultimate authority. It is more esoteric than secret, perhaps, but—"

The Colonel looked puzzled. "Excuse me?" he said.

Jones was baffled by the apology. The Colonel had not, to his perception, belched, broken wind or sneezed.

"I said," he restated himself, "that that which I propose to propose I can expound only to the person capable of conclusive decision, at the risk of appearing boorish or pretentiously cryptic."

The Colonel looked at the Lieutenant Colonel, who shook his head. Then he sat down, slowly, groping for the chair behind him.

"It sounds like it makes good sense," he murmured.

Jones was elated. "It is good sense, young man, and I am glad to find somebody at last in these interminable chains of command who has the intelligence to comprehend it. Now, then, may I speak to the General for no more than five minutes—although I shall place myself at his disposal for as much longer as he may wish."

"Yes," said the Colonel. "You better speak to the General. He went to Harvard."

"So did I," Jones exclaimed joyfully.

"That explains it," said the Colonel. He rose again, and walked to a door in the otherwise blank wall. There he turned to regard Jones thoughtfully for several seconds, before rapping on the panel and entering the General's retreat.

He emerged a few minutes later and beckoned to Jones, who wormed through the maze of desks to the doorway. The Colonel gestured for him to precede, and then followed him into the windowless cubicle where sat a young man with a silver star on his collar, five rows of ribbons below the silver wings to the left of the precisely tucked tan necktie.

"General Bullblank," said Colonel La Fesse, standing straight and stiff as a stick of molasses candy, "this is Mr. Jones."

"Please be as brief as you can, Mr. Jones," the General said. "Sorry I can't ask you to sit down, but this organization grows faster than we can procure chairs. It will be different, by God, when the Air Force takes over the War Department! We will eliminate all this wasteful duplication and inefficiency. Ask for a chair and what do you get? Excuses! Labor shortage! Shortage of material! What the government ought to do, sir, is to put some of the excess troops to work. Send 'em into the forests to cut timber. Put 'em in the factories to make chairs. But no! I suppose it would offend the woodchoppers' union and the chairmakers' union. It makes a man wonder where this democracy is that we are supposed to be defending when in the middle of a war one cannot even obtain essential military materials because the labor unions have to be allowed to do things in their own sweet way. This is the Air Age, Mr. Jones, the Air Age! But by godfrey, sir, you wouldn't know it. We are still geared to mile-a-minute thinking in a mile-a-second era. I think, sir, you will

184

see a change after the war. We in the Air Force, Mr. Jones, will be returning to civilian life by the millions. We will be in Congress, in the state legislatures, in industry. We know our mission. Today it will be to defend America against aggression. Tomorrow it will be to rescue America from obsolescence. But we are even hampered in doing our present job. Who sets the pace in the war? The foot soldier! Just think of it, sir, as you undoubtedly have or you wouldn't be here. In the Air Age, we are still geared to a pedestrian army. Our bombers can make three round trips between England and Berlin in the time it takes the Ground Forces to advance one lousy mile. The waste of it! Thousands of lives wasted every day of the Air Age because the dominant military thinking is still back in the age of Château-Thierry and Gettysburg. Jee-zuss! When I think of the factories that are making shoes for infantrymen when they should be making aircraft, I—I—well, I don't know, I get downright rebellious."

The General stopped to fetch a sigh that strained the ribbons on his breast, and Jones eagerly took advantage of the pause.

"As you say, sir," he said, "the waste of life is appalling, and that is indeed the reason for my insistence upon seeing you. The Navy . . ."

General Bullblank emitted a deep, throaty chuckle.

"The Navy," he jeered. "The Navy! There's an outfit for you. Who is the Navy's big hero? A guy they call 'Thirty-Knot' Burke. Think of it! In the Air Age, in the era of mile-a-minute transportation, the Navy gets all revved up over a poor bloke who manages to move at the rate of a mile in two minutes. You know, Mister—ah—Mister Smith, that's one thing that makes me worry about the time when the Air Force takes over. We'll have to absorb the Navy. We can use some of their aviators, I'm sure. You may think I am sentimental. You may think I am prejudiced in favor of aviators, even if they are in the Navy. You think we ought to make a clean sweep and junk the Navy the way we did the cavalry. But it can't be done. You may not believe it,

185

but it will be impossible. We'd have one hell of a fight on our hands. The shipbuilders' unions, the political machines in seacoast cities like New York and Philadelphia and Newport, they'll fight like hell to keep the mucking Navy afloat so they can continue to rake in the taxpayers' do-re-mi. Good God, it's enough to make a man see red. No, I take that back. That's what my old man used to say when he lost his temper. It's an old-fashioned phrase that has nothing to do with communism, believe me. Where would the Navy be today if it weren't for the Air Force, hey? Answer me that? Where—"

"Schofield Barracks?" Jones suggested, recalling that that was where he had been assured something would be if it were not for something. But the General did not reward his answer with so much as a nod.

"Where would the Navy and their musical comedy Marines be in the Pacific if it were not for the Fifth Air Force? And the Seventh? And the Thirteenth? Who keeps the goddam Panama Canal open for the Navy's ships? Bill Butler's Sixth! Do you know how many Flying Fortresses you could build for the price of one stinking battleship? Hundreds! The Navy sits around on its fat ass eating steak three times a day fried in butter and for a tenth of the money spent on it you could have the war won with air power, and the next war, too, because we would smash Germany and Japan so flat it would scare the living spit out of the Russians at the same time."

"I know you are a busy man," Jones said as the General came to a meaningful pause. "I only wished to ask your assistance in laying before the highest authority a certain technique of which I happen to have the sole possession . . ."

"The Colonel mentioned something about a new weapon."

"Yes, sir. It is not exactly a weapon . . ."

"Well, what is it, then? Are you the inventor or the manufacturer or what?"

"Neither one," Jones replied. "That is to say, well, I suppose I would be the manufacturer, I guess."

"Who holds the patent?"

"There isn't any. I don't think it is patentable."

"Well, what is it, Mr. Smith? A bomb? A gun? Do you have a model of it? Do you have a factory?" His voice grew bitter. "Have you priorities for materials? Have you made arrangements with the War Manpower Commission and the unions?"

"It isn't a gun," Jones said. "And it isn't exactly a bomb, although the effect is even worse, I should imagine."

"Worse? What is its dispersal area at point of impact?"

"I am afraid, sir, that I do not quite follow you."

"Excuse me," the General said curtly. "You said you could state your business in three minutes, the Colonel told me. You have been here nearly half an hour already, and I still don't know what you want."

"Would you be interested in a method to immobilize or destroy, as you chose, every living thing within range of vision?" Jones asked, suppressing a smile that anticipated the General's certain astonished assent. But Bullblank only looked bored.

"What's this?" he asked. "Another death ray, for God's sake?"

Jones frowned with vexation. "It is a force for which there is no adequate definition. I suppose you could call it a ray or a beam. At least, it is more nearly like one than it is like anything else."

"Come here a minute," Bullblank commanded, starting for the door. He held it open, and detained Jones on the threshold.

"Do you see that bank of filing cabinets against the wall there? Well, they are full—gut-full—of diagrams and descriptions of death rays brought in here by inventors," the General said, almost indignantly. "And not a single, goddam one of them will work. Not a clucking solitary one of 'em."

"Why should that interest me?" Jones demanded.

"Just this much," the General said. "We have set up three simple requirements which every death ray has to meet before we will even begin to consider it. Will this gadget of yours kill a small animal at five thousand feet in three seconds?"

187

"You can't see a small animal at five thousand feet," Jones protested. "It will kill an elephant at five thousand feet, I'll warrant."

"The Air Force isn't hunting elephants," Bullblank snorted. "Okay! Can you burn a half-inch hole in a four-inch plank in five seconds?"

"That's silly," Jones protested. "I could kill a—"

Bullblank held up an admonitory hand.

"Okay," he said. "So far, so good. Can you burn a six-inch live tree two miles away in three minutes?"

Jones slapped his hands together in exasperation.

"I am no Boy Scout setting fires without matches," he cried. "If you want to burn holes in planks and burn up trees I suggest you get yourself a pyrography set. I can't burn holes in planks and I can't burn pretty designs in leather, either. I can't even light a cigarette with my technique. But I can knock down a man behind a tree or—"

"I'm afraid we can't do business," Bullblank said. "I'm very sorry, Mister—ah—um! Very sorry, indeed. But those are our minimum requirements, and if you cannot meet them —well, we are doing pretty well with what we have, as far as we are allowed to, that is. You mark my words, this war will be stalled along until a Ground Forces officer receives the surrender. They'll cheat us out of it. Well, by God, we won't leave a sucking soul alive in Germany to surrender. That's what we'll do." His hand reached for the button on his desk, found it, and pressed. "By jee-zuss and General Jackson, sir, it is enough to make a man see—ah—purple! Oh, yes, Colonel, will you show Mister—ah—this gentleman how to find his way out?"

The General sat down at his desk; Jones, jaws clenched, followed La Fesse out of the room.

To La Fesse's unconcealed surprise Jones refused to wait for a guide, preferring to trust the acute instinct for orientation which had served him so well on the trackless deserts of Asia Minor to guide him to the Pentagon's perimeter. But no discovery of an uncharted oasis had ever thrilled him as much as the sight, fifteen minutes later, of a row of taxicabs snuffling in the basement tunnel. He climbed aboard the nearest.

"Take me to the Navy Department," he said.

He leaned back against the sticky imitation-leather cushions. "Burn holes in planks," he snarled. "Kill small animals at five thousand feet."

The driver gave him a quick, apprehensive look over one polo-shirted shoulder. "I'll go as fast as I can, boss," he said. "But I don't aim to burn up nothin' or to kill nobody."

"Not fast," Jones commanded. "I detest fast driving. I don't even like to ride on a camel."

"You said the Navy Department, didn't you?"

"You heard me."

"Well, I thought maybe you wanted Gallinger Hospital."

26

JONES REACHED the Navy Department just as the evening exodus was approaching its peak.

With difficulty properly badged, and begrudgingly escorted, he strode the now-familiar path to the precincts of Public Information. The office to which he admitted himself was shockingly empty, and for a moment Jones stood there damning a military operation that kept union hours in wartime, when he heard voices in the inner office. He crossed the room and pushed the unlatched door.

The Commander was sitting on the edge of his paper-drifted desk, chatting laughingly with a stocky, shock-haired civilian of early middle age, who sprawled in the visitor's chair. The Commander was saying: "So I said to the dumb bastard, 'Admiral,' I said——" when he looked up and saw Jones.

"Hello, Dr. Jones," he called out. "Come on in! I didn't expect you back quite so soon, or so late either. Meet Dr. Alford Hendrix. How did you make out with the War Department?"

Jones confined his reply to a snort, and the Commander went on:

"Dr. Jones, here, has invented something so secret he——say, by Jove! This is a bit of luck. Hendrix is just the man for you, Doctor. He is chief analyst for the National Board of Scientific Advertence and Perlustration, Doctor. That's no secret, is it, Al? Anyhow, Doctor, it's safe with you, if it is.

SAP looks into all sorts of inventions the military don't think they can use, or don't understand, but still may be of value to the war effort. SAP has rescued some pretty good stuff from oblivion, like the star-shaped toilet seats originally offered the Navy so a man wouldn't be thrown off in rough weather. He was supposed to grip one point between his knees and the two others with his hands. Well, the Army has adopted 'em now for standard equipment in its privies to identify the General's seat. And then again there's the stunt of fastening little radio broadcasting units to electric eels and turning them loose to fool enemy subs. Don't worry, Al. Dr. Jones here is working on an invention more secret than that."

"I am not working on it," Jones snapped. "It is completed and ready to be put to use. My difficulty is in gaining access to the proper authorities."

"How far did you get with the War Department?" the Commander asked with an anticipatory grin. "Not as far as the doorkeeper, I'll bet."

"Far enough," Jones replied. "I followed your advice and asked for the commanding officer of aviation. Well, at first they wouldn't let me see the General, but I made it plain and emphatic that it was to his benefit, not mine, so I was taken in, and—"

"You got in to see General Arnold—'Hap' Arnold?"

"No, that wasn't it. His name was Bullfiddle or something like that. Bullblank, that's it."

"Never heard of him," the Commander said, fumbling through the papers on his desk and extricating a thick pamphlet. "Let's look him up. Bull, Bullard; here it is. Bullblank. Whoops! I win the bet. A brigadier general. You did *not* get as far as the doorkeeper!"

"Then the obfuscatory tactics of the War Department are even more unconscionable than the Navy's or the White House," Jones raged. "And meanwhile I am being thwarted by bureaucratic myopia from applying the only technique that can stop this appalling waste of life, this enslaving waste of money, this profligate and destructful waste of resources, this waste of time—"

191

Hendrix snorted now.

"You argue from a false premise, Doctor," he said. "Scientifically there is no such thing as waste. Wait a minute; wait a minute, please. I know what you are going to say. But you're confused by the same fallacy that has shaped our political and economic thought for generations, until the New Deal got us at least looking in the right direction. Waste? Why, God Almighty, man, if it weren't for what you call waste this country would be at the social and economic level of the Stone Age. And that's just about where we got back to in nineteen-thirty-two, thanks to you conservatives. And if it were not for what you call economy, this country would be ten times richer and a thousand times happier. The margin of progress is measured by what you foolishly call waste, and the rate of progress is in inverse ratio to the success you conservatives have in applying your unnatural theories of economy."

"Now that is palpable lunacy," cried Jones. "And I am not a conservative, goddam it!"

"Oh, yes, you are," Hendrix declared. "A conservative is one who wants to conserve. It is as simple as A, B, C. You are against what you call waste. So I say you are a conservative, which is to say an evangelist of the gospel of disuse."

"And I say you are crazy," Jones said flatly.

Hendrix ignored the insult. "You are too subjective, you conservatives. You think that what money is to an individual it is to the nation, that what possessions are to an individual they are to the nation, and there is no more relationship between them than there is between a suit of clothes and a suit for damages.

"Look here. I'll prove you are wrong by examples even you can understand. You will admit that the cigarette business in this country is rich, profitable and expanding. Yet it thrives on waste. Walter, shove that ash tray over here. Look, Doctor, there are ten butts in it. Let's measure them. Got a ruler? Thanks."

He measured, he jotted down figures, scribbled a calculation. "Now then," he said, "the butts average three-quarters of an inch. A cigarette is—let's see now—two and three-quarter inches long. So, by your standards, three-elevenths or better than twenty-seven per cent of every cigarette is wasted. The butt contains just as much tobacco, just as much paper, as the first three-quarters inch. Suppose cigarettes were so made that they could be consumed down to the last shred. You see what it would mean? The cigarette industry, the tobacco industry, the paper industry, would immediately be reduced by more than twenty-seven per cent. I doubt if the margin of profit is that large. Say it is ten per cent. If what you call waste could be avoided, the industry would be operating at a loss of seventeen per cent at present prices.

"Look at mustard. Most of it is waste. At home or in a restaurant, what do you do when you help yourself to mustard? You put a little scoopful on the side of your plate, and you never, never use it all up. At least a quarter of it remains on your plate to be washed off down the drain. Suppose everybody used only exactly as much mustard as he actually consumed. Why, the price would have to be so high that mustard would become strictly a luxury item for the rich.

"These are only two very homely little examples, parables almost, but they prove my point."

He lit the borrowed cigarette he had been measuring, and Jones charged through the breach in the monologue.

"I have neither the time, the patience, nor the ingenuity to argue cigarettes and mustard," he cried. "But what about the war? I am speaking of the waste of time, that creates waste of human lives."

"The identical fallacy," Hendrix puffed. "You regard human life subjectively, individually. And time! Hell, there is no such thing as time. It is a human invention. Time does not exist. Clocks do, of course, and calendars. But you might as well argue that thermometers cause the changes in temperature. One of the basic causes of war is overpopulation. Hence the German appeal for *Lebensraum*. Their way of getting living space is to kill their neighbors and occupy their space. We, in fighting the Germans, and the Japanese, are by that act subscribing to the belief that there are too many Germans,

193

too many Japanese. So we kill Germans, or Japanese, and the more we kill the more room we make for the survivors, and the more we postpone the next war. At the same time we relieve an incipient population pressure in our own country. You, Doctor, sentimentally think of life in terms of individual human beings whereas from a military and economic point of view a human life has to be considered as a mathematical symbol which is a fraction of the total population per square mile of arable land. On that basis, we have more lives at our disposal than our enemies, consequently we will win the war. But if you suddenly appear with an invention that will, as you put it, save lives by ending the war prematurely, don't you see that you will be saving German and Japanese lives as well as American lives?

"In short, my dear Doctor, if you have, as you say, a means of ending the war tomorrow you are a menace to civilization."

Hendrix robbed his accusation of rancor by ornamenting it with a most affable smile. He stood up, shook hands with the Commander and pledged the mutual necessity of "getting together again soon," and with an all-inclusive "so long" let himself out.

"Well," sighed the Commander, "I used to know that guy when we were kids together and he hasn't changed much in thirty years. We used to trade cigarette cards, and he convinced me that one Sweet Caporal flags-of-all-nations was worth five Mecca actresses because there were more actresses than there were nations. And his father smoked Sweets."

That observation made less sense to Jones than anything Hendrix had uttered, and so he sighed. "I am," he said, "utterly discouraged."

The Commander paused in the act of putting on his khaki blouse.

"Look here," he said. "It is after hours, and anyhow we have got to know each other well enough so I can speak plainly. You just aren't going to get anywhere, Jones, not in the Navy or the Army or any branch of government. And you wouldn't get any for'arder if you tried to see the head of General Motors or the boss of the A & P or the publisher of the Chicago *Tribune*, either, by the tactics of refusing to state your business."

"Then what am I going to do?" Jones cried. "I tell you, I cannot state my business. I would not be believed, to begin with, even if I dared risk it. But it is business of so—how can I explain it?—of such conclusive and definitive importance that if it is shared with more than two or three of the persons who alone can initiate and utilize it the whole thing is best left unstated and undone."

"Then you have got to see the top man, Secretary or President or whoever, by pretext. Tell 'em you want to talk about oil fields you found in Persia," the Commander advised. "Nobody can, and likely nobody will even want to try, to get you into the front office for a secret reason. But you can get in to see any politician to discuss a triviality, because—" He snapped his fingers. "That's an idea," he exclaimed. "Look! You go to your congressman or your senator, and tell him you damn well have got to see the Secretary on urgent business. I think a senator would swing more weight, but he will only go to town for you if he is up for re-election. Yes! Forget about going through channels. By-pass the chain of command and get in at the top. The fact that you are a voter is a damn sight more important right now than the fact that you are an inventor. But don't tell anybody I told you."

"Why can't you obtain the audience for me on that basis?" Jones demanded. "I'm just as much a voter here as I am anywhere else."

"Oh, no! I am a naval officer. At least, to the naked eye, I am. As such, I have to fight shy of politics, except office politics, of course. Try your senator, like I said."

He locked his desk, dogged down the casement window, and walked to the door. Jones, however, did not move from his perch on the stenographer's chair, where, hands awkwardly thrust into pockets, he seemed lost in critical contemplation of the shine on his shoes.

"And I hope you get there," the Commander observed, "because, unofficially and off the record, I sure as hell would like to know what in blazes this scheme of yours is."

Still Jones made no reply. He got up from his chair and walked to the window, where he rocked back and forth on his feet as he contemplated the deepened shadows outside. The Commander fidgeted with the spring lock on the door.

"I am," Jones finally said, without turning his head, "still deeply discouraged. It is abhorrent to me to have to use subterfuge or to appeal to partisan political privilege, to gain what I believed was the inherent right of an American citizen, which is to have immediate access to a public servant, no matter how exalted his position. Of course, the President and his Cabinet cannot conduct their business in the market place. Despite what your learned friend has to say, too much time would be wasted.

"You have been very kind to me, Commander. Kind, and courteous, and patient. You have adjusted yourself to the inexorable pattern of bureaucracy without becoming a bureaucrat yourself. I am a lonesome man, by necessity and latterly by choice. Come what may, I want you to be my friend."

Jones turned around to face the officer, and stood silhouetted now against the graying oblong of the window.

"I have confessed to you that I am a discouraged man and a lonesome man," he went on. "Let me describe myself to you also as a worried man and a frightened man, a very frightened man."

"Oh, hell," said the Commander awkwardly, torn between embarrassment and impatience. "There's nothing to be scared about."

"Come here a minute," Jones said, turning back to the window. "Your friend this afternoon demonstrated his theories by what he called parables. I will do the same. Do you see that fly? Catch it."

"Now what in the devil," the Commander protested. "All right. But let me get a folded newspaper to swat it with."

"No, catch it in your hand," Jones directed.

The Commander made a few ineffectual swipes at the agile insect, and then Jones laid a hand on his arm.

"That's enough," he said. "Now watch me."

He cocked a forefinger at the fly. The insect froze on the

196

sill. Jones brought his finger close to the immobilized creature, and then picked it up. Presently the fly stirred, and began to buzz in his grasp, while the Commander looked at it in perplexity. Jones released the fly, and it soared to the ceiling.

"Now watch again," Jones said. Again he pointed at the fly, which was crawling erratically but happily upside down twelve feet from the floor. As Jones's finger came in line with it, the creature plopped to the Commander's desk.

"Well, I'll be damned," he said.

"No, you won't, but I am afraid I am," Jones said. The fly stirred, and, limping on four of its six legs, began to crawl under a mimeographed sheet stamped "Confidential."

"And the final demonstration," said Jones, pointing again. "Zotz!"

The fly gave a little leap into the air and fell back. It was, the Commander discovered when he poked it with a pencil, dead. Under his prodding, the insect began to disintegrate.

"How did you do it?" he asked, and the face he turned to Jones gleamed very white in the gloom.

"That," said Jones, "must remain my secret for the time being. But what happened to the fly I can make happen to every or any living thing, in any quantity. And that you will please keep secret yourself. But now you see why I am most anxious to talk to ultimate authority."

The Commander was slumped, gray-faced, in his chair. His clammy fingers skimmed the cold sweat from his forehead.

"Okay," he said. "That does it. Come back tomorrow. I'll get you in to see the Secretary if it means my court-martial. And now, please, let's get the hell out of here. I have a terribly important meeting right away."

He did have. It was with George, the bartender in the Press Club Taproom. Much of the Navy's reputation for unruffled two-handed drinking was lost that night by its most diligent press agent. Even before his first glass of Virginia Gentleman and plain water was even half consumed, it was noticed that the Commander returned all greetings with a glassy stare and a strangled hiccup that sounded like "Zotz!"

197

27

THE COFFEE had not even begun to percolate in the filing-cabinet drawer next morning when Jones, properly badged this time, was back in the Navy's Office of Information, and clutching a paper bag.

Miss Goldstein told him that the Commander was answering the morning mail, a ritual which brooked no interruption, and that the coffee would be ready as soon as Lieutenant Le Coq came back from washing the cups. Chief Sudol took his hat. Lieutenant Stafford offered him the back half of the morning *Post*. The cordiality contracted somewhat automatically, when Jones opened his paper bag and took from it his glass mayonnaise jar containing a white mouse.

"I hope you don't mind," Jones apologized. "I know that mice are nocturnal animals, but I do feel sorry about keeping him shut up."

"Oh, no, we don't mind," Lieutenant Commander Miller assured him. "We keep roaches ourselves. What is the mouse's name?"

"I haven't named him," Jones said, shaking the jar a little. "I have quite a few of them. You don't know anybody who would like some mice, do you?"

"Well, I don't know, offhand," Miller said. "That is, *I* haven't heard anybody mention a yearning to have white mice. But if I do, I will be glad to let you know."

Jones thanked him, and when the conversation thereupon

seemed to languish he returned politeness for politeness by inquiring after the office roaches.

"I understand they are really among the cleanest and most intelligent insects," he volunteered. "I have heard that prisoners often make pets of them in their cells."

"Yes," Miller replied. "That's where we got the idea."

Silence descended anew, but just as its weight became uncomfortable the door to the inner office opened and Miss Clark entered the room with an armful of notebooks, whereupon Chief Sudol snatched pad and pencils and scurried to the door.

"Honestly," Miss Clark exclaimed. "The darn-fool questions people ask! Eek! Is that a mouse?"

"Honestly, the darn-fool questions people ask," Miller observed. "Of course it isn't a mouse. It's a dehydrated rat for use on small craft, invented by Dr. Jones. To leave the ship, you know, when it is sinking."

Whether Miss Clark was ever set aright on that canard Jones never knew, because the communicating door opened again to reveal the Commander himself.

"I didn't know you were waiting, Dr. Jones," he called out. "Come in, please. Bring us some coffee when it's ready, Marion, will you? Sit down, Doctor. For God's sake, what's that, a mouse?"

"Yes," Jones replied truthfully, putting the jar on a stack of dusty papers bearing the terse word "ACTION" in red rubber-stamping. "I brought him along to demonstrate with, you know."

"Gosh, the poor little fellow," the Commander said, tapping the glass. "Hello, little martyr to science. Oh, don't go, Sudol, I want you to take a confidential memo. You know, Doctor, I damn near couldn't sleep thinking about that show you put on last night. It's beyond belief."

"Would you like another demonstration?" Jones asked.

"Hell, no! Sudol, take a memorandum for Captain Pelznickel in the Secretary's office."

"Via Captain Chumbley, Commodore Yarder and Admiral Baker?"

"Via nobody!"

"Via nobody? But what about channels, sir?"

"To hell with the channels!" The Commander's face was very red, but his assertion of defiance made the Chief Yeoman's turn white.

"But Commander," she protested, stiff-lipped. "You know, sir, what—"

"Yes, I know," the Commander said hoarsely. "Nevertheless—let me see, now. This has to be worded discreetly. Hm! Yes, Memorandum for Captain Pelznickel. Paragraph 1: I—ah—no, let's see. Cross that out. I mean belay that. Paragraph 1: 'Only the urgency of the situation impels the undersigned to address you directly on a matter of—(What's another word meaning 'urgency'? Okay!) —matter of pressing necessity. There is in my office Dr. John Jones, presently of the faculty of—(What's the name of the joint, Doctor?)—St. Jude's (jay-you-dee-ee, Sudol) Theological Seminary who is very anxious to place himself at the disposal of the Navy, and who, I respectfully suggest, should be granted an interview by the Secretary, as soon as possible.' Paragraph 2. (This is the tough part. No, don't put that down.) Paragraph 2. 'Dr. Jones possesses the power and the ability, to my certain knowledge, to knock people over with a word. (How's that, Doctor? Okay? I don't want to say too much, and I don't want to say too little.) (Okay, Sudol. Make it 'with a word and a gesture.')

"Paragraph 3: 'Dr. Jones, however, properly insists that he can deal only with the ultimate authority, and I agree with him that he will be subjected to delay and misunderstanding if his approach is through channels. He is a man of no small fame in other pursuits as a glance at Who's Who will demonstrate, and I most respectfully urge that his request be given top priority.' Sign this one 'Very Respectfully,' Sudol. Whew!"

The Commander leaned back, and wiped his brow with a shaking hand. The Chief, stark disapproval in her every gesture, turned to her typewriter, as the door was pushed open to admit Miss Goldstein bearing two mugs of steaming, blue-black coffee. The Commander gulped his avidly, as if in need of every drop. Then he signed the sheet the Chief put before him, with the command: "Take this upstairs yourself, please, and see that Captain Pelznickel gets it himself."

"Aye, aye sir!" The Chief stalked out of the room, no mean accomplishment for a person of five feet two. In the main room she tossed the pink, green and yellow carbons to Miss Clark for filing. A few seconds later the room was buzzing with shocked comment and hushed speculation.

While some held that it was just that sort of airy defiance of procedure that gave the Reserves a bad name with the Regulars, others said that the Commander's action took just as much guts as steering a submarine into a Japanese harbor and he ought to be given the civilian Legion of Merit. But all hands agreed that there would presently be a new laundry officer on Funafuti Island.

Meanwhile the unhappy iconoclast, having glumly told Jones that he would sure as hell hear from the memorandum very quickly, had asked his caller to wait. "Grab the extension telephone when I give you the high sign," he counseled. "You might as well hear what the Captain will have to say with your own ears."

They had not long to wait for the response.

"Hey, Karig! This is Pelznickel."

"Yes, Captain. Thank you for calling, sir."

"What the hell is all this about? It's damn irregular, you know."

"Yes, sir. I know it isn't regular."

"Damn right it isn't."

"But, sir, it is much more important than I could put on paper—"

"Why, you lecherous old lush, you! When the hell did you get so interested in theology?"

"My personal habits, sir, have nothing to do with this case. And it isn't a religious matter at all. Will you—would you—ask the Secretary if he can give Dr. Jones just five minutes?"

"Yeah, sure! This guy is an Episcopal, can really knock 'em dead, you say?"

"And no fooling. Literally, just that. I mean, dead. Can you get him in this morning?"

"This morning? Are you nuts? There's a line of people here longer than in the cafeteria right now."

"When can he get in, sir?"

"Hell's bells, he's got to take his turn. Maybe tomorrow, maybe next week. And I'm only doing this as a favor to you."

"Captain, it isn't a fa—"

"Call me back tomorrow or the next day."

"But, sir, if the Secretary only knew—"

"Yeah, I know. Well, I do happen to know that the Secretary is interested in the subject right now. Call me up."

The instruments clicked a period to the dialogue.

The Commander smiled, a little wanly. "Well, it looks as if you are going to get in," he observed to Jones.

Jones gave him a level and unsmiling look.

"Thank you," he said. "I will keep in touch with you."

He took the paper bag from his pocket and wrapped up his mouse jar. With a bow between the curt and the courtly, he left the room.

Jones went away in bitterness. If he could not get in by front door or back, then his only recourse was to come down the chimney, no matter how befouled he might become. In other words, he would petition political influence. He would, as the Commander had shamefacedly advised him, go to his senator or congressman—

But who was his senator? Who was his representative?

The waitress in the Eighteenth Street lunchroom didn't know. "I'm a stranger here myself," she said. "Just killing time waiting for a job as entertainer with the Red Cross. Have your coffee now? White?"

Jones decided he could use some counsel as well as information. He would go back to the Holy Hollow and ask Alfred.

Once aboard the big blue bus, Jones settled himself in a seat by a window prepared to spend the ninety-minute ride in planning his interview with the politician Alfred would designate. It was just another hodful of frustration, then,

202

that was laid on his shoulders when a woman's voice exclaimed: "Why, Dr. Jones! I haven't seen you in a coon's age!" and, as the bus started, the source of the voice lurched into the seat beside him.

It was Virginia Finster, explaining that she was returning from an errand to the Congressional Library.

Jones contracted his skinny thighs and flattened himself against the bulkhead.

"How do you do," he said politely. "And how is the book coming?"

"How nice of you to ask," Virginia replied. "I shall have the revision finished in another fortnight, and may I dare ask you to look at it again, before I ship it off?"

Jones replied with a noncommittal mumble.

"And how is your war work coming along?" Virginia asked, dropping her voice. "Or shouldn't I ask?"

"To answer your questions truthfully," Jones answered, "my war work is making no progress, although the Dean was kind enough to permit me to devote my entire time to it. It almost seems, at times, as though I were the victim of a subtle plot, and that intangible forces were at work to prevent me from fulfilling my mission."

He uttered the last sentence with his eyes focused sharply on Virginia's face, but he could detect there no masking of guilt, no sparkle of satisfaction. To the contrary, her big brown eyes softened with sympathy and her full, rutile lips drooped at the corners.

"Oh, that's really too bad," she cried. "But you simply mustn't give up. Don't let yourself get discouraged. Surely someplace there must be just exactly the vacancy you can fill superbly. I wonder, now!" She caught her lower lip between her teeth, and focused her eyes on her clasped hands, falling into a musing silence as the bus rumbled with a vibrating grinding of gears that sent her bosom into provocative saltation.

"I wonder," Virginia resumed, "whether Mr. McJavert could help."

"So?" Jones stirred uneasily. He had been wondering if

Mr. McJavert might not have been taking a too active interest already.

"He is with the government, you know. Confidentially, because he does not want it generally known, he is with the FBI. Maybe this will amuse you, but he came to the Seminary to investigate me!" Virginia uttered a deep, throaty chuckle. "Maybe he still is. But I could ask him, if you wish, if there isn't some chance the FBI could use you."

The FBI! Now, that explained everything, Jones assured himself with delight. Of course Virginia was mistaken. McJavert had visited Holy Hollow to investigate *him*.

"No, thank you," he said warmly. "I think I am on the right track now. But why should you be under investigation?"

"Paxton has never told me," Virginia said, her eyes bright with amusement. "He said he would, some day." She gave a little giggle. "Do you remember coming in one day and suddenly warning me against strange men? Well, that was the day Paxton first came into the Library. And do you know, before long he was warning me against faculty men!"

"Specifically?" Jones demanded. "Anybody in particular?"

"Oh, no! But it's too delicious." She gave him a sidelong glance. "You men always laugh at how suspicious women are of each other. Anyhow, I feel very well taken care of. But, honestly, don't you want me to ask him about you?"

"I have an idea that Mr. McJavert is already fully aware of me," Jones smiled. "You see, I was also under investigation."

"Oh, Dr. Jones! Really?" Virginia turned in her seat toward him.

"It was nothing extraordinary," Jones reassured her. "I understand it is routine procedure when one is under consideration by the White Ho—under consideration for—well, I mean, it is necessary, of course, to establish proof that when a man says he is John Jones, he really is John Jones and not an impostor."

"Ooh, I think that's fun," Virginia crowed, cuddling up

to Jones and taking his nearer hand in both her own. "We are both being shadowed together. That's delicious!"

Jones smiled, but did not withdraw his hand. He felt curiously lighthearted, and he choked back the correction he was about to make, that he was not now being "shadowed." The investigation was completed, so far as he was concerned. That was patent. But it was so delightfully silly to pretend with Virginia that they were parties to a benevolent sort of melodrama. He squeezed the palm that lay against his, and launched into reminiscence of the time he had been trailed from Qal'a Shargat to Basra by Iraqi assassins who thought a case of cigarettes labeled "Fatima" contained the remains of Mohammed's daughter. And that reminded Virginia of the time she was under surveillance in Haiti, being suspected by a wrinkled black crone of having matrimonial designs on her shriveled, inky voodoo-priest husband. And so the journey was made short and merry. Now walking with their heads together, then stopping to face each other laughing ("—the Khifri word for nursing mother is pronounced almost like the Druse for deep well, so when I asked if they had a deep well because my camels needed refreshment—").

Virginia's laughter ended in midtrill, and Jones followed her gaze to see, approaching them and only a few paces distant, the Dean and a tall, stoop-shouldered, dour-looking man whose unwinking blue eyes were deep-set under shaggy iron-gray brows. Both men looked unhappy. The Dean had taken Mr. Grimper of the Trustees on a tour of the grounds to see for himself that the sharp-edged holes in the macadam drive should be filled ("No, that's unnecessary. Just close the driveway to all traffic; too much gasoline being wasted these days anyhow") and that the leak in the septic tank serving the dormitory was a menace to community health ("When I went to college my boardinghouse had an outdoor privy; all that water leaking there is a sign of waste, waste").

"Mr. Grimper," said the Dean, "I think you have met Miss Finster, our assistant librarian, and Dr. Jones?"

"Hrgh," said Mr. Grimper. "Grk."

Jones, still ebullient, said: "I could not help overhearing

205

you saying something about waste. I had a most interesting conversation with a government official yesterday who claimed there is no such thing as waste."

"Hrgh! No such thing as waste? Grx!"

"He had some interesting statistics about cigarettes, for example. Said that twenty-seven per cent of them were wasted—"

"A hundred per cent," Grimper said loudly and clearly. "Narcotics! Waste of money. Waste of time. Waste of health!"

"Well, he also mentioned mustard," Jones said, a little weakly.

"Mustard! Grf! Causes ulcers. Only people whose stomachs are jaded by alcohol need mustard. Bad for 'em, though. Serves 'em right. Waste!"

"I think," Virginia said, "I shall have to run along. Will you excuse me, please?"

Grimper eyed her retreating figure.

"No corsets," he said. "Might as well be nekkid."

Jones, a little desperate now, bethought himself of a prime way to change the conversation and to appease the curmudgeon by a request for advice.

"Mr. Grimper," he said, "I find I have to consult either a senator or a congressman on a matter of importance. I am afraid I am not as familiar as I should be with our representatives in Washington. The strategy of the situation requires that I consult one whose term is about to expire and who seeks re-election, and who has influence at the White House."

Grimper's eyebrows went up like two Angora cats arching their backs.

"White House? White House? Red House, you mean, sir! We have not had a man of honor and courage in the White House since James Buchanan! Good day, sir."

Jones shrugged his shoulders at the abruptly turned back of Trustee Grimper. It is likely his gesture might have been more emphatic had he heard Grimper's grumble: "That's the fine pair that made us so much trouble getting their names in the papers. Carrying on in broad daylight. Telling me to my

206

JONES THOUGHT OF A WAY TO APPEASE THE
CURMUDGEON

face there is no such thing as waste. Cigarettes. Grx! Mustard! Argh! And trying to get into New Deal politics! Ga-a-a!"

"But a very great scholar, Mr. Grimper," the Dean said. "A bit eccentric, perhaps, as a probable result of living long alone and remote from civilization. But about that septic tank . . ."

Jones posed his problem to Alfred that evening.

"Well, now, John," said Alfred, polishing his glasses vigorously, "I must say I am glad to see you take an interest in public affairs. Yes, indeed. People are too prone to condemn politics as a sordid business and to avoid any part in it, not realizing that they are thus responsible for the very evils they condemn. If every practicing Christian would take an active part in politics, we could soon purge the government of corruption. I have long held that our forefathers made a mistake in not making membership in a religious organization a prerequisite to the franchise. It would have strengthened religion and kept politics pure. Election day should fall during the Lenten season, too. . . ."

"Nevertheless, who is our representative?" John insisted.

"I know his name as well as I do my own," Alfred said, smiting his forehead. "A Baptist, I remember. Oh dear! It seems to me he is named rather poetically. Angela! Oh, Angela! Angela, do you remember the name of our congressman?"

"Goodness gracious," Angela said, appearing at the living-room door. "You ask me for somebody's name like that, point-blank, and——"

"That's it! Blank! Thank you, my dear. Orvil Blank."

"What's poetic about that?" Jones asked. "It sounds the opposite."

"Oh, just my little system for remembering. 'Blank' like in 'blank verse.' Hullo, there is the phone. Who can be calling us up, I wonder."

He trotted off to appease Dr. Bell's intrusive invention. "John, for you," he called back. He met Jones at full length

209

of the telephone cord, his eyes round. "It's Mr. Grimper," he said. "You know, the president of the bank. The trustee."

"Wants to apologize," Jones guessed aloud, taking the receiver which Alfred seemed on the point of dropping at that remark.

"Dr. Jones?" gobbled the instrument in John's ear. "Grimper. I wish, sir, that you would arrange to meet with the Committee on Faculty of the Trustees tomorrow afternoon at four o'clock sharp in the Deanery. Thank you."

The instrument clicked. Jones, wordless, stared at it a moment and then thoughtfully replaced it on its cradle.

"Why didn't you speak to him?" gibbered Alfred.

"I will, tomorrow," Jones said.

28

NEXT MORNING Jones repaired to the Capitol, where he was directed to the House Office Building a block distant, only there to be told there was no such person as Representative Orvil Blank.

His insistence shook the guard's faith in the red-bound Congressional Directory to the extent of appealing to a colleague of obviously maturer years.

"Orvil Blank?" The blue-uniformed gaffer shook his head, and then his oystery eye brightened. "Oh, Orvil Blank! Let's see. He quit to run for governor back in 'twenty-eight, I think it was. Or maybe 'thirty. It must of been 'thirty, because that's the year the Democrats took over, so I wasn't here in 'twenty-eight. Been here since 'thirty-one, and expect—"

"Well, who took his place?" Jones interrupted.

"Starling," the old man said promptly. "The Hon. Peter Starling. A great man, too. Yes, sir! A great congressman. Why, he—"

"Where do I find him?"

"Well, sir, you take the elevator yonder to the sixth floor, and it will be about halfway down the second corridor on your left."

Surprisingly enough, it was. But the Congressman, it seemed, was busy. Would Dr. Jones wait? Would he like to see the paper? And here was a reprint of a speech that Congressman had made last Friday on victory. Even a lot of senators had come over to listen to it.

Jones took a seat, hands in pockets and one of them clutching the jar in which his chosen mouse martyr reposed. He was only third in the line of waiting supplicants, none of whom was aware that the business that engaged the Congressman at the moment was breakfast. By the time the first one was summoned into the presence, the office contained at least two dozen constituents and the room was radiant with the hope that shone in every countenance, for Peter Starling was a power not only in the nation but in the state and if a deserving citizen couldn't be added to the payroll of the WPB or OCD he could be sure of a job as an oyster warden or courthouse cop.

Jones did not know that, and it would have made no difference if he had. He did not know, either, that there were those among his own neighbors who said that, although Washington had a billion starlings and their state but one, Washington was the cleaner.

Seated at last beside the Congressman's desk, in an office whose walls were decorated with a portrait of Jefferson, crossed American and Confederate flags and tinted photographs of bucolic scenes, Jones listened to an oration of welcome delivered in rich Tidewater accents by the stocky, red-faced statesman. The welcome was well larded with quotations from the Old Testament, for Starling had been succinctly briefed that this Dr. Jones was practitioner for bodily ills of neither man nor horse, but of the faculty of St. Jude's.

Jones recognized some of the Talmudic phrases and wondered briefly. Then he inserted his own speech into a pause in the Congressman's salutation.

"I have no desire to intrude upon a busy man," Jones declared, "especially so because I, too, am pressed for time. I have been advised that you can obtain an audience for me with the President."

Starling jerked forward, bringing his cocked-up foot to the floor with a slap like the sound of a breeching strap on the back of a well-roped Negro.

212

"I be dogged," said Starling. "I be dogged! Who mought ha' told you that, now?"

"An officer in the Navy," Jones replied. Who was he? Jones told him. Where did he live? Jones didn't know.

"You know," Starling said, "me an' the White House, we don't get along so well. They ain't my brand of Democrat. Now, why did you want to see the Pres'dent fo'? Whut can he do fo' you that Pete Starlin' can't do?"

"It's a long story, and much of it I cannot relate," Jones began, but Starling interrupted him with an admonitory hand.

"Just you give me all the time you can spare," he said graciously. "You warned me you were pressed for time, suh, but fo' a distinguished visitor like you, suh, I got jest a little mo' time than you have!"

"I'll make it brief," Jones promised. "I want to contact the President on a matter vital to the war effort. I wrote him a letter, and received a cordial reply from his secretary. On the strength of that I went to the White House where I was received, but did not see the President. He was not there. However, I was sent to New York to see a—a certain personage—but he wanted to employ me in a local operation of particular interest to himself, so I declined. Since then I have tried to obtain interviews with the Secretary of the Navy and the Secretary of War, but I get no farther than generals and commanders."

"I declare!" Starling said, with a sympathetic shake of his head. "Well, suh, that's the kind of gov'ment we got these days. Yes, suh! A bunch of self-seekin' bureaucrats. Just what kind of job are you lookin' fo'?"

"I'm not looking for a job," Jones replied passionately.

"I certainly beg yo' pardon," Starling hastened to say. "That's just a phrase we learn to use in politics. Now, this contract you aim to get—"

"Not contract. Contact! I am offering my services to my country, without salary, without compensation of any kind."

Starling shook his head again.

"The laborer is worthy of his hire, as the Good Book says,"

he observed. "In gov'ment, suh, especially, you'll find that people will accept you at yo' own valuation. If you want nothin', you are worth nothin'. Politics is a practical business, Reverend. I don't say that that's the way it should be, but the way it is. And yet, it is the democratic way. Otherwise politics would be run by the rich people for the rich people."

"I am far from being wealthy," Jones quickly interjected. "I receive a small salary but I have a few hundred dollars saved. If I am willing to give my life to my country, I should not hesitate to give my money. Therefore I propose to make a will, so that if I lose my life in this enterprise, my savings will be bequeathed to the government. Of course, if I am not killed, I shall need my savings."

Starling stared blankly.

"Look here," he said, "you ain't tryin' to get into uniform!"

"No, no," Jones replied. "But I am trying to participate actively in the war. I am sorry that the risk is too great to permit me to give you either detailed explanation or demonstration, but I am in possession of a technique, thoroughly tested, by which I could end the war in a very few days by virtually immobilizing the enemy's forces."

"Do you think that would be good?"

"Good? Good? Why wouldn't it be good?"

"Well, it would cinch the election for the administration, to begin with. Does this here process kill people?"

"It can, and it can't," Jones said. "As you like. Either way."

"What is it? A gas or something?"

"Call it 'something,'" Jones answered. "It isn't a gas or an explosion or a death ray. It is noiseless and invisible."

"Well, I be dogged," Starling mused. "How long would it take to manufacture this apparatus?"

"Only inexhaustible natural forces are used," Jones said cannily. "I can put them to work tomorrow, if need be."

"I tell you what," Starling said. "The war is goin' along fine, just fine. The Germans can't last through the winter. Then it will be a cinch to knock off the Japs. That will give

214

business a chance to reconvert, and for the country to get back to normal by degrees. If you could, as you say, end the war in a few days, we'd have plain chaos, suh. Chaos, that's what. Every factory would stop producin'. Millions would be thrown out of work. The soldiers would clamor to come home, adding more millions to the unemployed. Suh, we just ain't ready for peace. It ain't practical. We are going to have unemployment anyhow, and the doggonedest labor troubles and strikes you ever saw. And sure as hell we'll have to fight the Russians. We simply got to. The Communists will try to take over this country, and the only way we can prevent it is to use up what's left of our big war production to smash the Russians. Now, that's where you should come in. Not now. Everything is dandy right now. But if you can do what you say, we'll need you bad to keep down the revolution in this country and to lick the Bolshies in their own country. And then, by the Almighty, the Democratic party will be returned to the hands that created it and kept it alive since eighteen-sixty. How does that appeal to you?"

"It presents an entirely new thought to me," Jones admitted. "But I still think it is my duty to offer my services to my country now."

Starling leaned back in his chair again, drumming on its arms. He smiled inwardly. He knew exactly how a request from him would be received at the White House.

"Very well, suh! That's yo' decision, and I honor you fo' it," he declaimed. "I will call the White House and try to make an appointment fo' you with the President. All I ask is, that if—as I confidently expect—the gang up yonder does not permit you to employ yo' God-given genius, that you come back to me and we will plan together to combat the bigger crisis to come. I repeat, suh, that victory is perched upon our banners in this war. We have nothing to fear, so far as the Germans and Japs can go. But we have nourished the viper of communism in the process. We have given to our real enemy, the Antichrist of Marxism, the tools and the techniques which will be turned against us, suh, just as sure as God made green apples. You will see this country paralyzed by strikes, suh, with Jewish-led mobs marching on the Capitol, and at the chosen moment Russia will strike. That is when you will be needed."

"Nevertheless," Jones said doggedly, "I wish you would get me an audience with the President."

Starling allowed himself to smile openly. He reached for his telephone: "Get me General Popkins at the White House. Yes, you heard me! The White House."

He smiled again, and then became suddenly serious.

"Don't think I am against labor," he said. "I believe in labor's right to organize, too, in fraternal organizations to work for civic improvements like the Kiwanis Clubs and the Lions, but not to strike against the public interest. There's no law that says a man has to work on a job where he thinks he is underpaid, or the conditions ain't right. But dog me, suh, if we don't have a law now that says an employer has to hire people he knows are overpaid. I believe in the law of supply and demand and—"

The telephone interrupted him.

"Hello? Hello? White House? This is Representative Peter Starling. I'd like to speak to General Popkins. Hello, Pop? What? Who is this? Farm—what? Famulus? Who are you?"

"I know him," Jones whispered, leaning over the desk. "President's secretary."

"President's secretary!" Starling growled huskily, covering the mouthpiece with a freckled hand. "That's like talkin' about General Eisenhower's privates. He's got a million of 'em." Then, into the telephone: "This is Representative Pete Starling talkin'. Do you reckon you can get an appointment with the President for a constituent of mine, a very important and famous gentleman—"

Reedily through the instrument Jones could hear Famulus's "I'm sorry, Congressman, I'm very sorry, but the President—"

"A very important and famous gentleman named Dr. John Jones of St. Jude's Theological Seminary. Do you hear me?"

216

The instrument was silent. Then, thinly over the wire, came the query: "Did you say Dr. John Jones, Congressman?"

"Yes, I said Jones. Jay as in Je—as in Jefferson, oh as in—as in—"

"Ophiolatry," Jones whispered.

But Famulus's voice was shrilly audible.

"We know all about Dr. Jones, Congressman. We are planning a very important spot for him. He can expect to hear from us in a very few days. The President wants to meet—"

The receiver dropped from Starling's hand, dragging the whole instrument to the floor with a tinkling crash. The Congressman picked it up, and silenced the pipings it still emitted.

"Well," said Jones. "That's fine! That's great! Thank you, sir."

"Yes, that's swell," Starling said without conviction. "Good-bye, suh. Any time I can help you out in any way, remember this office . . . well, good-bye, suh!"

29

INSTINCTIVELY, BLINDLY, Jones took the bus for home. His long quest was almost ended.

The exaltation that permeated Jones in body, mind and spirit rescued him from the thralldom to time. He could envision himself years hence, a Cincinnatus delving among books and suddenly called upon to fly to Africa or Asia or South America where evil against the peace and dignity of humanity had emerged, there to blast and destroy it with its own captive bane.

The bus driver's hoarse proclamation of arrival at the crossroads where one descended the curving path to the Seminary brought Jones back to the sorry and evil-infested world of today. Clutching his mouse jar in his pocket, he stumbled from the bus to the red-clay shoulder of the highway and stood blinking in the sun, surprised to find himself on the familiar ground.

The weather had turned cool and a fresh breeze flirted with the oaks and honey locusts, for it had rained up the valley. There was much for Jones still to ponder, dreams to be prepared for translation to substance, and all this on a universal scale impossible to achieve in Angela's tidy household wherein no plans were consummated of stature larger than a tea party for twenty.

Jones turned his back on the Seminary, following the pink gravel that led to the river and, crossing a rather weedy railroad track and the river road beyond, led to a long and weather-beaten pier. Here, once upon a time, sailing barges had tied up to take on crates of chickens, bawling calves and hog-tied shoats from the farmers of the region for delivery to the Washington produce markets, the barges themselves loaded with oysters from the Chesapeake and melons from the Eastern Shore.

Jones walked out to the end of the pier and sat down on the rain-scoured planking, his back against a bollard and his feet dangling over the roiled and rolling current. Evidently the storm up the valley had been deluginous. Jones took the mouse jar from his pocket, and set it on the edge of the silvery bleached stringer, so the little animal could have the benefit of sun and repose.

Round and green as a mermaid's thighs the hills of Virginia and Maryland sloped down to the river. Upstream the green-blue was smirched by sooty fumes which marked Alexandria's leprous waterfront, above which, in symbolic triumph, the high white tower of the Virginia Theological Seminary (parent, and to some of the scion's faculty, rival of St. Jude's) reared against the sky. In the stream's channel a few sailboats scudded, dipping up and down like feeding ducks, and a small boat in the war paint of Navy or Coast Guard tried to look ferociously determined.

Jones turned his eyes inward. How to use himself after the immediate task was accomplished? Could a man offer himself to the government with reservations? "I shall invoke this power only against those whom I deem to be evil." If he had the right to say that, had he the wisdom to make such decisions? He would need advice, indeed he would; advice from somebody who was a friend of humanity, that most nearly friendless of the world's tenantry. Nobody thought in terms of humanity, particularly.

And yet, civilized or savage, people were essentially unselfish once they were secure from fear, Jones reasoned. The world was full of good Samaritans, remembering that "Samaritan" was to Christ's hearers a term of obloquy, and the epithet more paradoxical than a "good whore" would be to a Carmelite nun. Men fled fear or fought it according to their natures. Fear put gyves on the wrists of charity. Fear blinded Americans and Germans and Spaniards and Britons to the fact that *humanity* had to inherit the earth, not democracy or fascism or Catholicism, or, for that matter, the meek. Well, he, Jones would remove one fear—

"How's tricks, Professor?"

Jones's head jerked on his shoulders. Leaning against the opposite bollard was a man who, he could have sworn, was a stranger; and yet the intruder's ready identification of Jones argued that they must be known to each other. It was hardly probable that he could have met on any social or professional plane a creature whose fat and flabby form should be draped in a grease-spotted blue polo shirt, earth-stained seersucker jacket and trousers, and a grimy hat with contour lines of sweat above the faded band.

So Jones nodded, affably enough, and turned his face back to the river.

"If you're headin' south, you gotta cross the river. This jerk line don't go nowheres, and the brakies are as mean as if it was the Nickel Plate. What the hell is that in the goddam bottle? A mouse?"

Nor was that question worthy of reply. Jones wondered how he could rid himself of the unwelcome companionship.

"What's the gimmick, Professor? You a med worker? I never tried that racket. I've pitched ink-sticks, genuine facsimile Brazilian diamonds, cundrums and, last time, a line of bullet-proof breast-pocket Bibles. That was the real larry, though. Wouldn't stop a mosquito's stinger, but how the gals went for 'em to give to the soldiers! God, the geedus I raked in! But pitchin' isn't my regular line. I got ideas. All I need is a partner with a little moola. Bulletproof jock-straps, now. They'd outsell bulletproof Bibles by ten to one. Did you ever meet up with Professor Nooky Sloper on the road? There's an operator for you. Ideas? Like a toad has warts. They come natural. When everybody was talking about the new sulfa drugs that's supposed to cure clap in one night, he gets a lot of slips of paper printed up, see? And puts 'em

220

in envelopes, like headache powders. That's how I got acquainted with him. I'm a printer. That's my regular line. Got my card here in Detroit Chapter. In good standing, you'll see for yourself. It's always good to have a union card on you. Well, anyway, Doc Sloper goes around whisperin' to the young fellas—mostly he worked the cans in the better saloons—that he had a new sulfa drug to keep you from knocking up your gal. Absolutely guaranteed, see? For only a dollar. Inside of five minutes he'd have ten customers and scram. And when the guys opened the envelopes and unfolded the papers inside, there was printed one word—*sulfadenial!* Oh, cripes! But I got an idea better than that."

He waited for the invitation to explain. When Jones remained silent, the stranger spat into the river and continued anyhow.

"This is bigger than the Ku Klux," he said. "It's the biggest thing that ever was, but it will take a front to start it. All it would need is a clean shirt, a couple of case notes and some smooth, fast jawbone. Here it is, brother! Who's the biggest guy in America today who drags down the most dough for the least work? You know who. Not the President. Not John D. Rockefeller. It's John L. Lewis. How come? All he did was organize the coal miners. I know how the labor organizer racket works. Give 'em a gripe, give 'em a good time, and collect a buck a month from every damn one of 'em the rest of your life. All you do is tell 'em how wonderful they are and how they're gettin' a dirty deal but you'll get 'em out of it, and a free-beer picnic once a year.

"You know the biggest bunch of people that aren't organized yet and are just hanging there like peaches on the vine for somebody to organize 'em? It's these Civilian Defense rubes.

"Every goddam little town in the country has a Civil Defense. They run around wearing helmets, turning out lights and squirting water on make-believe bombs and having themselves a hell of a good time making like soldiers. The boys and girls have good clean fun giving each other artificial inspiration or something and bandaging each other's behinds, but it just isn't organized. So here's my idea, and if you're interested, we'll go partners because you got what I ain't got. You look like a goddam parson and you can be the front man.

"We'll organize the Civilian Defense Workers Veterans Society. They can't join the American Legion, you see, and this will be their own Legion. It will cost ten bucks for a charter, and we'll have lapel badges made in the shape of little stirrup pumps which I can get stamped out five hundred for a dollar and sell 'em for two bits, or a dollar silver-plated. And we'll have a convention once a year, like the Legion, with big cities bidding against each other and payin' you and me yards of moola for being the convention city. And we'll have memorial blackouts, and every dip in the country will have to pay us ten per cent of what he lifts during the blackouts. We just sit back mailing out badges and charters and the money rolls in like nobody's business, and no income tax on account of we'll incorporate as a charitable, benevolent co-operative society.

"What do you say, cull? Are you with me?"

Throughout the incredible recital Jones's ire had risen until he felt suffocated, and his fingers twitched in his pockets. At the final question he struggled to his feet and looked down on the stranger, his lips writhing in anger and anguish.

"No," he spat. "I am emphatically not with you. Most of your jargon has been unintelligible to me, but I understand enough of your uncouth talk to be convinced that you are a scurrilous, low, vile, vulgar and thoroughly offensive parasite. It has been my lot recently to suffer more anger and disappointment than I thought a human could endure, but it becomes negligible compared with the disgust and wrath your loathsome scheme inspires."

The stranger, with considerable and noisy effort, scrambled upright, but the face he turned on Jones was unclouded by resentment or displeasure. Instead, admiration shone there, and he voiced it:

"Professor, that is the most god-lovely line of jawbone I

ever heard pitched. I take it you don't like my scheme, but that's on account of you're mad at the whole world. You'll come around okay. With your come-to-Jesus looks and that line of chin-music, we will make a million dollars. A million dollars each, I mean. Why, we'll make the Ku Klux look like grifters. Ku Klux? We'll make the Masons and the Knights of Columbus and the Boy Scouts look like—"

"Silence!" Jones bellowed, and then his voice fell to a choked, chesty rumble. "You don't know what you have done to me, and there would be no way of explaining to your cannibalistic little soul, but if I could invoke the curses of every deity from Allah to Zeus upon your pediculous head it would not be adequate compensation."

"Take it easy, bo," the stranger said nervously. "I see a guy sittin' here lookin' like he's plannin' to do the Dutch act, and I offers him a partnership in the biggest racket since Al Capone, that's all I done to you. I give you a chance to make a million bucks, and I don't like to get pushed around for it."

"Anything you don't like is my great delight," Jones cried. "You and your vulpine scheme. Ferine perversion of—"

"Now, wait up, my friend," the man snarled. "Enough is enough, and nobody can call me a fairy an' a pervert, by God. Why, you lousy little mouse-lover, you! I'll show you."

And with that the gross creature thrust out a shabby foot and kicked the jar from the projecting stringpiece. For a moment it teetered on the edge of the joist, its wee occupant making frantic efforts to escape by tearing at the glass with small pink feet.

A groan rose from Jones's chest, and he reached for the toppling jar. The smooth glass slipped from his finger tips, and in a final lunge at rescue Jones felt himself lose his balance. The swirling, foam-flecked, coffee-colored waters seemed to rush up to meet him as, mouth opened in a cry of despair, he plunged head first into the river.

He was lost in an evil-tasting and fecal-hued element where there was no up, no down, and yet a tremendous sense of uncontrollable motion. He was a leaf in a typhoon, a meteorite in space; he was benumbed with cold, cramped from shock, and as he tried to flail his arms and legs in an instinctive attempt at swimming he found his limbs pushed and pulled in contrary directions by the eddying waters.

Suddenly he was thrust by those forces above the river's surface. He had a blurred glimpse of the distant pier and of a blowzy figure galloping landward and, as the eddy whirled him, a panoramic view of hills and brown water, blue sky and bright horizon; then he was sucked down again into cold darkness. Writhing tentacles seemed to be groping and stretching for him, to entangle his arms and legs as he tried desperately to move them in some sort of synchronized up-thrust. Hard and slime-surfaced objects poked and butted him, slithering under his fingers, rubbing obscenely against his face, but again he gained the surface long enough to draw a few agonizing bubbling breaths. The air only made his heart beat harder, until his breast was one searing flame in an envelope of ice.

Jones was dimly conscious of a new and contentious force wrestling the flood for possession of him. The white-hot pain ripped and thrust inside of him until it burst through and escaped, leaving him pleasantly numb. Into the gaping apertures made by the escaping pain, heat began to seep into his body. Strange faces, wavering of outline and distorted by the water, floated close to his, their mouths working like fishes. Bells tolled far off, and voices bubbled in the distance. Invisible hands strove with his inert body, lifting him and thrusting him down, quarreling over him. He felt the yielding mud of the river bottom against his shoulder blades. It was strangely warm.

30

PRESENTLY Jones discovered that, while he could not move head nor limbs, he could open his eyes. But all he could see was whiteness, in any direction. It was like being inside of an egg. Pain tugged at his lids, and he slid back into warm blackness, barely aware that a chalky white arm had stretched over him, barely sensing the contact of a warm, dry palm upon his brow. Out of the hidden depths of childhood memories came the recollection of Big Klaus and Little Klaus and the people who lived with their flocks on the river bottom. . . .

The yacht's mahogany was concealed under gray paint, and her brasswork was hidden under the double shroud of twine and canvas seamen call "worming and parceling," but none of the habiliments of war could hide the grace and beauty of her. Of all the works of man that ply the sea today, only a schooner-rigged yacht deserves to be called "she." All other craft have evolved into contours of sturdy masculine utility; they are bald, broad-thewed things of planes and muscles and tendons, filled with hoarse rumblings and a thrusting assertiveness. Only the yacht under full sail is feminine in curves that describe the rise of breast and flexure of thigh, feminine in voice as the shrouds sing alto to the breeze, feminine in motion as they lean away from the ardent wind and yet embrace it and move with it.

The tall and tired-looking man half swathed in a togalike cloak of blue had said, somewhat fretfully: "No, I shall not make a campaign. It would not be becoming and it will not be necessary."

There had followed a silence, then, among the small group lounging on the deep-cushioned wicker chairs. Then one of them spoke, raspingly: "I agree with you, Chief, that it is not going to be absolutely necessary, but—" he cleared his throat noisily—"but just the same— My God!"

Slack-jawed, he pointed shoreward.

"I'll swear I just saw one man push another off that pier," he cried. "See, the fellow is running back to shore."

Binoculars were trained.

"There's a guy running, all right . . . Legging it as fast as he can go . . . But I don't see anybody in the water . . . Do you see anybody in the water? . . . Look at that cuss make for the woods . . . Maybe we'd better make sure. . . . Joe! Joe!"

The yacht's lovely breast dipped and rose; her sleek body rolled on the brown waters; she turned into the wind, and as her sails drooped and trembled a boat splashed into the river like a child jumping from its mother's lap. All but the blue-cloaked man crowded to the yacht's rails to watch the questing dinghy, to make exclamations when the small boat suddenly backed water, and careened dangerously to the dead weight of him who was dragged aboard.

"He's still alive, anyhow . . . Yes, just barely though . . . Elderly chap to be brawling on the waterfront . . . Take him below and I'll go over him as soon as you've rubbed him dry. . . . Hot blankets . . . How about some of this bourbon, Doc? . . ."

Chairs creaked again. Muddy brown water and green slime on the white teak. As the unconscious man was carried off, his head rolled and he spewed the contents of his indignant stomach on the deck.

"Must be a Republican."

Laughter.

"This will make a grand story for the papers . . ."

"No!"

"No?"

226

"No! I don't care who he is. They'll revive that old gag about walking on water. The opposition will say it was planned that way. No!"

"Well, to get on with what we were saying. We'll have to blanket the country with speakers. We'll have to coax every big name we can on to committees."

"Speaking of that: Funny thing! Starling called up this morning, Famulus said, to—"

"Starling! Not Starling! Why, he—he—"

"Yes, siree, Starling. Called up in behalf of this man Jones we were talking about only yesterday. You don't know about this, Chief. The boys almost pulled a bloomer on that one. This Jones is a big-shot explorer and also something fancy in religious circles, and we are weak in both. A little over-zealousness almost lost him to us, but . . ."

The talk went on. Put Jones on the Committee of Churchmen, but make him chairman of the Explorers' Committee. The one who had absented himself rejoined the group and was asked: "How is your patient, Doc?" and answered: "Pretty close call but he'll be okay in a couple of hours. I did thus-and-so and gave him this-and-that."

The yacht two-stepped down the river in the arms of the wind.

Jones opened his eyes again. Still the dismaying whiteness above. Whiteness below. Whiteness to the right. Whi— No, a face on his left, a face on a level with his own, a seamed and careworn face. And floating above it another face. He himself was only face. He could not feel his body. Three faces floating in an eggshell.

"How do you feel, old-timer?"

It was the lower face. Jones smiled at it. "Heard of people losing their heads," he whispered laboriously. "Seem to have lost our bodies." He chuckled, exhausted by the speech.

"Out of his head, do you think?" the lower face turned toward the upper one.

"No, no," Jones wheezed. "Head is here. Three of them in an eggshell. That's a yolk."

He thought to guffaw at his shameless pun, but could emit only a rattle in his throat. The higher face floated down to his level. It produced hands that felt him, prodded, smoothed.

"He'll be all right. Here, Pop, swallow this."

Sliding head first into darkness was the most marvelous sensation of Jones's experience. It was like being embraced by a dark woman. Like being embraced by a dark woman. A dark woman. The dark woman. The dark woman of the storm. The dark.

He awoke to darkness.

Where was he? He was lying on his back; in warmth and utter silence and in darkness. He sat up, fighting against deep-tucked sheet and blankets, bumped knees and head against a wall on his right, found emptiness on his left and, extraordinarily far below, a floor revealed to him that he was bare of foot.

Bare of foot? Bare of body. Stark naked.

He gripped the side of his high couch for mental, as well as physical, stability and groped as far as he could reach with his free hand. There was a bureaulike thing at the bed's head, with a metal railing. His groping hand knocked over a glass, and liquid pattered and piddled to the floor.

Where—ah, the pier; the pier and the repulsive, pulpy creature who had besmirched Jones's dream of an unselfish world; the mouse, the cruel blow of foot, the plunge.

"Hey! Hello! Help!" Jones cried. His chest hurt, and he had to pant for air before he could shout again. "Halloo! Somebody! Hey!"

An oblong of yellow light appeared at the end of the room, and a silhouette within it, and then there was a click and the oblong became a cube of light, containing Jones. He was in a small, white-paneled room, and a white-coated figure came toward him. It had a brown face.

"You feeling all honky-dory now, sir?"

"Where are my clothes?" Jones demanded. "Where am I, for that matter?"

"Yacht basin, sir. Clothes coming now very quickly."

He backed from the room. Jones looked around again. Two

228

curtained windows, small and high in the wall. A high bunk-bed, built on top of a locker of sorts. A chair. The bureau, with a narrow brass railing against which a half-drained tumbler was tilted. Green rug, green chair.

The door opened again. It was the brown-faced one, burdened. On the green chair he spread shirt and shorts, top shirt and necktie, all clean and smooth and still redolent of the iron. Shoes. On a hanger, his suit, fresh-pressed.

"No hat, sorry," said the brown one. "Would you like a highball, sir?"

"A highball? Great belly of Bacchus! What time is it?"

"Five o'clock, now," the roomboy answered, drawing back the curtains from round, brassbound portholes. He took assorted objects from the pocket of his white jacket. "Here your money, knife, watch. Knife okay, watch no good. Too long in water."

He was, Jones thought, as he drew on his freshly laundered clothes, a Hawaiian or some such South Sea Islander; a servant, not the owner of the ship. And when the steward returned with a very tall glass in which ice floated in a brown and bubbling fluid, Jones set to work to fill the blank in his life.

"Whose yacht is this?"

"Belong U.S. Navy, now."

Jones took a long gulp of the drink. His throat was parched and raw, and his every muscle ached. The liquor stung and choked him, but he swallowed it gratefully, alternating his sips with questions. Yes, somebody had seen him fall into the water. Sailors went off in the dinghy and picked him up. The Captain Doctor put him to bed, gave him medicine, gave him whiskey. Himself, the roomboy, Hilario, had rubbed him with alcohol and put hot blankets on him.

"Well, it's a lucky thing for me you were out cruising," Jones said, shaking his watch ruefully. "I thought I was dead."

"Not cruising," Hilario said proudly. "Taking President to catch destroyer down bay."

The watch dropped on the floor, spewing cogwheels.

"The President? The President? You mean, the President?"

"Yes, sir. We put him on destroyer. Destroyer take him to cruiser, maybe. He gone away someplace. He come in for to see you. You don't remember?"

"No," Jones gasped, drooping against the bunk. "He was in here?"

"Oh, sure. You talk to him. He talk to you."

"Oh, ye gods!" Jones groaned. "What did he say? What did I say?"

"He say, 'How you feeling, old-timer?' and you talk about eggs."

"About eggs? What about eggs?"

Hilario shrugged.

"Just eggs," he said. "And heads. I don't know what about. Captain Doctor, he give you another pill."

"I wish to Aesculapius he had given me a lead pill," Jones choked, beating his brow with his fists. "Oh, Zotz! Your cunning is great, and your powers are far-reaching, but I'll beat you yet. Ealario, or whatever your name is, I have to get out of here."

"Yes, sir. Skipper, he gone ashore. You tell officer of the deck your name for log. Come this way, please, sir."

Jones followed the steward through narrow door and tiny passage to a steep flight of steps, and emerged on deck where a white-clad naval officer, a single gold bar on his black shoulder-boards, shook him violently by the hand and made loud inquiry into Jones's present outlook on the world. And Jones answered with words of gratitude, gave his name correctly, and stepped to the concrete jetty where two taxicabs were waiting to transport liberty-bound bluejackets to the public library or any other of Washington's diverse places of education and/or entertainment.

Only when he mentioned the address did he remember that he had had an urgent appointment with a committee of trustees for four o'clock.

He would be at least two hours late.

He was, plus five minutes.

Now the Deanery, like the head of MacGregor's table, is wherever the Dean lives, and for all its Gothic title it was the most modest building on the St. Jude campus, as befitted its tenancy by the most modest man on the faculty. In fact, the Deanery (at the time this story describes) had originally been designed as a gardener's cottage. The Dean, being a bachelor, had given up the gambrel-roofed submansion to which he was entitled to the Professor of Pentateuchal Genealogies (who had nine children) and choosing for himself the four-room cottage on the edge of the campus.

It was to there that Jones directed the taxicab. His rap at the door was answered by the elderly colored woman who washed, scrubbed, mended and guarded for the Dean. To Jones's inquiry she replied, no, the Dean had left a few minutes ago to preside at dinner in the Refectory, implying that the Professor might have known as much and probably did.

But the other gentlemen were still in the library.

At that, Grimper himself appeared in the hall.

"Argh," he said. "Urk! Come in."

He stalked ahead of Jones and preceded him into the book-lined room where two other men sat, one of them stuffing sheaves of paper in his scuffed briefcase, the other chewing gum. Grimper seated himself behind the desk, and forthwith addressed Jones:

"Huck! Gr! Mr. Jones, as you know, this is the time of year we argh prepare to renew our contracts with the teaching staff. Urk. In some cases we deem it huck expedient to interview the members. We expected you, sir, at four o'huck. Clock. Your tardiness delayed and inconvenienced not only the Committee and the Dean but others scheduled at exact hours for argh consultation. I hope your excuse is adequate."

Jones returned Grimper's stare until his temper was under control.

"I believe it is adequate," he said. "I regret very much having inconvenienced the Dean and my colleagues. My tardiness was unpreventable."

231

Grimper glowered at him as if he believed that no tardiness was unpreventable. He tapped on the desktop with a pencil.

"As a matter of fact," Jones went on, "I was unconscious most of the time. You see, I fell—or was pushed—into the river and nearly drowned. By great good fortune the President's yacht was passing, and I was rescued and taken aboard, nearly dead. When I recovered consciousness the boat had docked, and it was nearly five o'clock. I took a taxicab all the way from Washington, and came directly here."

"Urgle," said Grimper. "Grix!"

One of the other men laughed a short, sharp yelp. The third one cracked his gum.

"You mean to huck," Grimper choked, "that you fell in the argh river and were fished out by the President and came straightforth here urgle?"

"I didn't say the President fished me out," Jones snapped back.

Grimper rose and stepped around the desk to face Jones, demanding, as he came, to know what Jones was doing at the river and how he happened to fall in.

"I don't see," Jones said, "that this has any bearing on the renewal of my contract. You asked why I was late. I told you. I will voluntarily add that I went down to the river to meditate, and I was there accosted by a low character who wished me to participate with him in a dishonest enterprise. When I stood up to denounce him he kicked my mouse into the water, and I either fell in or was pushed in trying to rescue it."

"Eek!" cried Grimper. "Then can you tell me, if this preposterous story is true, why your clothing is so urk immaculate?"

"Oh, that!" Jones looked down at his sharply creased trousers and glistening shoes. "A Hawaiian named Eelsomething laundered my clothes while I was in bed. He even ironed out my money. I gave him two dollars."

"A mouse!" raged Grimper. "A Hawaiian. An eel. Argh! Do you know how much of your story I believe, sir? I believe that you were down by the river in conversation with a low character. That's how much I believe."

He stood hunched before Jones, arms crossed, rocking on his heels. Jones thrust his face forward.

"And do you know what difference it makes to me whether you believe me or not?" he snapped. "Nothing. Less than nothing. Minus zero—and Fahrenheit, not centigrade."

Grimper reeled back. "Ug!" he exclaimed. "Grgh! I knew it. You are drunk. Your breath reeks of alcohol."

Jones retreated a pace, nonplussed, and Grimper turned to his fellow committeemen, arms outstretched.

"This man is intoxicated," he snarled. "He is uggle the influence of liquor. His story is an alcoholic delirium on the urg face of it. And it is not the first time. A few days ago I saw him prancing and giggling along the road with a young woman. He had the urgh effrontery to stop me to announce there is no such thing as waste and to chatter about a scheme to meet that man in the White House. It is an obsession with him, a drunken obsession. I move that Mr. John Jones be not offered a contract for the next term and that he stand suspended from the faculty as of this huck moment."

He turned and glared at Jones. Jones said: "Gentlemen, one moment.

"I do not doubt there is the odor of liquor on my breath. I was given a stimulant on the President's yacht. I am, however, no more under the influence of alcohol than—than Grimper, here, is under the influence of the Christian religion."

"Arx!" squawked Grimper. "Urgle! I'll have you huck—"

"Shut up!" Jones roared. "You've had your say! You have had it too much around here. To my way of thinking, it is time that the money-changers were again driven from the temple, instead of piously blaming the waning influence of the church on the motion pictures, the radio, the automobile, and what other silly scapegoats I can't recall. Stop gargling, Grimper. I told you you had had your say.

"Gentlemen, excluding Grimper here, I resign. I had

233

planned to resign under pleasanter circumstances and with a properly phrased statement of my affection for this institution, which has served me better than I served it. I am resigning to dedicate what is left of my life to a higher purpose than teaching a group of bewildered young men the rudiments of languages which they will never use and cannot learn."

"He can't resign!" Grimper shrieked, pounding the desk. "He huck! He can't! He uggle not do it. I demand that his resignation be not accepted, and that he be forthwith argh suspended and his contract be torn huck, and by Jupiter, Sam Doolittle, you better vote my way. I do now hereby move that John Jones be suspended forthwith and his contract not renewed!"

"Gentlemen," Jones intoned ironically, "you have heard the question. How do you vote, Mr. Doolittle?"

Doolittle took the gum from his mouth and stared at the pink, tooth-marked wad. "Vote aye," he mumbled.

"And you, sir?" Jones bowed to the man with the briefcase.

"I am not beholden to my friend Mr. Grimper for anything, not note nor mortgage, and my name is Walton Q. Gaylord, Colonel United States Marine Corps, retired, sir. And I admire your guts. I do indeed. Your story is so outrageously fantastic I admire your courage in sticking to it. And I don't think you're drunk. I've had more experience with drunks than Mr. Grimper has. And I vote no."

"Thank you, Colonel." Jones smiled, with another brief bow. "And now—" he turned to the smugly grinning Grimper "—and now, you, sir?"

He pointed a rigid forefinger at the smirking banker, and with that Grimper's face turned the color of cold oatmeal. His jaw sagged, his eyes bulged, and sweat stood on his forehead like the warts on a cucumber.

"Come, Mr. Grimper, how do you vote?" Jones insisted, his finger sternly and unwaveringly pointed.

But Gimper only writhed in his chair, clutching at the top of the desk, drooling and yammering in the back of his throat.

234

"The man is palpably drunk," Jones said, thrusting his hands in his pocket. "The vote is a tie and the motion, I take it, is defeated. I think Grimper will be better after he has had a little black coffee. Good night, gentlemen, and, Colonel, again my thanks."

31

JOHN JONES strode blithely down the curving path to his residence, where he found Alfred and Angela at the table over remnants of fried eggplant, yam patties and braised chard.

"Oh, John, I was so worried," Angela exclaimed. "Sit right down. I put a plate in the oven for you."

"I'm not so late, am I?" Jones reached for his watch, and winced as he recalled its loss.

As he sat down the telephone shrilled its vehement code.

"Was that our number?" asked Alfred of nobody. "I have never heard the line so busy as it has been for the past ten minutes. Seems as if every party on the line is being called."

And, his curiosity thus brought to focus by his own remark, Alfred went into the hall to listen in. He returned to the table grave-faced just as Angela came in from the kitchen with John's dinner.

"The plate is hot," Angela warned. "What kept you, John? You have been gone since early breakfast."

"I was out on the river yachting with the President," John grinned teasingly. Although his chest ached abominably he had never felt so sportive and carefree. "I'll tell you about it later."

"Oh, John, you weren't," Angela cried, vexation outweighing amusement in her voice.

The telephone drilled into their ears again.

"That's the Dean's number," Alfred said. "Mr. Grimper had a heart attack there a few minutes ago."

"He didn't have a heart attack," John declared, munching his chard dutifully.

"Oh, yes, he did," Alfred insisted mildly. "I—er—I answered the telephone by mistake a moment ago, Angela. It was the nurse at the Infirmary. She is calling up every known cardiac case in the Neighborhood for some digitalis until the doctor can get here."

"Bah!" Jones's snort eclipsed Angela's murmur of compassion. "He will be all right before the doctor arrives. I know. I just came from there. Personally, I think he was drunk."

"Why, John! How scandalous of you," Angela exclaimed. "Mr. Grimper has never touched liquor in his life. He is the most ardent dry I know."

"One doesn't only get drunk on liquor, Angela."

Alfred stared at Jones from across the table, his eyes wide, his head thrust forward, his palms flat on the cloth. And as Angela carried out the plates, he whispered hoarsely: "John, did you have anything to do with this?"

Jones leaned back in his chair and smiled. "Well, it is possible I contributed to his shock. You see, I resigned from the faculty."

His announcement was punctuated by a crash. Angela stood in the kitchen doorway, a shattered dish at her feet and applesauce splattered over her skirt and the floor.

"John, you didn't! You didn't resign!"

"Oh, yes, I did."

"Why did you do such a thing? Why? Why?"

"Because it was the thing to do," John replied, kneeling at her feet to pick up the gummy shards. "Alfred, get a newspaper and a knife to scrape up this stuff."

Vacant-eyed, Angela sat down and dabbed at her skirt. "Oh, you must reconsider," she moaned. "It is all this silly idea of yours about getting into the war."

"It is not a silly idea," John said sharply.

237

"Well, has the Army taken you, or the Navy?" quavered Angela. "Is that why you said you were out sailing with the —with the Pup-pres—"

Now she was interrupted by a shrill, tinny voice plated with good cheer that cried from the front screen door: "Any body home? Yoo-hoo! Are you still eating?"

Instantly Angela composed herself, gave her skirt a final scrubbing with her napkin. Alfred resumed his habitual look of benevolence and amiability, and bustled to the door crying: "Come in! We're just finished. Why, it is Mrs. Jay!"

The librarian strode angularly into the dining room:

"Angela, my dear! Have you heard? Oh, Dr. Jones! Good evening." Her voice went flat and then rose again. "I'll just have a cup of coffee with you, Angela, and then I'll help you do the dishes. You men are excused. Angela and I want to gossip."

Angela looked as if she preferred bleeding to gossiping, but John lost no time in quitting the room with the news-paperful of wrecked dessert. Alfred lingered to ask if Mrs. Jay had heard anything about Mr. Grimper's condition.

"The poor dear man," the librarian shrilled. "I just came from there. He is perfectly all right, you will be happy to hear. The doctor said it wasn't a heart attack or a stroke or anything like that. He said it was probably indigestion or maybe gall stones."

Alfred went thoughtfully into the parlor, where Jones had already taken roundabout refuge; he put on his glasses and picked up a book, but sat regarding John over them both. John affected a tremendous concentration on his lately neglected notebooks. Neither one could insulate ears or mind against the penetrating voice from the dining room.

"—I know Negras. They will listen at keyholes. Well, why should that black wench know more about our business than we do ourselves? I ask you! So I just went to her. 'Genesis,' I said, 'Genesis! You know right well you're going to have that black ear of yours against the door.' She just grinned and scraped her foot, the way darkies do, so I told her there would be a dollar in it for her if she (Well, yes, just half a cup, Angela) told me what happened when they called that woman before the committee. And do you know what? Do you know what! She was never called in. Mr. Grimper was all for firing her. But the Dean pleaded for her. Actually pleaded for her. And that Colonel person, he did, too. Well, not pleaded. He argued. And when it came to the vote, that little feist Doolittle who drinks like a fish, everybody knows, and ogles women out of his drugstore window, he voted to give her a new contract. Well, Mr. Grimper nearly exploded. I wish they would have consulted me! I could have put a flea in their ear, those two. I tell you, when men get to a certain age! Well, I don't have to stand for it. I reckon I should have some say-so as to who my assistant—"

Jones smiled, despite himself. Well, so Virginia was safe for another year, anyhow. She could publish her book, and if it were a success she would probably resign her job anyhow.

His musing and the nasal monologue in the next room were both brought to a halt by a clatter of feet on the porch steps, and a formidable pounding on the doorframe. With a twitter of surprise Alfred put his glasses between the pages of his book, and scurried to answer the summons. The three heard Alfred's surprised: "Why, good evening—" and its harshly interruptive response: "Is Jones huck? I want to see him."

Fury surged through Jones as he recognized the voice, and he leaped to the encounter. The two women, Jay to the fore, came into the hallway, too, to share with Jones the sight of Grimper looming dourly on the doorstep, and Alfred, holding the door, wide, as flat against the wall as his cylindrical shape could be pressed.

"Argh! I just came by to tell you," Grimper snarled, his dentures gleaming from the darkness. "Jones, you are fired! Your resignation was voted down two to one, as soon as I recovered. And you stand huck suspended, sir, till your contract geek expires, do you urgle understand? Don't interrupt me! Suspended for drinking and common brawling gargh huck. I won't be interrupted. There is nothing you can say

239

that interests me. You admitted that you had been drinking. Even Gaylord admits you admitted it. You're through. You are fired."

Still bellowing to circumvent any audible retort, Grimper stamped down off the porch and along the path to where his glistening 1932 Ford stood parked. Jones watched him go, his fists clenched, striving against a torturing urge to raise his hand against the departing back and to blast his enemy into eternity.

White-faced and shaken from the struggle against himself, he turned back into the hall. Alfred rolled bloodshot eyes at him from a face gray and flaccid. Angela clung to the dining-room door, mouth open, eyes a-stare, one hand clenched at her throat. Mrs. Jay, although pale, showed the only animation.

"Well, I must run along," she cheeped. "You folks have private matters to discuss."

She jerked through the door.

"John," Angela moaned through stiff lips, "how could you?"

"How could I what? I couldn't say a word or do a thing to choke off that madman."

"Oh, oh, oh, and in front of that woman, too," Angela sobbed, cheeks and chins quivering. She dabbed at her eyes with the napkin she had carried from the table. "Oh, what did you do, what did you do?"

"Damn it, I did *not* do anything," Jones shouted. "Excuse me! I am sorry," he continued, lowering his voice with an effort that hurt his still aching throat. "Here is the whole story. I happened to come home on the bus the other day with Miss Finster . . ."

"Oh, I knew that harpy was mixed up in this somewhere!" Anger dried Angela's tears.

"Don't talk nonsense," John rudely told her. "As I got off the bus I was telling her some anecdote or another. We had been swapping stories. ("I can imagine what kind of stories!" Angela murmured.) We were laughing. And there, all of a sudden, is this toad Grimper. The carrion crow! I tried to be pleasant to him. I told him something ludicrous I

240

had heard. I even asked his advice. I tried to flatter the old vulture. And he maliciously distorted the whole affair."

"I'll never be able to hold up my head in the Neighborhood again," Angela moaned. "He said you admitted having been drinking."

"God's teeth! Do you want to hear me out or not? This afternoon I came home early from Washington. Everything had gone well. I had to straighten some things out in my mind, in anticipation of—well, what is going to happen. Then I was recognized by a rogue I don't remember ever seeing before. He tried to interest me into becoming party to a gigantic swindle. I denounced him. Somehow I fell or was pushed into the river. I nearly died. When I revived, hours later, there I was on the President's yacht which had rescued me and returned me to Washington. I had been given medical care, my clothes had been dried and ironed. I came here directly by taxicab to meet the committee. Grimper was insolent and dictatorial. He demanded an explanation of my tardiness as if I were a schoolboy. Nevertheless, I told him the story, politely and truthfully. He called me a liar. He thrust his foul beak into my face and said he smelled liquor. I did not admit drinking, as he calls it. I explained that I had been given a stimulant. So he proposed that I be suspended and discharged. The Colonel took my side. The other man, that cud-chewing little cockroach, voted against me under an open threat from Grimper, but before he could vote himself, he fell over in a fit. And that's the whole story."

"John," Alfred asked huskily. "Did you—did you—you know?"

Jones looked at him from under arched brows.

"I only shook my finger at him," he said. And then he winked.

Alfred made a sound like a pinpricked toy balloon and sat down heavily on the nearest chair.

"It is all a dreadful misunderstanding," Angela gulped, wiping away an oozing teardrop. "I am sure if you will apologize to Mr. Grimper—"

"What in the name of Midas's marbles have I got to

apologize for?" John choked. "What should I say? That I regret I didn't drown in the river?"

"Don't be sarcastic, John," Angela sighed. "I am sure Mr. Grimper would have been more reasonable if only you had been rescued by somebody else than the President. Mr. Grimper hates him worse than he does liquor."

"I had no choice in the matter," Jones said. "And I don't think I would have exercised it if I had had the chance."

"I asked you not to be sarcastic," Angela said, her self-composure regained. "We have to be practical and realistic."

" 'We' have to? No, this is something between my conscience and me."

"Don't behave like a stubborn little boy," Angela said firmly. "Don't you see that it's an issue that involves not only you and Mr. Grimper, but Alfred and me and the Seminary as a whole? Phoebe Jay is already involved. So is that other woman. I declare! Every single bit of our troubles dates from her."

That was palpably true, John thought, biding his silence.

"You must realize this, John," Angela said earnestly. "Mr. Grimper has the upper hand. He is in authority. You must make the first move, for the sake of us all. You must go to him and apologize, or we will never get the septic tank mended. He will be generous, and, no doubt, renew your contract."

"But I don't want my contract renewed," John protested.

"If you are dead set on this harebrained scheme of going to war, having a new contract with the Seminary won't stop you," Angela argued. "You can always resign or ask for leave of absence. But as matters now stand, you are in disgrace. What will people say?"

"I don't care what people say," John retorted. "Anyhow, it is up to Grimper to apologize, not me. He has something to apologize for. I have not. Apologize? I'll punch his nose, that's what."

" 'Resist not evil,' " Alfred murmured. " 'Pray for them which despitefully use you and persecute you.' "

242

"Tell that to Nimitz or Eisenhower," John snapped. "Tell it to the Marines!"

"Oh, you do behave just like a stubborn little boy," Angela said, sharp impatience in her voice. "Well, we won't get anywhere arguing in your present mood. I suggest we go to bed and sleep on it. You will see the situation clearly when you are calm and can think sanely."

"Who isn't calm?" Jones felt his face grow hotter, and hoarseness grip his aching throat. "Pluto's pants! If I hadn't been calm, that marplot would not have left here alive. See the situation sanely? Am I crazy because I won't apologize to that limgam of Lucifer for objecting to slander? Oh, well, as you say, there's no point in arguing. Let's call it a night!"

"There," said Angela with a smile's ghost on her lips. "I knew you would come around to my way of thinking. Let's sleep on it, and tomorrow when your pride has healed a little, and we are all calm and rested, we can talk it over together quietly. But something has to be done to stop the gossip before the Store opens."

"Good night!" Jones made the words more an exclamation than a valediction. "I'm going to sit outside awhile and cool off."

"It is pretty chilly," Angela observed. "Put a coat over your knees."

Alfred thoughtfully went about his locking-up duties as Jones betook himself to the porch. His throat ached, and his head throbbed; his hands felt hot and dry in his pockets. He rose abruptly and strode off, head bowed, hands clasped behind him. He could not marshal his thoughts. He tramped blindly, shifting back to gravel whenever he felt turf beneath his feet, but otherwise caring not what path he followed.

He would be damned if he apologized to Grimper. To hell with Grimper! To hell with the whole ridiculous controversy. It was a sour anticlimax to the bitter and ironic farce that the day's puppet play had enacted. He had achieved his meeting with the President and had babbled in delirium when, in as many syllables, he could have unfolded his great plan to bring eternal peace to the world. Maybe the world was not worth it. A world in which Grimpers triumphed and grafters schemed to convert good-willed men to dishonest profit. Let Zotz triumph! Humanity deserved—nay, humanity craved—no better fate than to be in bondage to the lord of selfishness who was served in cruelty and honored with dishonor. He might as well abase himself to the Grimpers, bow to the bureaucrats, truckle to the Bullblanks who saw in the world only the passive target for their bombs, and bide his time to use the Word and the Gesture to gather for himself all the power and the wealth and the glory. They would serve him gladly, admiringly, these little people; they would fawn upon him, worship him, strive for his favor by betraying the charitable and denouncing the benevolent.

He was dimly aware of footsteps that echoed his own, and he quickened his pace, for he was done with human companionship and his head hurt abominably. But hands reached out and plucked at him, and a voice spoke his name: "John Jones, John Jones, John Jones."

He wasn't John Jones. He was Zotz. He stopped and whirled in a half-turn, right hand upraised, finger rigidly poised.

"John! I heard what they did. I'm sorry, so sorry. But don't let him get you down. Oh, my dear!"

A hand was on his raised arm, another rested on his opposite shoulder. He blinked aching lids to dispel the burning sparks that whirled before his eyes and darted at them like Lilliputian arrows.

"John, it's me, Virginia."

He dropped his arm, and it embraced her. His head fell on the fragrant cushion of her hair.

"I heard. And I couldn't sleep, I couldn't rest. Oh, John!"

His heart should have been racing, but instead it sang in his bosom a song of sweet repose.

32

JOHN FELT Virginia's hands clasp behind his back, and within that girdle of living compassion he suddenly felt secure and disburdened.

"You are shaking! You must have caught a chill."

But Jones shook his head and clasped her closer to silence her, so she had to brace herself against the weight of him trembling on her bosom; and he, drooping against the resilient cushion, seemed to feel strength surge into him, an osmosis of solace and confidence and composure.

All at once he dropped his arms and stepped back from the embrace she as instantly loosened.

"You found me," he whispered. "And you have brought me back. How did you know? How did you know, Virginia?"

She looked up at him, her eyes lustrous in the starlight.

"I don't know," she said. "I listened on the telephone. I do it lots. And I heard all about the excitement, and then a little while ago Mrs. Jay got on the line telling her cronies about old Grimper coming to the house and, oh, horrid things. I just had to get out. Golly, I was mad! And there you were."

"If you had appeared just as I was about to fall into a volcano you would not have come in better time." There was awe in Jones's voice. "And to think that once I suspected you, and feared you, and thought you had been sent to destroy me."

"But, John, where did you get such crazy ideas?" cried

Virginia. She put her hands to his face, and he did not flinch. "Golly, but you're feverish. I'm sure you caught a chill. Come into my house, and let me give you something to drink."

"Your house? But where do you live?"

"Right here, in this funny little place. It used to be the porter's lodge to the Macandle estate."

John looked, only now realizing where his unseeing flight had carried him. He stood opposite the one wonderful example of the architectural onanism of the eighties the Neighborhood possessed, the turreted brick-and-bluestone mansarded Macandle mansion; night gave it a certain brooding Gothic dignity, as he saw it framed in the arch that spanned the entrance to the box-bordered driveway. One pillar of the arch was thickened into a sort of magnificent sentry box, or, to be more accurately descriptive, a miniature silo, all overgrown with ivy. Virginia led him to a narrow door in that squatty tower.

"I don't think I had better go in," Jones demurred, halfheartedly. "It will only cause worse scandal."

"Oh, piffle," Virginia laughed, drawing him after her by the hand. "There's nobody to see, and what do I care, anyhow! This is the night to defy the smug and it would be silly for you to postpone it for lack of a chaperon."

She pushed him ahead of her into a cave-cool circular room of twelve-foot diameter. Against the opposite wall a narrow flight of stone steps curved upward; on the red-tile floor was a single large, threadbare but lustrous, Muskhabad rug. The only furnishings were a sofa in the Duncan Phyfe tradition, behind which a reading lamp's parchment shade glowed upon the candy-striped upholstery, and a leather armchair of scurfy brown upon which a fat black cat was curled, unless one counted as furniture a bookcase improvised from two orange crates painted black. There was a tiny fireplace, containing a potted fern now, and the sole garniture on the walls was the big square of crudely woven cotton whose border in barbaric green and yellow proved on second look to be a highly conventionalized serpent.

"A Zulu medicine man's cloak," Virginia explained. "If

you remember my manuscript, the Zulus believe that snakes are descended from people, while most all other religions have it the other way around. Zulus think bad men are reincarnated as poisonous snakes, good men as harmless snakes, and women as lizards."

"A tenable belief," Jones replied. "But some people acquire the character long before the form."

"Well, now, sit down, sit down," Virginia urged. "The couch is more comfortable, even if Diana would be polite enough to get off the chair. All I have is some sherry. I'll go upstairs and get it."

"No, don't go yet, Virginia. I'm still too close to the precipice to be left alone."

She looked down upon him as he leaned back on the sofa, and then seated herself on the edge.

"Phooey," she said. "You're all right! Don't let them get you down. What do you mean, precipice!"

"I had just about made up my mind to make my salaam to Grimper, biding my time until I could revenge myself adequately. And it would not have been long. A most subtle revenge it would have been, but an evil triumph, and a triumph for evil."

"Oh, nuts to old Grimper," Virginia scoffed. "You are ten times the man he is. He's just jealous of you, that's what."

"Thank you!" Jones smiled and patted her shoulder. "Child, you give an old man new courage to forge his own destiny."

"Old man indeed! How you do talk! Why, half the student body would give anything to be as straight and lean and sharp-eyed as you are. Or maybe they wouldn't, because they'd be in the Army."

"I'm over fifty," Jones said. "There is not too much time left for me to do what I must do."

"I'll bet there's another fifty years!" cried Virginia. "Anyhow, whatever it is you think you've got to do, go ahead and do it! That's been my motto."

"I wish you would tell me about yourself sometime," Jones said, letting his hand fall, palm upward, between them on the couch. "Then, later on, perhaps, I will tell you the weird biography I invented for you."

Virginia drew his hand into her lap, pulling her skirt down over round knees as she did so.

"Look at the messy old skirt I grabbed up in the dark," she said. "I really ought to go up and put on something more suitable."

"Oh, clothes," John said impatiently. "What difference do they make?" And as he saw her color deepen in recollection of their first meeting he made awkward effort to repair his blunder, feeling his own cheeks burn as he cried: "To me you will always be clad in the robes of a rescuing angel."

And that, too, was a rococo bit of rhetoric, he thought in silent self-reproof. But the gaucheries were best left unrepaired. He wanted to tell Virginia that she would appear charming to him if she wore Jeanne d'Arc's armor or Quaker habit, and thus conscious for the first time what her attire was, felt half his fifty years fall away. For she was barelegged; between her feet, thrust into scuffed moccasinlike slippers, and her knees, where the hem of a tight and threadbare, paint-spotted tweed skirt made scant covering, was twin expanse of smooth, tawny, sculptured flesh. There was no other word for it. They were functional legs, slender and lithe but muscled. Above the close-clinging rust-colored skirt there was a slender revelation of identical golden hue, where her tan sweater had wrinkled upward; but that telltale was unnecessary to demonstrate that Virginia wore no other garments. The thin wool, only a shade or two darker than the body whose contours it covered without concealment, appeared to John's feverish eyes to be like a natural pelage, now that he scrutinized her. And he thought it was a wonderful and a beautiful and an exciting thing to possess a woman delicately furred, like a mouse.

He freed his hand from hers and raised it to one fictile breast. Virginia inhaled sharply, but remained motionless as painted marble except for the parting of her lips.

"Truly you have restored to me a youth I never had," Jones said gently. "Although I fought against myself by

248

THE BEAST ADVANCED A NOISELESS STEP
AND HISSED

means both cruel and foul, I know now that I have long loved you, Virginia. Do you still say I am not old? Can you love me?"

"Bu-but—but Angela," stammered the dark woman, and as John's hand fell inertly from her bosom and the ardor in his eyes became glazed with doubt and hurt, she suddenly threw herself forward across his thighs and reached up to draw his face down to hers. Her lips were cool and moist against his hot trembling mouth. Under his gentle hands her skin grew taut as she yearned toward him with all her body, and then, quickly as a trout, she was out of his grasp. A pace distant, she stood facing him.

Her hair was a thundercloud, electrically vibrant, from which her face, half veiled, looked down upon him with the bewilderment of an Astarte taken captive by a mortal. Mechanically she smoothed her skirt, pulled down her sweater, and groped with one foot for the fallen slipper that had bared it.

"I must—I've got to—I—I—" she gasped. "I'll be back!"

Clutching sweater and skirt together at her hips, Virginia ran up the curving stone steps. Jones leaned back on the sofa, arms limp by his side, his mouth and palms burning in memory of contact but his ribs like separate knives to the effort of his breathing. Under his lids his eyes smarted from fiery pinwheels but when he raised them the circular room seemed to spin like a juggler's platter.

Something in the room gave a heavy thump, and the sound was followed by another; a sharp and sinister and an inquisitive cry, thin but demanding. Jones lifted burning lids to look into two greenly gleaming eyes that glowed from the depths of an amorphous blackness in the deep shadows. A triangle of scarlet appeared below the green disks, and the cry was repeated.

Jones stared, blinked, and remembered.

"The cat," he said aloud. "Pussy! Nice pussy!"

The beast advanced a noiseless step into the perimeter of lamplight, and hissed. It took another step, and a third; stood there, one black paw lifted, its mouth like a blood clot, staring unwinkingly at the intruder. The brushy tail twitched as the creature flattened its haunches.

"Why, the cursed thing is going to attack me," Jones told himself. He thrust out a foot as far as he could stretch his leg, offering it in caress or rebuff as the animal preferred to take it.

With a strangled yowl the cat flattened to the floor, claws digging into the carpet. It writhed for a moment, and then lay inert, but with its glaucous eyes still rigidly gleaming hate.

My God, it's having a fit, Jones thought, sitting up to focus his hearing on any sounds of Virginia's return. All was quiet in the little tower.

Suddenly the cat twitched, and then abruptly stood up, back arched, tail swollen and upstanding. It emitted a throaty yowl which merged into a menacing sizzle of pain-goaded hatred, and this time Jones again thrust forth a toe-pointed foot wholly in gesture of self-defense.

And again the cat jerked and fell as if electrocuted. Jones's chin dropped to his breast, and cold sweat stung his eyes while nausea crawled in his belly and clamored in his throat.

"The gesture of Zotz!"

Horror plucked at his heart strings with bony fingers.

No matter with what member of his body he pointed, paralysis and death would flow from it! No matter with what intent; with no intent at all: whatever he reached for, whatever he reached with, though he groped in the dark for love, the lethal thrust of Zotz was sped forth like an invisible electric bolt.

Then the sickening realization of all the implications in that discovery shook Jones like a man on the gibbet.

For him there could be no love. In the very gesture of the consummating embrace he would pour forth anguish upon his beloved, converting the sweet tremor of ardent expectation to a spasm of paralyzing pain.

The cat clawed at the carpet, sobbing and cursing.

With a groan that wrenched him so that his gullet was salty with the taste of blood, John Jones leaped from the sofa and ran stumblingly to the door. At the head of the curved stone stairs, Virginia stood staring in fear and wonder. Her hair hung down in a soft midnight cloud over a long silken robe of ivy green, beneath which her toes tensed to preserve her balance against the shock of the vision below. The tall glasses on the copper tray she held clattered to her trembling, spilling the pungent brown wine.

"John!"

He did not turn, but wrenched open the door and raced down the graveled drive to the reaching shadows of the Grove.

33

THE NEXT MORNING the first person to report to the Office of Information found Jones waiting at the door. He was hatless and unkempt, his eyes red-rimmed, and a faint stubble like a mold on cheeks and chin.

He accepted the invitation to enter without word of assent or thanks, and sat mutely in the chair nearest the door of the inner office as the room gradually filled with those who worked there. They stared curiously at his uncharacteristic untidiness.

When he was offered coffee, Jones started up from reverie and then dumbly accepted the cup, which cooled untasted in his hand. And when, tardiest of all, the Commander announced his arrival by the slam of his corridor door, Jones put the cup on the chair beside him and entered that room unbidden.

"Why, hello, Dr. Jones," the Commander hailed him cheerfully. "Up with the lark, what? You look a bit on the seedy side, though."

Jones swallowed. "Listen," he said in a hoarse whisper, his hands deep in his pocket. "Something is about to happen. I came here to tell you—excuse me, but do you mind if I stand with my back to the window?"

"Hell, no! But sit down, instead. Does the light bother your eyes?"

"No, it isn't that. It's just that accursed big obelisk. I can't stand the sight of it sticking up there."

The officer looked wonderingly over his shoulder at the Washington Monument looming over the opposite roof-tops.

"Look here, Dr. Jones," he said anxiously, "you aren't well. Why don't you let me get you an aspirin or an APC tablet."

Jones jerked his head in impatient refusal.

"What was it I wanted to tell you? Oh, yes! My apprecia-tion. You have been very considerate and courteous, and you have tried to be helpful."

He looked blankly at the floor while the Commander made cheerful protest that he hadn't done anything at all, and anyhow, that's what the Navy paid him an exorbitant salary for doing. Wait a minute, he didn't mean that, exactly. He had just done what his job called for and—

"No, don't say that," Jones muttered. "Look, I want you to do one thing more. Someday when—when things are ac-complished, or finished anyhow, I would like you to put it all down. In a book."

"Well, I'd be awfully happy to try," the Commander said, "and I am deeply honored, sir, but how—I mean, just what—?"

"Thank you," Jones said gravely. "I'll be back at the proper time. I went to the Congressman, as you advised. He called the White House. They said they had an important commission for me. Said the President wants to see me."

He threw back his head in a short, explosive laugh that ended in a strangling cough. "And I did see the President, but he didn't know it and I didn't know it. I—oh, well, that can wait, too."

He turned and walked to the corridor door.

"Doctor," the Commander said, following him, "how about a cup of coffee? I'm sure you're coming down with some-thing."

"Oh, yes!" Jones stood with his hand on the knob. "There is another thing. If I don't come back—there is always that chance, you know—there is the manuscript of my book on the Semantics of Dionysius of Halicarnassensis. If you will try to get it published."

He jerked open the door and left.

The Commander went into the adjoining office.

"Hey," he said, "that old geezer was sick. How long was he here?"

"*He* was sick? He gave *me* the willies! Coffee, sir?"

It was an hour later that the Commander received, in the batch of interoffice memoranda, the carbon copy of a letter to which was attached a note from Captain Pelznickel: "Karig —Hope this takes care of your friend."

The letter was addressed to Dr. Jones at St. Jude's. It offered him a commission as a lieutenant in the chaplains' corps of the Naval Reserve, depending upon certain requirements first to be met.

"God—how does he say that again?—God bite me?" the Commander murmured. "I hope he doesn't come back *here*."

Nor did he. For a long, long time.

First there was difficulty in identifying the unkempt, unshaved middle-aged man who tried mutely and stubbornly to push his way past the guard at the White House. He was obviously drunk, because he fell flat on his face from no more than just a little push the policeman gave him. When he did not get off his pallet in the precinct cell for his supper that night, the sergeant called a doctor to pump him out. It looked to him like a wood-alcohol coma, no matter what the two other lushes in the cell said.

But the police surgeon, after a whistle-punctuated check of the man's temperature, diagnosed pneumonia and a plenty bad case.

On the morning of the second day after Jones's departure from the Navy Building, the Commander received a telephone call from the District Hospital. There was a patient there; not expected to live. No laundry marks, no identification except some indecipherable cards in a wallet that had evidently been water-soaked, and a notebook in which the only readable notation was, they were sure, the Commander's name and room number. Would the Commander mind dropping in?

"My grief, it's Jones," was the officer's identification of the emaciated figure noisily fighting for breath behind the curtained ward bed. "Look, Nurse: This is an important person, a very famous man. Can't you move him out of here into a private room?"

"Even if we had one," the nurse said, shaking her capped gray head, "he's too sick to move. I'd say if he's moved at all it will be to the icebox downstairs. Who is he, now?"

Jones did not know that the Dean came and knelt on that spotless, carbolic-scented floor day after day to wrestle with the Lord for the preservation of that fading life.

"If he has a lucid moment," the care-lined clergyman told the nurse, "please tell him right away that the Board voted unanimously to give him a new contract. Be sure to say unanimously. If you can remember it, tell him that even Grimper—gee-are-eye-em-pee-ee-are—voted, after the Colonel got proof from the Navy that he had really been rescued by the President's yacht. Can you remember all that?"

"Sure," said the nurse. "But I doubt if he'll ever learn it this side of Paradise."

Jones did not know, either, that Angela and Alfred, too, came to add their petitions to Heaven from the bedside, and that Angela begged to be allowed to labor in more material fashion for the stricken man. They told her she could come in as a nurses' aide if she wanted to, but when they discovered she could not rise from the floor after an hour with the scrub-brush because of her sciatica, the matron appreciatively but firmly told her that the best contribution she could expect to make was to continue praying.

"And it's about the only thing that will save him," she said. "He has every complication in the book, and a few others besides."

There was a younger woman who came frequently, too— an Amazon of a wench, one of the interns described her. "Except," he said, "she has both of them, and plenty. I understand the Amazons cut one off." But the black-haired one didn't pray. She cried a little, though. Two or three times she came while Angela was there, and the two women held hands as they looked around the corner of the screen at the remnant of John Jones, AB., MA., Ph.D.

But there came a day when Angela saw John's eyes focus on the unused call bell that dangled above his head, and she ran sobbing to call the nurse to come and see if he were conscious.

The nurse came briskly, but exuding doubt with every creak of her starched uniform.

"Where am I?" Jones whispered.

"John!"

"Why, it's Angela. Have I been here long?"

"Oh, yes. A long, long time."

"How are my mice?"

He didn't hear the sob-broken reply. Jones slept.

They got him into a private room sometime after that. He objected, saying he could not afford it and would certainly not permit anybody to subsidize him in luxury. But when he was told that the advance royalties from his book [1] more than covered the expense, and that the privacy and extra care would speed his recovery, Jones gave his consent rather eagerly, celebrating the move with a Christmas dinner of jellied chicken broth, minced turkey, a mashed potato and ice cream.

It was some time later that Jones gave the physicians their first suspicion that all was not well with their patient.

"Of course a continuous fever of a hundred five might have—but, no, it's not in the book. A concurrent encephalitis, perhaps, that wasn't diagnosed because—well, humor him. It may be a psychic trauma that will pass . . ."

For Jones had demanded a live fly in a bottle.

"Or a wasp will do. Even a spider," he told the nurse.

"But why?"

"Never mind why. If it costs extra I'll pay for it."

"But there are no flies in this hospital. Not ever. And certainly not in the winter."

"God's teeth! Go out and hire somebody to catch one."

So they decided to humor him. The Dean prayed again, outside the door, and Angela's eyes were often red, which Jones told her came from reading to him too much. But she

[1] *The Semantics of Dionysius of Halicarnassensis* (2 vol. 8mo.). Murray Hill Press, N. Y. ($50).

knew better, of course, and so he patiently continued to bear the boredom of her monotonous recitals from the *Saturday Evening Post* and other journals of equally baffling content to him.

He would eye his captive fly, as it buzzed about in its crystal cage or twiddled its paws over the feast of sugar and crumbs spread for it.

Every once in so often Angela would look up to see Jones pointing a clawlike and trembling finger at the insect.

"What is it, John? What is your pet doing?"

"Not a goddam thing," he would sigh, and Angela would blow her nose.

So it was suggested that John should go to a sanatorium in Arizona for a leisurely convalescence. It surprised everybody with what alacrity he accepted the idea. He wanted to see desert again.

Under the Phoenix sun, which he soaked up greedily under the watchful eye of a muscular young man in white (he had a glass eye, which he took out when he left the sanatorium in silent explanation of his civilian status), John slowly gained in body. But his apathy worried the medical director.

"All he does, Doc," the cyclopian nurse would say, "is sit there looking at his damn fly in the bottle. First thing he asks me every morning is how is the war coming, and the better the news the glummer he gets. Do you reckon he's a Nazi-lover?"

"It's a strange case," the doctor said. "I'll give him the Rohrschach test tomorrow."

The doctor emerged from that attempt, white and shaken, with Jones's shrill denunciation pursuing him down the corridor.

"And stay out of here with your damn kindergarten ink blots! You can take your asterisk fortunetelling cards and you know what. With a hot poker, too!"

Then came the day when Jones could walk around the courtyard with a cane, the orderly close behind him—in case he should fall, it was explained.

"You know the way he's gloomy when the war news is good?" the attendant reported. "Well, I thought when I'd tell him the President passed away, I sort of expected he'd be happy as a bedbug. But do you know, he almost fainted! You should of been here, Doc. I was scared as all hell."

Presently Jones was walking without a cane.

"Doc, he is getting along swell in every way but—" The orderly twirled a forefinger at his forehead. "This morning he lets out a yell. He's laughing, and waving his arms with his fists all balled up. And do you know why? *His goddam fly is dead!*"

"As soon as I can discharge him in good conscience, he is going out of here so fast they'll think it's a dust storm up in Flagstaff."

"Yeah, but that ain't all, Doc. He asks me to get him another fly! And he sits there grinning at it, with his fingers twitching."

"Maybe—hm! I'd want a consultation on it, before I tried it. Shock treatment. Insulin. I'll write to his people."

Jones's improvement accelerated. He ordered books. He ordered technical magazines. He ordered more flies, as many as three or four a day. It was astounding how the insects perished. The orderly could put a fat, saucy bluebottle in the jar and no sooner was his back turned, the creature was dead on its back. And Jones, mind you, clear across the room all the time!

Then Germany surrendered, and Hitler's charred corpse was dug out of the ruins.

"I tell you, Doc, the guy almost had a stroke. He sits there saying: 'All in vain, all in vain.' I think you ought to tell the FBI about him, and no kidding. He's a bastard Heinie-lover."

"That's none of our business. We'll have him out of here in two weeks. I'm notifying his people today."

"That ain't all, either. He doesn't want flies any more. He wants lizards. They don't die so quick, that's one thing. But they sure get unhealthy fast."

One day in early August the door of Commander Karig's office crashed open just as he was in the middle of dictating a letter advising a Chicago importer of Christmas-tree lights that the war with Japan would probably last two years more.

The officer rose slowly from his chair, unbelief in his eyes, which are 8/20.

"It isn't Dr. Jones, is it?" he addressed the sinewy, suntanned figure that advanced briskly toward him.

"Jones indeed," chuckled the visitor.

"Last time I saw you, I wouldn't have given a one-yen occupation note for your chances," the Commander cried, groping for Jones's hand. "Come and sit down and tell me all about yourself."

"That can wait," Jones said. "I am coming right back to where I started. How long is this war with Japan going to last?"

"I don't know. My instructions are to tell clients it is bound to last a long time yet. That's top government policy, not just Navy. It's to keep up the bond sales and industrial production, naturally."

"Well, what do you think?"

"I have nothing to base any thoughts on, except from what I read and from having been in Japan once. I think they'll fight to the last man. I think the Battle for Germany was a strawberry festival compared with what the Japs will put up. Look at the Kamikazes."

"All right, then," said Jones. "Now I want to see the Secretary."

"Hm-m-m, well, if you will tell me——" the officer began, and then he laughed ruefully. "Look here, I thought you had everything fixed with the White House away back last fall."

"There has been a change," Jones reminded him. "So, I must see the Secretary. I insist upon it."

"Damn it, Doctor, I tell you——"

Jones reached across to the desk and picked the departmental telephone directory from its hook. He riffled the pages, found what he was after.

"All right," he said, with an inverted smile. "I'll just have to use another channel, that's all."

"I'm sorry as hell, Doctor, but you know how the saying goes. 'If you know a better 'ole, go to it.' "

"I shall take that advice from you, too," Jones said. "It should bring up your average. By the way, my warmest thanks for your help in getting my book on Dionysius published. It saved my life."

"I didn't do much," the Commander said. "Mrs. McJavert did the real job." But Jones was already through the door.

"If he can find a straighter channel than this dead-end corkscrew," the Commander muttered to Chief Sudol, "then I'll make captain, because it will prove anything can happen."

"I bet it will, too," the Wave said. "Well, do you want to go on with this letter?"

Jones passed out of sight and mind of the Office of Information, muttering a number to himself. He climbed a stair, and scanned the ground-glass paneled doors in a corridor the duplicate, even to the aroma of coffee, of the one below.

"Excuse me, sir."

Jones looked up to see a Marine barring his way. On the youth's shoulder was the blue, starred patch of service in Guadalcanal.

"Can I help you?"

"Oh, no," Jones said. "I know where I am going, thank you."

"I'm sorry, sir, but unless you have an escort—"

"Just let me pass, please."

"I'm very sorry, sir, but you can't—"

The Marine clutched his stomach and sat abruptly on the floor, his side-arm clattering on the cement. Jones stepped over his legs, took a few paces and turned sharply right. He opened a door and found himself flanked by two desks, from behind each of which another Marine rose smartly.

"How do you do, sir? Can I help you?"

"I would like to see the Secretary at once."

"Have you an appointment?"

Jones gestured, turned on his heel and repeated the stab of his finger at the second guard. Both men, eyes glassily bulging, sank out of sight behind their desks. Jones walked briskly into the room, surveyed an array of doors, and made his decision. He opened the one that looked most formidable.

It admitted him to a large room, dim in the filtered light from heavily shrouded windows. At a desk that would have made a handsome coffin for a mastodon sat an aggressive-looking man holding an earphone to his head. He shot a surprised look at Jones from beneath a deep-seated frown.

Jones nodded and smiled.

The man's cheeks twitched, and Jones thought a sudden pallor bleached the tan of his face. Slowly the earphone was laid down.

"We have just dropped an atomic bomb on Japan," the man behind the desk said slowly, looking over Jones's head. "The war is—over. But God knows what we have loosed on the world."

"At-om-ic *bomb*!" Jones had difficulty pronouncing the words.

"Yes. Who—what—who are you? How did you get in here?"

"I just opened the door," Jones said. "There are some soldiers outside who seem to be in distress."

Through the door, as in confirmation of this statement, filtered a muted hullabaloo of voices and of furniture being violently moved. Jones walked briskly across the room to a farther door, and let himself out. There seemed to be a considerable crowd of agitated persons in the corridor. It may have been Doris Fleeson's syndicated column a few days afterward that revealed a survey of the Navy cafeteria to determine the source of the sudden epidemic of acute indigestion which had filled the Department's corridors with writhing victims.

EPILOGUE

IT WAS NEARLY a year later that I met John Jones by appointment.

The rendezvous was on a Sunday night in the kitchen of the Cordon Bleu Tea Shoppe in Upper Massachusetts Avenue: "Come in the back door. The place will be closed."

I went wonderingly. Running a restaurant seemed to be the last vocation Jones would undertake. Calling it by so outrageous a name was of remoter probability.

"Have a seat, Commander," Jones said over his shoulder, indicating a chopping block of scrubbed whiteness. He was seated, himself, on a tall chromium stool in front of a shelf-like counter that ran the length of the kitchen.

"Captain now, sir," I said proudly.

"Hmpf! Is that better?"

"Yes, sir."

"Well, congratulations, if they are indicated. I'm nearly through for the night. Then we'll have a snack that I asked to be left in the icebox. There's cold beer, too."

"It sounds good."

I wondered why he had sent for me. It certainly wasn't for entertainment.

Jones kept sitting there, facing the counter. It was absolutely bare, except for what appeared to be a sifting of sawdust in a narrow band down its whole length. On the floor, at his feet, was an opened newspaper on which lay a heap of

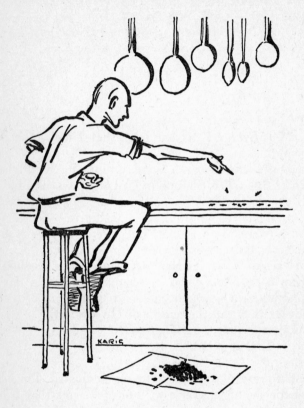

"ZOTZ," HE SAID. "ZOTZ, ZOTZ, ZOTZ, AND ZOTZ."

shiny brown things, something like watermelon seeds, that glistened in the dim light from a distant forty-watt bulb that gave all the illumination there was.

"I mentioned to you," Jones said at last, "and that many months ago, that I hoped you would be willing to write my story as a historical document. How do you feel about it?"

"As I said then," I replied, "happy to try, sir. But I have to know an awful lot more than I do now."

"I'll hold nothing back," Jones declared. "The whole truth must be told. Maybe but a few persons will read it, and maybe not many of them will profit by it. I dare say I could find better literary craftsmen than you, but none I would trust as much."

I said thank you.

"Well, then, can you arrange to spend a couple of evenings a week with me, while I supply you with the details?"

"Here, sir?"

"Oh, no! It will be a different place each evening. As you see, I am keeping in practice. The time is going to come when I shall be needed. I will be ready. And, I think, if you do your part as ably as I think you can, when the next time comes I will not have to beat in vain against the doors of government. They will come to me."

"Yes, sir," I said. What the hell? I was more interested for the moment in just what was going on in that kitchen than I was in an extracurricular job of ghost writing.

During our conversation I had watched half a dozen large roaches creep out of the crevice between table and wall. They twiddled their antennae, strangely like radar, before venturing far. Having surveyed the area, they trotted over to the table-long smear of what I had taken to be sawdust, and began munching at it.

Jones raised his hand.

"Zotz," he said. "Zotz, zotz, zotz. And zotz. And zotz."

The six roaches rolled over dead. Jones scooped them up and added them to the pile of insect corpses on the newspaper.

"This stuff is bran mixed with a little molasses and oil of cucumber," he said, brushing the bait into a paper sack. "I

267

use it over and over again. My overhead, you see, is very small. And I get a penny apiece for cockroaches, three cents for female roaches, and a dime each for mice. Must have ten dollars' worth in that pile. And, as I said, it keeps me in practice."

He washed his hands at the sink.

"Well, let's eat. And call me up when you are free to begin. Here is my card."

It read:

STAR EXTERMINATING COMPANY
Our Results Guaranteed
Tel: SOuth 3-0101

I guess I am the only person in the world who knows where John Jones lives.